BETTER *than* PERFECT

BETTER than PERFECT

SIMONE ELKELES

BLOOMSBURY

LONDON   NEW DELHI   NEW YORK   SYDNEY

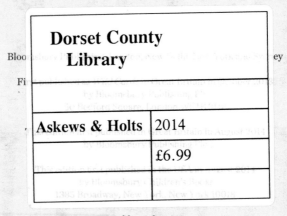

Bloomsbury Publishing, London, New Delhi, New York and Sydney

First published in Great Britain in March 2014
by Bloomsbury Publishing Plc
50 Bedford Square, London WC1B 3DP

Simultaneously published in the USA in March 2014
by Bloomsbury Children's Books

This electronic edition published in 2014
by Bloomsbury Children's Books
1385 Broadway, New York, New York 10018

www.bloomsbury.com

Bloomsbury is a registered trademark of Bloomsbury Publishing Plc

A CIP catalogue record for this book is available from the British Library

ISBN 978 1 4088 5299 6

MIX
Paper from
responsible sources
FSC® C020471

Printed and bound in Great Britain by CPI Group (UK) Ltd, Croydon CR0 4YY

1 3 5 7 9 10 8 6 4 2

To my #1 fan, Amber Moosvi

Your strength inspires me.
Your courage inspires me.
You inspire me.

I will never forget the three words you taught me
as I saw you go through chemo at age sixteen
and face the greatest battle of your life:
NEVER GIVE UP!

CHAPTER 1

Derek

Getting caught wasn't part of the plan. Pulling off a prank so epic that it'd be talked about for decades was. I'm standing with five of my friends in Headmaster Crowe's office listening to him rant for the past hour about how our latest prank embarrassed not only him but the trustees and teachers of this "prestigious boarding school" as well.

"Anyone want to fess up?" Crowe asks.

Jack and Sam are freaking out. David, Jason, and Rich are trying to hold back their laughter. I've been called into the headmaster's office more than a few times since I transferred here, so this is nothing new to me.

During finals week at Regents Preparatory Academy in California, seniors pull a prank on juniors. It's tradition. This year, the seniors managed to put blue dye in our showers and removed all the lightbulbs from the common areas of our dorm. It was only fair that we returned the favor, but on a bigger scale. The seniors had been waiting for us to raid their dorm, and you could tell they were on edge all week. They had lookouts posted at all hours, ready to defend their territory.

My roommate, Jack, came up with the brilliant idea of greasing three baby pigs from his uncle's farm and letting them run loose in the senior dorm. Sam said we should let the pigs run loose during graduation instead. I admit it was my idea to number the pigs . . . 1, 3, and 4. It took six of us to pull it off. The processional music was our cue to set the pigs loose.

I thought we'd gotten away with it, too, until all of us got summoned into Crowe's office an hour ago.

Crowe's assistant, Martha, peeks her head into the office. "Mr. Crowe, number two still hasn't been found."

The headmaster growls in frustration. If Crowe weren't such a dick, I'd tell him to call off the search because there is no pig number 2—that's part of the joke. But he's the kind of guy who doesn't give a shit about the students. All Crowe cares about is making sure everyone knows he's got the power to hand out detentions and fire teachers at his whim. I've seen him abuse that power more than once during the past year.

"I did it," I blurt out, exaggerating my Texas drawl because I know Crowe cringes at the thought of a redneck attending his precious school. More than a few times he's called me out for saying "reckon" and "y'all." I *reckon* I did it just to annoy the guy.

Crowe stands in front of me. "Which of your buddies here helped you?"

"None of 'em, sir. I did it all on my own."

He shakes his finger at me. "When your father hears about this he will most certainly be disappointed in you, Derek."

My spine stiffens. My dad, otherwise known as Commander Steven Fitzpatrick, is on another tour of duty. He's in a submarine for the next six months, completely cut off from the rest of the world.

I briefly wonder how my new stepmother, Brandi, is doing now that my dad is deployed. Our setup is perfect. I live here until I graduate, and my dad's new wife lives in a rented house near the naval base with her five-year-old kid she had with some ex-boyfriend.

News of my pig stunt isn't likely to reach my dad. And if Crowe thinks I'll be disappointing Brandi, that's a laugh.

Crowe hunches his shoulders and gives me one of his many practiced scowls that make him resemble an ogre on steroids. "You expect me to believe that you *stole* one of our school vans and transported *four* pigs to the graduation ceremony, greased them up, and set them loose all by yourself?"

I glance at my friends and signal for them to keep their mouths shut when I realize that more than a few of them are about to fess up. No reason all of us should get in trouble just because Crowe lacks a sense of humor.

I nod. "I acted alone, sir. But technically I didn't steal the van. I borrowed it." There were three pigs and it took all six of us to pull it off, but I'm keeping that info to myself. I wait for him to slap me with detention and order me to wash floors or bathrooms or something humiliating. Whatever. Detention during summer session will be a piece of cake since less than 20 percent of the school population stays on campus.

"The rest of you gentlemen are dismissed," Crowe declares. He takes a seat in his big leather chair and picks up his phone as my friends file out. "Martha, call Mrs. Fitzpatrick and inform her that her stepson has been expelled."

Wait! *What?*

"Expelled?" I practically choke on the word. What about a warning or detention or suspension? "It was a harmless prank."

He carefully hangs up the phone. "Expelled. Actions have consequences, Mr. Fitzpatrick. Despite numerous warnings about your cheating, drug use, and pranks, you have again disobeyed our rules and proven yourself unworthy to be a student at Regents Preparatory Academy. Obviously this also means you will not be invited to rejoin us for your senior year."

I don't move or say anything. This is not happening. I can count a dozen other students who've gotten caught pulling pranks and have escaped without so much as a warning. I accidentally left my notes on the floor during a test and Mr. Rappaport wrote me up for cheating. And the drug accusation . . . okay, so I went to a party with a few friends and came home wasted. I didn't mean to puke on the statue of Regents' founder after I found out someone slipped XTC into my drink, and I sure as hell wasn't the one to post pics of me puking on the school website. A certain senior on student council was responsible for that one, although he never got caught because nobody would accuse a guy whose dad donates a crapload of money to the school every year.

"Since you've already finished your finals, I'll be lenient and allow you to receive full credit for your junior year. As a courtesy to your father, I'll also grant you forty-eight hours to remove your belongings from campus." He starts writing on a piece of paper, then glances up at me when he realizes I'm not moving. "That will be all, Mr. Fitzpatrick."

Lenient?

I walk to the junior dorm as the absurdity of my situation sets in. I'm being kicked out of Regents and have to move back home. With my stepmother, who lives in her own, clueless world. This is bullshit.

My roommate, Jack, is sitting on the edge of his bed, shaking his head. "I heard Crowe say you got expelled."

"Yep."

"Maybe if we all go back there and tell him the truth, he'll rethink—"

"If your dad finds out, he'll make your life a livin' hell. The other guys'll be in the same boat."

"You shouldn't take the fall for this alone, Derek."

"Don't sweat it," I say. "Crowe had it in for me. This just gave him the excuse he needed to kick me out."

A half hour later Brandi calls. My stepmother's heard the news from Crowe and will drive the three hours from San Diego to Regents tomorrow. She doesn't yell or lecture me or act like she's my mom. Instead, she says she'd try to convince Crowe to change his mind about expelling me. As if that's gonna work. I doubt Brandi was a member of her high school debate team. I don't have much faith in her persuasion skills. To be honest, I'm not even sure she graduated from high school.

In the morning I'm still figuring out what the hell I'm gonna do when campus security knocks on my door. They have specific orders to escort me to the headmaster's office immediately.

As I walk across the quad with campus security flanking me, I'm all too aware of whispers from students I pass. It's not often someone gets expelled. I walk up the stairs to the front office, where photos of former students who became famous athletes, astronauts, congressmen, and business gurus are proudly displayed on the Wall of Fame. If it were two years ago, I might have imagined my own picture on the wall, but not anymore.

When the door opens to Crowe's office, my eyes focus on the woman sitting in front of his desk. It's Brandi, my dad's wife of eight months. She's fourteen years younger than my dad (which means she's twenty-five, only eight years older than me). Her orange stilettos match her oversize orange earrings dangling down to her shoulders. Her dress looks two sizes too big, which is definitely out of character. Every time I've seen her she's worn tight-fitting, low-cut outfits like she's about to go clubbing. She looks out of place in this office full of mahogany and dark leather.

Brandi glances at me when I walk in, then returns all her attention to Crowe. "So what are our options?" she asks as she fiddles with her earring.

Crowe closes the folder on his desk. "I'm sorry, but I see no options. *Heinous* crimes involving animals are not tolerated at Regents, Mrs. Fitzpatrick. Your son—"

"Stepson," I correct him.

Crowe regards me with disgust. "Your *stepson* has finally crossed the line. First, I'm told he's quit all extracurricular activities. Next, he's been rumored to attend parties with alcohol and drugs. That's in addition to the cheating on tests and defacing school property with vomit. Now this prank with live farm animals. We've been patient with Derek and sympathize with the challenges he's faced in recent years, but that does not excuse delinquent behavior. We have a duty at Regents Preparatory Academy to mold our young students into productive citizens and future leaders who are responsible for their community and environment. Derek obviously no longer wishes to be part of that proud tradition."

I roll my eyes.

"Can't you just assign him community service or have him, like, write some kind of apology letter thingie?" Brandi asks, her bracelets clinking as she taps her brightly polished fingernails against her purse.

"I'm afraid not, Mrs. Fitzpatrick. Derek has given me no choice but to expel him."

"By expelling him you mean, like, he can't come back for his senior year?" A speck of sunlight shines on her wedding band, a stark reminder that she's married to my dad.

"That would be correct. My hands are tied," Crowe tells her, which is a complete lie. He makes the rules and changes them on a moment's notice to suit his needs. I'm not about to call him out. It won't change anything, so why bother? "The decision has been made," Crowe continues. "If you'd like to appeal to the board, most of whom witnessed the debacle yesterday at the graduation ceremony, you're free to fill out the appropriate paperwork.

Although I warn you the appeals process is lengthy and a positive outcome is unlikely. Now if you'll excuse me, we still haven't located one of the animals that your stepson let loose and I have to do some very extensive damage control."

Brandi opens her lips in a last-ditch effort to persuade him, but closes them with a sigh when, with a flick of his wrist, Crowe motions for us to leave his office.

Brandi follows me back to my dorm, her stilettos clicking on the sidewalk. *Click, click, click, click.* I didn't notice back in the office, but she's definitely gained weight since I last saw her. Doesn't she care that everyone is staring at her and her ridiculous outfit and big blond hair with overly long extensions? Knowing her, she probably doesn't even realize the scene she's causing.

My dad sat me down before he announced they were getting married and said Brandi made him happy. That's the only reason I haven't completely written her off.

"Maybe," Brandi says, her cheery tone carrying across the quad, "this is for the best."

"The best?" I give a short laugh as I stop and turn to her. "What's *the best* about it?"

"I've decided to move back to Chicago to live with my family," she says. "Since your dad's gone for six months, I figure it's the best thing for Julian. He'll be starting kindergarten in the fall, you know." Brandi gives me a big smile.

I think she expects me to jump up and down clapping in excitement at her big relocation news. Or smile right along with her. None of those things are about to happen.

"Brandi, I'm not movin' to Chicago."

"Don't be silly. You'll *love* it in Chicago, Derek. They've got snow in the winter, and in the fall the leaves are, like, the *coolest* colors—"

"Come *on*," I say, interrupting her Chicago-is-all-that speech. "No offense, but we're hardly family. Y'all can move to Chicago. I'll stay in San Diego."

"Yeah . . . about that . . ." She bites her bottom lip. "I canceled the lease. Another family is moving into the house next week. I was gonna tell you, but I knew you had finals coming up, and since you'd already planned to stay on campus all summer I, like, didn't think it was urgent."

A feeling of dread settles in my stomach. "You're sayin' I, *like*, don't have anywhere to live?"

She smiles once again. "Sure you do. In Chicago, with me and Julian."

"Brandi, come on. You don't honestly think I want to move to Chicago for my senior year." People move from Chicago to California, not the other way around.

"I promise you'll love Chicago," she gushes.

No, I won't. Unfortunately, there's no one I can stay with in California. My dad's parents are dead and I heard my mom's dad died a while back. My mom's mom . . . well, let's just say she lives in Texas and leave it at that. No chance in hell I'm living with her. "I don't have a choice, do I?"

"Not really." Brandi shrugs. "Your dad left me responsible for you. If you can't live at the academy, you'll have to stay with me . . . in Chicago."

If she mentions the word "Chicago" one more time I think my

head might explode. This is not happening. I hope I'm living in some kind of realistic nightmare and I'll wake up any minute.

"There's one more thing I haven't told you," Brandi says as if she's talking to a toddler.

I rub the back of my neck, where a knot is starting to form. "What?"

She puts her hand over her stomach and says in a high-pitched, excited voice, "I'm pregnant."

No. *Fucking*. Way.

She can't be.

I mean, it's physically possible, but . . . the knot on the back of my neck is throbbing in earnest now, threatening to burst out of my skin. This is definitely a nightmare.

I want her to tell me she's kidding, but she doesn't. It was bad enough my dad married the bimbo. I expected him to realize eventually that marrying her was a mistake, but now . . . a baby permanently seals the deal.

I'm gonna be sick.

"I wanted to keep it a secret until you came home for the Fourth of July," she explains excitedly. "Surprise! Your father and I are expecting a baby, Derek. I think your being expelled is a sign that we're all supposed to be together in *Chicago*. As a *family*."

She's wrong. My being expelled is a sign, all right, but not that we're supposed to be together in *Chicago* . . . it's a sign that my life is about to implode.

CHAPTER 2

Ashtyn

I've been the only girl on the football team at Fremont High since freshman year, so it's not a big deal when Coach Dieter shouts a warning to the guys to make sure they're decent as I head into the boys' locker room for the first football meeting of the summer. My coach pats me on the back as I pass, just like he does to the guys.

"You ready for senior year, Parker?" he asks.

"It's the first day of summer break, Coach," I answer. "Let me enjoy it."

"Don't enjoy it too much. Work hard this summer during practice and at that football camp in Texas, because I expect a winning season come the fall."

"We'll take State for the first time in forty years, Coach!" one of my teammates yells out. His words are met by enthusiastic cheers from the rest of the team, including me. We almost made it to State last season, but we lost in the playoffs.

"All right, all right. Don't get ahead of yourselves," Dieter says. "Let's get down to business first. It's that time of year to vote for who you consider the player most deserving of leading this team. Think of the player whose talent, hard work, and dedication to this team is undeniable. The player who receives the most votes will be chosen as captain for the coming season."

Being voted captain is a huge deal at my school. There are a bunch of clubs and sports teams, but only one counts—football. I glance proudly at my boyfriend, Landon McKnight. He'll be voted captain. He's the first-string quarterback and expected to lead us to the Illinois state championship. His dad was in the NFL, and Landon is all set to follow in his footsteps. More than a few times last season Landon's dad even brought college scouts to watch his son. With his talent and connections, there's no question he's going to get a scholarship to play in college.

We started dating at the beginning of last season, right after Coach Dieter moved me up to first-string kicker. I perfected my technique the summer before my junior year and it paid off. The guys on the team would watch me practice, making bets on how many field goals I could make in a row.

I used to be self-conscious about being the only girl on the team. Freshman year I stayed in the background, hoping to blend in. The guys made comments to intimidate me, but I laughed them off and threw comments right back. I never wanted special consideration and fought to be treated like another teammate who just happened to be a girl.

Dieter, wearing his trademark khaki pants and polo shirt with

FREMONT REBELS embroidered on it, hands me my ballot. Landon gives me a nod. Everyone knows we're dating, but we keep our relationship on the down low at practice.

I write Landon's name on the ballot, then hand it in.

Dieter goes over our brutal practice schedule while the assistant coaches count the ballots.

"You don't win games by sitting on your asses," Dieter says during his lecture. "And besides, we're expecting to attract more college scouts this year. I know more than a few of you would like to play college ball. Seniors, this is your year to prove yourselves." Dieter doesn't say the obvious, that the scouts are coming to see Landon but we'll all benefit from their presence.

It would be amazing to play college ball, but I'm not delusional enough to think scouts will be knocking down my door. Only a handful of girls have been chosen to play for collegiate teams, and almost all of them are walk-ons without scholarships. Except Katie Calhoun. She was the first female to get a Division I football scholarship. I'd do anything to be like Katie.

I've watched football with my dad for as long as I can remember. Even after my mom left and he checked out of being a parent, we still watched the Bears together. He was a kicker for Fremont High forty years ago, the first and last time our high school won the state championship. The lone championship banner hangs on the gymnasium wall.

I guess going out for football freshman year was a way for me to try to connect with my dad . . . Maybe if he saw me kick enough goals he'd be impressed. Freshman year, I hoped my dad would come to games and cheer me on. He never did—he still hasn't, and I'll be a senior in the fall. My mom hasn't seen me play, either. I think she's living in some high-rise apartment in New York, but I haven't heard from her in almost a year. One day I'll prove to my parents that they're missing out, because it sucks feeling like your family doesn't care if you exist.

Luckily I have Landon.

As Dieter winds up his big pep talk and lecture, one of the assistant coaches hands him the voting results. He reads the paper silently, nods his approval, then writes on the whiteboard:

CAPTAIN
ASHTYN PARKER

Wait . . . what?

No way. I read that wrong.

I blink a few times as I feel pats on my back from my teammates. My name is clearly written, no mistake about that.

Jet Thacker, our star wide receiver, gives a hoot. "Way to go, Parker!"

The other guys start chanting my last name . . . "Parker! Parker! Parker!"

I glance at Landon. He's staring at the whiteboard. I want him to look at me, congratulate me, or make me feel like this is okay. It's not. I know he's floored. I am, too. I feel like the earth just tilted on its axis.

Dieter blows his whistle. "Parker, meet me in my office. The rest of you are dismissed," he says.

"Congrats, Ash," Landon mumbles, barely pausing as he walks past me on his way out. I want to pull him back so I can tell him I had no clue how this happened, but he's gone before I have a chance.

I follow Dieter to his office. "Congratulations, Parker," he says as he tosses me a patch with the letter *C* on it so I can sew it onto my letterman jacket. Another one will be sewn onto my game jersey. "Starting in August you'll have weekly meetings with me and the coaching staff. You'll have to keep your GPA at or above a 3.0 and continue to lead this team on and off the field." He talks to me more about my responsibilities and ends with: "The team is counting on you, and so am I."

"Coach," I say as I run my fingers over the smooth embroidery on the patch. I place it on his desk and step back. "Landon deserves to be captain, not me. I'll step down and let him take my—"

Dieter holds up a hand. "Stop right there, Parker. *You* were voted captain, not McKnight. You got more votes than any other player. I don't respect players who quit when they're asked to step up by their peers. Are you a quitter?"

"No, sir."

He tosses the patch back to me. "Then get out of here."

I nod, then walk out of his office. Back in the locker room, I lean against a locker and look down at the patch with the big *C* on it. *Captain.* I take a deep breath as reality sinks in. I was voted captain of the football team. Me, Ashtyn Parker. I'm honored and thankful my teammates voted for me, but I'm still in shock.

Outside, I hope to see Landon waiting by my car. Instead Victor Salazar and Jet Thacker are talking in front of my old beat-up

Dodge that needs a new paint job . . . and a new engine, for that matter.

Victor, our middle linebacker with more sacks than any other player in the state of Illinois, doesn't talk much. His dad practically owns this town, and Vic is expected to do whatever his father orders. Behind his father's back, Vic is reckless and a daredevil. It's as if he doesn't care whether he lives or dies, which is why he's so dangerous on the field.

Jet drapes an arm over my shoulder. "You know Fairfield is gonna have a field day when they find out their rival is about to have a girl captain. Those motherfuckers egged Chad Young's house the day he got voted captain last year, so we retaliated and tp'd their captain's house. Watch your back, Parker. Once word gets out, you're a target."

"I've got your back," Vic says in a gruff voice. He means it.

"We all do," Jet says. "Just remember that."

Target? I convince myself that I can handle being a target. I'm strong, tough, and nobody is going to get the best of me.

I'm not a quitter.

I'm the captain of the Fremont High football team!

CHAPTER 3

Derek

My muscles are tense when we pull into the driveway at my stepmother's childhood home in a small suburb of *Chicago*. I drove my dad's SUV and followed Brandi in her new white Toyota with blinged-out rims. We drove for six days. As soon as we step out of the cars, an older man I assume is Brandi's father appears on the front porch of the two-story redbrick house. He's got brown hair just starting to gray at the temples, and he sure isn't smiling. The dude is staring at Brandi as if she's a stranger. It's a standoff, with neither willing to make the first move.

I don't know what went down with Brandi and her old man. She didn't explain much, except to say she left home right after her parents' divorce and hadn't been back . . . until now.

Brandi grasps Julian by the hand and tugs the tired kid up the porch stairs. "This is my son. Julian, say hello to Grandpa."

Brandi's son is a cool kid who can talk your ear off. But he's acting shy right now and doesn't say hello to his grandfather. Instead, he keeps his eyes focused on his sneakers. Brandi's old man does the same.

"And this is my stepson, Derek," Brandi finally says as she waves her hand in my direction.

Her father looks up. "You didn't say anything about a stepson when you called."

I'm not surprised Brandi didn't prep her father about me. Common sense is not her strong suit.

Brandi cocks her head to the side, her big red hoop earrings reminding me of those ring-toss things at the carnival. I think she's got a set to match every color in her wardrobe. "Didn't I? I'm such a flake I must've forgotten to tell you, with all the moving and packing and . . . other stuff. Derek can stay in the den."

"The den is filled with boxes," he tells her. "And I gave the old couch that was in the den to charity a while back."

"If you'd rather, sir," I drawl, "I can sleep on the porch. Just give me a blanket and toss me scraps of food every now an' then and I'll be just fine." It's times like these that I'm wound so tight I can't turn off the natural twang in my voice even if I want to.

Brandi's dad narrows his eyes at me. I have the feeling if I let three greased pigs loose in his yard he'd shoot 'em, eat 'em, and then attempt to skin me alive.

"Nonsense," Brandi says. "Derek can stay in my old room with Julian, and I'll sleep on the couch in the living room."

"I'll move the boxes and put a blow-up bed in the den," her dad says, reluctantly giving in when he realizes that I'm not about to hightail it back to California.

"I'm cool with that," I say.

It's not like I plan on hanging around the house all that often.

"Derek, can you and my dad bring our stuff in the house while I put Julian down for a nap?" Brandi asks. "I'm exhausted from the trip and need a nap myself." I note she doesn't spill the beans to her dad that she's pregnant, not that she can keep the secret for long.

Before I can answer, she slips through the front door with Julian, leaving me alone with her grouchy old man.

Her father scans me up and down. He doesn't look impressed.

"How old are you?" His gravelly voice carries down the steps and across the yard to where I'm standing near the packed SUV.

"Seventeen."

"I don't expect you to call me Grandpa."

"I wasn't plannin' on it."

"Good. I suppose you can call me Gus." He sighs in frustration. I'm about as thrilled to be here as he appears to have me here. "You gonna come in, or are you about to stand there all day and wait for an invitation?"

He disappears inside. I'm tempted not to follow, but I have no choice. The house is old, with dark wood floors and well-lived-in furniture. The floorboards creak as I walk, reminding me of a haunted house.

He leads me down a hall to a back room and swings open a door. "This'll be your room. I expect you to keep it clean, do your own laundry, and make yourself useful."

"Do I get an allowance?" I joke.

The guy looks at me with a deadpan expression. "You're a real comedian, aren't you?"

"To people with a sense of humor, yeah."

He makes a *harrumph* sound in response.

I follow again when he makes an about-face and heads back to the car. I don't expect him to help unload the boxes, but he does. It doesn't take us long to lug everything into the house. We put Brandi's and Julian's stuff in her room upstairs and mine in the den. There's no conversation. This is definitely going to be an interesting living situation—not in a good way.

I'm moving boxes to the corner of my room to clear space when Gus reappears. Without a word, he hands me an air mattress and leaves me to figure out how to inflate it. I have no clue why Brandi would want to come back and live with a father who obviously doesn't want her here.

My dad is the opposite of Brandi's. When I was younger and my dad came home on leave, he was all smiles the second he saw us. He'd hug me and my mom so tight we'd pretend we couldn't breathe.

Brandi's dad didn't even hug her, when I know they haven't seen each other for years. Hell, they didn't even bother to shake hands or pat each other on the back. And he hardly acknowledged his own grandson.

I shove my suitcase behind the door and take in my new room. Faded wood paneling is on the walls. Boxes are scattered everywhere. There's an old fireplace in the corner that looks like it hasn't been used since the Civil War. At least there are two windows to keep the place filled with light. This place doesn't feel like home—not by a long shot. It doesn't remind me of Regents, either, surrounded by friends. I remind myself I'm here because I have to be.

Suddenly this house feels like it's suffocating me.

I head to the backyard. It's hot and the sun is shining, so I strip off my shirt and tuck it into the waistband of my jeans. The grass is so tall I wonder if it's ever been mowed. I walk through a small garden of weeds to a big wooden shed. The paint is chipping, obviously having been neglected for years. An old padlock on the latch is open, so I push back the door. Rusty garden tools hang on wall hooks, spray-paint cans and bags of weed killer are scattered on the workbench, and little metal buckets crowd the floor. I kick a bucket aside, then pick up a second one, thinking about everything that's changed in the past two years.

I swear under my breath and whip the bucket across the shed, the sound of the metal hitting the wall echoing in the small space.

"Stop or I'm calling the police!" demands a girl's voice from behind me.

I turn to find a hot chick about my age with blond hair in one long braid snaking down her chest. She's blocking the doorway and holding a rusty pitchfork. She looks like she's ready to stab me to death, which lessens her hotness factor, but not by much.

"Who're you?" I ask, taking in her black T-shirt and matching hoodie. If she weren't threatening to stab me, I could imagine her being one of those sexy warrior girls in a video game or action flick. And while it'd be damn cool to fight her in a video game, in real life that's never gonna happen.

Next to her is a monstrosity of a dog with short gray hair and gunmetal eyes that match hers. The beast barks at me as if I'm fresh meat and he hasn't eaten in months. Streams of drool fly from his mouth with each bark.

"Quiet, Falkor!" the warrior girl orders. The beast goes silent, but his lip twitches in a menacing snarl as he stands next to her like a soldier, prepared to pounce at her command. "You thugs from Fairfield think you can come here and—"

I hold up a hand, halting her tirade for the moment. Me, a thug? That's hilarious. This girl's thug radar is way off. I don't think I've ever been called a thug before. "I hate to break the news to you, sweetheart, but I've got no clue where Fairfield is."

"Yeah, right. I'm not stupid. And I'm not your sweetheart. I don't even fall for that really bad fake southern accent." Rustling in the garden captures her dog's attention. He abandons his post and leaps toward some unlucky critter. "Falkor, come back here!" she orders, but the beast ignores her.

"Put the pitchfork down, honey." I take a step closer to her and the exit.

"Not on your life. I'm warning you . . . take one step closer and I'll stab you." One glance at her shaking hands tells me she doesn't have the nerve to go through with her threat.

I put my hands up in mock surrender.

I wish this girl had an on/off switch so I could permanently shut her down. I'm standing directly in front of her now, the points of the pitchfork an inch away from my chest. "You *really* don't want to stab me," I tell her.

"Yes, I think I do." The warrior girl blinks her fierce eyes. For a second I'm sure she's about to lower her weapon, until I hear something creak behind me. As I glance over my shoulder, a bracket holding a bunch of tools on the wall crashes to the ground. The sound startles the girl and she drops the pitchfork. On my foot.

What the—

She stares at the pointed tine sticking out of my left shoe and her mouth opens in shock. Before I know it, she backs up and slams the door shut. I'm swallowed by darkness as I hear the padlock snap into place. Two thoughts cross my mind: she thinks I'm a thug and I think she's a wackjob.

One of us is right, and it's not her.

CHAPTER 4

Ashtyn

I can't believe I just stabbed someone! A thug from Fairfield I've never seen before. He's too cute for his own good, and he's tall, with shaggy brown hair peeking out from a knit cap. If that isn't bad enough, he isn't wearing a shirt and is totally ripped. If I didn't know any better, I'd think he was posing for a magazine spread. Did he actually think he'd get away with vandalizing our property with those old spray-paint cans he was hovering over? Those jerks from Fairfield are always causing trouble on our side of town. Jet's warning is still fresh in my mind. I was voted captain and became a target as soon as word got out.

I run as fast as I can toward my house, refusing to panic but not doing a great job.

"Dad!" I yell as I rush inside, hoping he's home and not at work. "There's a guy in the . . ."

My voice trails off as I catch a glimpse of a strange woman in our kitchen standing in front of the open refrigerator. She's wearing a red sundress and big red earrings to match. I think she's about to steal our food, but when she smiles brightly and says, "Hi! Wow, my baby sister's all grown up!" my mind focuses and I'm stunned.

The woman standing ten feet away from me isn't a food burglar. She's my sister, Brandi. In the flesh. I recognize her now . . . an older and bigger version of the eighteen-year-old who left when I was in fifth grade.

"Umm . . . hi," I say, dumbfounded.

My dad said Brandi was coming to stay with us for a little while. I didn't believe it, because my sister hasn't called or written or e-mailed or texted me since she left when I was ten. Not even to tell me she'd had a son with her ex-boyfriend Nick, or that she'd recently married some random Navy guy. I found that out when I ran into an old friend of hers.

I haven't seen my sister in seven years. With her bright and cheery "hi," she's acting like it was yesterday.

"Where's Dad?" I ask, postponing our reunion because there's an intruder in the shed with a pitchfork sticking out of his foot.

"I think he went to work or something."

"Oh no. That's not good." I bite my bottom lip as I worry about the boy in the shed. Will I be arrested? Coach Dieter won't be happy to find out that within an hour of being voted captain I stabbed someone. Forget maintaining a 3.0 or higher GPA. Stabbing people in the foot isn't exactly role-model material, but I have a good excuse. I was defending my house . . . or, more precisely, my shed. What am I supposed to do? Should I call the police or ambulance . . . or both?

"What's going on?" Brandi asks.

"Umm . . . there's a little *situation* out back." I cringe at the thought of what I just did.

"Like what?"

"I locked a football player from Fairfield High in our shed. They're animals," I explain quickly as I gesture toward the backyard. "I told him to leave, but he wouldn't. I didn't mean to stab him."

My sister's eyes go wide. "*Stab* him? Oh, my gosh. Umm. Umm. Umm. What should we do? Umm . . . I got it!" she says frantically. "Derek will help!" My sister slams the refrigerator door and hurries toward the den, yelling, "Derek!"

"Who's Derek?"

Finding nobody in the den, she runs to the living room, her long bleached blond hair flying behind her. "Derek, you in here?"

"Who's Derek?" I ask again. I thought her husband's name was Steve. Supposedly he's deployed and wasn't due back for a while. Did Brandi dump him and already move on to a new guy? I wouldn't put it past her. My sister was never known as the stable type.

"Derek's my stepson, Ashtyn." I follow as she heads upstairs calling, "Derek, we need your help! Where are you?"

Stepson? What is she talking about? She's got a son named Julian, but I hadn't heard about another kid. "You have a stepson?"

"Yes. He's Steve's son."

"How is Steve's little kid gonna help us, Brandi?"

Brandi whips around to face me with furrowed brows. "Derek's *not* a little kid, Ashtyn. He's seventeen."

Seventeen? My age?

I get a sinking feeling in the pit of my stomach. No, he couldn't be. But what if he is?

"Is he tall . . . with blue eyes, a southern accent, and a knit cap?" I ask, my heart beating so fast I wonder if it's going to burst out of my chest.

My sister's eyes go wider. We both realize my horrific mistake and race to the shed. I get there first. Falkor barks like crazy, his long tail wagging back and forth excitedly.

Brandi pounds on the door. "Derek, it's me, Brandi. Please tell me you're, like, not bleeding to death."

"Not yet," comes the guy's muffled voice from inside the shed.

Brandi yanks on the padlock. "Ashtyn, we need the key."

Umm . . . "Key?"

More wide-eyed stares. "Yeah, *key*. You know, those oddly shaped metal things you use to unlock stuff. Where is it?"

"I don't know."

"You've *got* to be kiddin' me," Derek moans.

"Don't worry, Derek. We'll get you out in a jiffy," Brandi cries out. "Ashtyn, where does Dad keep those big sharp cutters?"

"In the shed," I answer weakly.

Brandi picks up a rock and starts slamming it against the padlock, as if that will somehow magically unlock the thing.

"I can break the door down if you want me to," Derek yells through the door, "but I can't guarantee the roof won't collapse."

"No!" I yell. I don't want to be responsible for Brandi's step-son being stabbed in the foot *and* the shed collapsing on him. He could get crushed. There are too many sharp tools inside, ones that could cut off really important body parts. I rack my brain, trying to think of where the key might be. That door hasn't been locked in years.

"Wait!" I call out. Brandi stops her rock assault. "Let me think a minute."

I ignore the frustrated snort from inside the shed.

I get an idea. "Derek, see if you can find a watering can in the shed. My dad used to hide a spare key in there. If you find it, you can push it through one of the slats. I know it's dark, but—"

"I'll use my cell phone light." I hear Derek rummaging through the shed. "Found it."

I never thought those words would make me so happy.

Derek pushes the key through a gap in the slats. Brandi unlocks the padlock and opens the door as I peek around her at her stepson. Derek and his abs are leaning against the workbench. He looks relaxed and maybe a little irritated, but he's definitely not bleeding to death.

"Derek, this is my sister, Ashtyn," Brandi says as she rushes up to the guy. "Your, um, step-aunt. Isn't it funny that you guys are the same age?"

"Hilarious." He shakes his head like he can't believe he's in this situation. He's not the only one.

Brandi glances down at the pitchfork lying next to him, then stares at his feet. There's a hole in his left shoe.

"O'migod," she says, eyeing the hole. "You really did stab him!" She kneels down like a concerned mother hen and examines his shoe.

"Not on purpose," I say.

"At least she's got bad aim," Derek says in a sexy drawl. "It just grazed my toe."

Brandi gnaws on her lip. "What about lockjaw? Julian's pediatrician said you could *die* if you're cut from something rusty."

"Don't worry, little guy," Derek says to someone behind me. "I had a tetanus booster last year."

Little guy? I turn around to see who he's talking to. An adorable little boy with blond hair has joined us, obviously my nephew, Julian. He stares at the hole in Derek's shoe, then looks up at me with fear, as if I'm the Grim Reaper here to collect humans on earth and bring them back to Hell with me.

Brandi pats her son's head. "Ashtyn, this is Julian. Julian, meet your auntie Ashtyn."

Julian won't even look in my direction. Instead, he looks up at Derek as if he's his hero for life.

"Don't be afraid of her," Derek tells Julian. "Your aunt's not mean. She's just crazy."

CHAPTER 5

Derek

I manage to stay away from Ashtyn the rest of the day, hoping to avoid the crazy warrior girl who locked me in the shed. Apparently she doesn't feel the need to avoid me, though, because as I'm talking to my old roommate, Jack, on my cell and giving him props for managing to stuff my suitcase with random poker chips as a good-bye prank, she stomps into the den without knocking or an invitation. Her guardian watchdog tags along.

"I have a bone to pick with you." She crosses her arms on her chest. Her dog flops down on the floor next to her. I bet if he could cross his front legs on his chest to imitate her, he would.

I raise an eyebrow, amused. "Jack, I'll call you back." I slide my cell into my pocket, lean against the wall, and prop my feet up on the box labeled WINTER CLOTHES I'm using as a mock coffee table. "What bone do you want to pick?"

Her eyes narrow. The girl doesn't miss the double meaning as I throw her words back at her.

She ignores my joke and instead lets out a burst of irritation. "First off, you need to tell my nephew I'm not crazy. The kid won't even look at me."

I wag my foot. "I'm not the one threatenin' innocent people with pitchforks and accusing them of bein' thugs."

"Yeah, well, maybe you should've told me who you were right away . . . and stop wearing knit hats in the middle of the summer. Obviously my sister didn't tell us she had a stepson, so I wasn't expecting you."

"She didn't tell me she had a sister, either. And it's called a beanie."

"Whatever. It threw me off."

"Why are you so serious? Loosen up." I wag my foot again. "If it'll make you feel any better, you can rub my foot for ten minutes and we'll call it even."

She eyes my toe as if I have a fungus. "You think this is funny, don't you?"

"Entertaining is more like it." I look down at my foot. "So I assume the foot rub is out?"

"Let's just get one thing straight, Cowboy." She eyes my collection of boots lined up in the corner. "You might be used to getting girls to rub your feet or do whatever you want by flashing that smile or showing your six-pack, but it's not gonna work with me. I'm around football players all day, so seeing a fit body is like seeing a statue. It doesn't do anything for me."

"Tell me, then. What does it take to get your attention?" I ask.

"Wouldn't you like to know."

Yeah. And I have a feeling I'm gonna find out real soon.

I can tell Ashtyn is a girl who plays by her own rules and refuses to acknowledge that there's some kind of electricity flying between us. The more she protests, the more I know I've gotten under her skin. I'm about to say some cocky comment until Falkor groans, then stretches out and starts lapping away at his balls. "Your dog has issues."

"We all have issues." She stares me straight in the eye. "But don't try to figure me out or get into my business."

"Ashtyn, the last thing I'm gonna do while I'm here is get into your precious business. Or your issues, whatever they are."

"Good." She tosses her braid back. "Then we're on the same page."

Brandi peeks into the room, her big earrings swaying from side to side. "Derek, how're you feeling?" she asks, concern laced in her voice.

"Ashtyn was just about to give me a foot rub. Why didn't you tell me your sister was as sweet as sugar pie?"

Brandi puts her hand to her heart. "Aww. It's *super* cool that you're so forgiving, Derek. I made dinner and it's ready whenever you are."

When Brandi leaves, Ashtyn puts her hands on her hips and raises a brow. "Sugar pie, my ass," she says, then storms out.

In the kitchen, Brandi's dad sits at the head of an oak table surrounded by six wooden chairs. Julian is stuffing his face with mashed potatoes I'm sure are processed and probably don't have actual potatoes in them. I don't think Brandi has ever made anything that hasn't come from a box. Ashtyn is sitting across from

Julian. She glances up and our eyes meet. When I raise a brow, she quickly gazes down at her food.

"Have a good nap, buddy?" I ask Julian as I wash my hands in the sink and pretend Brandi's sister doesn't make me want to find out what it would take to get her attention just for the satisfaction of knowing I can.

Julian nods. I catch a tiny hint of a smile on his face when I mess up his hair and slide into the chair next to him—and across from Ashtyn.

I scan the food on the table. Chicken fingers that don't look like they actually came from a chicken, "just add water" mashed potatoes from a box, and corkscrew pasta smothered with canned Alfredo sauce. I've got to go grocery shopping with Brandi and introduce her to vegetables and chicken that aren't processed to death. Obviously eating healthy is not part of the Parker household plan.

Neither is conversation.

It's silent except for the sound of silverware clinking on the plates and the occasional cough. Is this typical? My dad always has crazy stories to tell and will yank conversation out of you even when you don't want to talk. It's a talent he was born with, or maybe it's some interrogation technique he learned in the military. Either way, it's a skill I don't have. I'm tempted to fling mashed potatoes across the room to liven up the evening, which is more my speed. Would Ashtyn follow along, or would the warrior girl try to stab me with her fork instead?

Ashtyn is the first to speak. "I was voted captain of the

football team today," she says. I detect a quiet, almost unrecognizable pride in her voice.

"Wow!" I nod, impressed.

"You play flag football?" Brandi asks. "That's cute. I played on the powderpuff team when I was in—"

"It's not flag football," Ashtyn interjects. "I play varsity for Fremont. You know, the one without the flags."

"Your sister has become a tomboy," Gus chimes in.

"Are you a lesbian?" Brandi whispers loudly.

I try to hold in my laughter, but I'm not doing a great job.

"No, I'm not a lesbian," Ashtyn says. "I have a boyfriend. I just . . . like to play and I'm good at it."

"Derek used to play football," Brandi says.

"A while ago," I say quickly, hoping to cut Brandi off before she elaborates. Ashtyn doesn't need to know the truth, because the truth doesn't matter. Not now, anyway. I hope Brandi doesn't blab my entire history. "I was average," I mumble.

The girl wielded a pitchfork, so I shouldn't be surprised she plays football. But I am.

Brandi waves her hands excitedly, getting our attention. "Ashtyn, I have the *best* idea. Why don't you, like, take Derek out and introduce him to your friends tonight?"

Ashtyn's eyes lock on mine. "I kinda have plans, but, umm . . ."

"You don't have to entertain me. I'm not really up for a late night after drivin' for the past week, anyway. I'm fixin' to go for a run and knock out early." I don't need to be babysat, that's for damn sure.

"Lake Michigan isn't far," Brandi chimes in. "You can run on the beach. It'll make you feel like you're back in Cali."

I'd bet my left nut that Chicago beaches are nothing like the beaches in Cali.

"Or the school track," Ashtyn pipes in too enthusiastically. "Everyone runs on the school track. The beach gets *crazy* crowded at night. You definitely *don't* want to go there."

Uh-huh. She's definitely going to be hanging at the beach tonight.

"What's your plan?" Gus asks Brandi. "You don't expect to sit around here all day, do you?"

Time for her to break the news that she's prego.

"I'll apply for a job at Debbie's salon after Julian starts kindergarten and Derek starts his senior year at Fremont." Brandi stabs her fork into a piece of chicken. "I figure Debbie will hire me to do nails after I get certified this summer."

Her dad shakes his head in disapproval. "Seems to me like you should apply to the community college and take some real classes so you have options besides making minimum wage doing nails. This marriage of yours might not work out, you know."

Gus doesn't hold back anything. While I might have had the same thought before I knew Brandi was pregnant, I wouldn't have mentioned it. I look over at Julian, who's got his attention squarely on his food. In an attempt to make sure he doesn't pay attention to more of the conversation, I balance a piece of chicken on Julian's knee and watch as Falkor eats it off him and licks him. Julian giggles.

"I'm not good at *real* school, Dad. You know that." Brandi bows her head. Her usual optimism might be irritating, but now she looks like her spirit is broken as she mumbles, "And my marriage is just fine, thank you very much." Brandi doesn't spill the news about her pregnancy. Instead, she shakes her head and looks defeated.

Nice going, Gus. I motion for Julian to feed Falkor more table scraps, hoping the dog doesn't mistake his little fingers for mini hot dogs.

"You weren't good at school because you didn't apply yourself," Gus continues. "If you'd spent half as much time studying as you did chasing boys and getting in trouble, you'd already have a college degree."

Ashtyn slaps a hand over her eyes and shakes her head, completely embarrassed.

Brandi puts down her fork and stares at her dad. "Are we going through this again? 'Cause we can walk out that door and never come back, just like practically everyone else in your life."

Gus stands, his chair scraping the kitchen floor so loudly Julian covers his ears. Gus storms out of the kitchen. The front door slams and his car tires squeal a minute later as he drives off.

One look at Brandi and Ashtyn is enough to make me want to escape from the room like Gus just did. Julian doesn't seem to be faring any better.

Ashtyn stares at her sister accusingly.

"What?" Brandi says innocently. "Dad started it."

"Maybe you started it when you left seven years ago," Ashtyn tells her. I can feel her resentment from across the table. Man, I'm in the middle of some civil war here.

"That's not fair," Brandi says.

Ashtyn rolls her eyes. "Whatever, Brandi."

I catch a tear running down Brandi's face. She swipes it away, then leaves the table. Julian runs after her, leaving Ashtyn and me alone.

"Y'all should audition for the new reality show where they eliminate the least dysfunctional family each week," I tell her. "I think you guys got a decent chance of winnin' the million."

"You're part of this dysfunctional family," Ashtyn shoots back.

I look at her, amused. "What makes you think that?"

"Otherwise, you would have stayed in California and not followed Brandi here. You'd be with your own mom. Your *biological* one, I mean."

"That's not really possible." I push myself away from the table. "She's dead. What's your excuse for not living with *your* mom?"

CHAPTER 6

Ashtyn

I didn't answer. I couldn't, because I've never been able to say out loud why my mom's not living here anymore. Truth is, she left because she got sick of being a wife and mother. I don't talk about my mom with anyone, not even Landon.

I should have known better than to ask Derek about his mom. I feel awful that I brought it up. If I knew his mom wasn't alive I wouldn't have mentioned it. His answer hung in the air long after he cleared his plate and left me alone in the kitchen. I wanted to call him back and apologize, but ever since I laid eyes on him my defenses have been up and my mouth has gone into overdrive.

Julian looks at Derek as if he's some superhero. I can't mention football without my sister mentioning that Derek played. Then she wants me to entertain him. Next thing I know my dad'll probably start watching football games with him.

I wanted to kick myself for attempting to look into his eyes more than a few times tonight. It's not because I'm attracted to him. It's because they're a unique color, that's all.

When my dad told me Brandi was moving back home, I hoped maybe we could become a family again. I imagined Julian and I would immediately bond. Instead, thanks to Derek, my nephew thinks I'm his crazy aunt. It's time I change that perception.

I find Julian in my sister's room, playing with a handheld video game.

"Hey, Julian!" I say.

He doesn't stop playing. "Hi."

"I know Derek said I was crazy, but I'm not."

Julian looks up from his game. "I know. He told me he was joking."

"Good." I sit next to him. Besides his blond hair, he's the spitting image of Nick. Supposedly Nick left my sister after he found out she was pregnant. I don't think she's seen him since, which means Julian has never met his biological father.

"Can I have a hug?" I ask him.

He shrugs.

"All right. Well, when you feel like giving me one, I'll be waiting for it. Okay?"

He nods, his attention still on the game.

I sit with him for fifteen minutes, until my sister comes in and tells him to get ready for bed. My sister acts like our argument in the kitchen didn't happen, but it's still fresh in my mind.

Landon hasn't called me, even though we're supposed to hang

at the beach tonight. I walk to my room, close the door, and call my boyfriend.

"Hey," Landon answers.

"Hey."

"Sorry I rushed out of Dieter's meeting and didn't call. I had to get home to help my mom with some stuff," he says.

"So you're not upset?"

"About what?"

"The captain thing. I totally expected you to get voted captain, not me." I know he did, too. I can't help but feel twinges of guilt, like I took his spot even though I had nothing to do with it.

"Whatever. It's not a big deal."

But it is. I guess I'm waiting for him to say I've worked hard and deserve to be captain just as much as anyone else, but he doesn't.

On top of the captain thing, my sister's homecoming and the argument I had with her are totally stressing me out. "Can we hang out alone tonight? My sister came home this morning, and I guess I'm just having a hard time with it."

"Everyone's meeting up at the beach," Landon says.

"I know, but I'm feeling kinda . . . I don't know."

"Listen, you were always pissed your sister left. Now she's back. You should be happy, Ash. You got what you wanted."

It doesn't feel how it should, though. "You're right." I don't want to be the whiny girlfriend. Landon told me that his ex-girlfriend Lily, who goes to our rival school in Fairfield, complained all the time. He'd said nothing was ever good enough for her and she smothered him to death. I told myself I'd never be like his ex. I'm the happy-go-lucky girlfriend, even when I don't want to be. "When will you be here?"

"I'll pick you up in fifteen," Landon says, then hangs up.

I rush to get dressed, knowing I can't very well go out with Landon wearing a T-shirt and hoodie. I try on seven different outfits before calling Monika. I'm not good when it comes to fashion, but my best friend is an expert. I text her pictures of each outfit and she picks one: jean shorts and a short, low-cut pink shirt that reveals cleavage and a hint of skin above the shorts' waistband.

In the bathroom, as I lean over the sink to put on my lip gloss, Derek strolls in.

"Don't you knock?" I ask him.

"No need to knock if the door's open." He leans against the shower door and focuses on me with his bright blue eyes. "Hot date?"

"Yes."

"With your boyfriend?"

"Yes."

"He play football, too?"

"Not that it's any of your business, but yes." I turn to face him and wish he had some blemish or imperfection, but I can't find one. Ugh, the girls at school are gonna have a field day when they take one look at him. I imagine a lot of drama and fighting over him. "Did you barge in here for a reason, or did you just want to rub it in that I have to share a bathroom with you?"

"I need to relieve myself. Do you mind?"

"Eww."

"You act like you've never done it before."

"I've done it. I just don't have the need to announce it." I grab my stuff and start to walk out, but turn back and say, "Don't you *dare* leave the toilet seat up."

"And if I do?" he asks with a smirk.

"Trust me, you don't want to find out."

In my room, I wonder if Derek has a girlfriend and imagine what she might look like. Not that I care. I'd actually feel sorry for the girl who has to deal with a guy who's too sarcastic, too witty, and too good looking.

The doorbell rings a few minutes later. I can't wait to see Landon's expression when he sees me all dressed up.

"Be right down!" I call out, then grab my purse and rush downstairs.

Landon is waiting for me in the foyer wearing jeans and a preppy button-down shirt that covers his dark-skinned body. I give him a peck on the lips just as Derek appears wearing long shorts with REGENTS PREPARATORY ACADEMY embroidered on the leg. I'm not surprised he comes from a fancy prep school with that ego of his. He's shirtless once again, showing off solid muscles and an air of confidence that rival Landon's. I'm not immune to him even though I said I was. There's just something about Derek that draws my gaze to him, even though I hate myself for acknowledging it.

"Who're you?" Landon asks, as if Derek's an intruder who needs to be kicked out of my house immediately.

"Just a thug from Cali," Derek says with a wink for me, then pushes open the screen door and saunters outside with a pair of running shoes in his hand.

Landon points to the door. "Who the hell was that?"

"He's Brandi's stepson." I wave my hand in the air, dismissing the importance of the guy living in our den. "Don't pay any attention to him."

"Stepson?" He glances at Derek through the screen. "I don't like it."

"Me neither." I grab Landon's hand and urge him out of the house. My boyfriend is competitive and definitely has a high testosterone level. He doesn't mind me hanging out with our teammates, but he's jealous of outsiders. Derek is definitely an outsider. "Come on, let's go celebrate the beginning of summer break. I need a distraction."

Outside, Derek is sitting on the stoop tying his shoes. "Y'all have fun," he calls out as we head for Landon's car.

"We will," Landon growls back.

From the car, I look over at Derek. Our eyes meet and I feel a jolt of adrenaline. I want to ignore him, to pretend he doesn't exist. So why do I have such a hard time keeping my eyes averted? I get a sense that there's sadness behind his eyes, something that I can relate to.

Landon's phone is in his cup holder when it rings on our way to the beach. Lily's name comes up on the screen.

"Why is your old girlfriend calling you, Landon?"

He glances at the phone but doesn't answer it. "Beats me."

"You never told me you still talked to her."

"We catch up every now and then. It's no big deal."

I wonder why he'd want to catch up with his ex-girlfriend when he always complains about her. I want to ask more questions about how often he talks to Lily and what they talk about, but he drives up to the entrance to the beach and hops out of the car before I can ask him to elaborate.

I thought Landon and I would find a nice quiet place to sit and talk in front of the bonfire, but he leaves me to hang with some of the guys. I could join him, but I'm getting a weird vibe from him tonight and decide to give him some space. I don't want to smother him like Lily did.

Jet has a six-pack in his hand as he stands by Victor's car with a bunch of other guys. The second Jet sees me, he waves me over.

"Hey, Captain," he says as he wraps me in a bear hug.

"Cut it out, Jet."

"You know you love me, Ash."

"No, I don't. Most of the time I don't even like you," I joke. "Get your paws off me and leave them for the poor, unsuspecting girls who buy your bullshit." I dig an elbow into his ribs. "Landon's right over there. Don't piss him off."

Jet laughs. "Why would I want to piss off our star QB, our pride and joy, the prince, the single most important person on our team, the only quarterback who can take us to State with one hand tied behind his back?"

"Lay off, Thacker," Vic chimes in, shutting Jet up for the moment.

After we lost in the playoffs, the local paper printed a quote from Landon bashing Jet about not catching his last two passes. Landon said they misquoted him, but Jet still took it personally. Ever since then, the two have been trading barbs and I've had to defuse a lot of it to keep the peace.

Jet points to a girl by the water's edge wearing a skimpy thong bikini. "What are the chances I get lucky with her tonight?"

"Better than most," I tell him. "Should I warn her that you just want a one-night stand so she shouldn't expect a call from you in the future?"

That gets an amused grin out of Vic.

"Hell, no." Jet doesn't have girlfriends. He likes to "spread the love" and hook up with as many hot girls as he can. Which also means he's pissed off more than a good share of the high school female population in Fremont and the surrounding communities.

A few times Jet has needed my help being rescued from clingy girls desperate to have a real relationship. I've reluctantly acted as his fake girlfriend too many times to count. I told him that one day he'll fall hard for a girl who'll break his heart, but he laughs it off. He thinks love is complete bullshit.

I walk to the bonfire where Monika is sitting and think about the conversation Derek and I had in the kitchen. And the fight my dad and Brandi had. And Derek's stupid abs he flaunted today. And the guilt I have for Landon not being voted captain. I want my brain to stop thinking. It's on overload.

"I can't believe my best friend didn't tell me she was voted captain," Monika says as she snuggles against her boyfriend, Trey, our star running back. "Congrats, girl!"

"Thanks."

Trey and Monika have been dating since junior high. They're completely in love and aren't afraid of PDA or talking about their future as if it's a given that they'll be together forever.

After my parents split, I gave up on finding true love—something manufactured in movies and books to make people believe in the impossible. Trey and Monika renewed my faith. He looks at Monika as if she's the only girl in the world. It's as if she's his lifeline and he'd be lost without her. Monika told me that Trey's her soul mate. They're both planning on going to the University of Illinois, although Trey needs a scholarship to the Big Ten school to be able to afford it.

When Landon sits next to me, I lean into him. "What are you thinking about?" I ask, getting my boyfriend's attention. "You look so serious."

"It's nothing," he says irritably before opening a can of beer and chugging the entire thing.

I put my hand on his chest. "Is it the captain thing? Because I didn't know—"

He swats my hand away. "Fuck, Ash, will you stop bringing it up? I'm just pissed off at the world right now, okay? So you were voted captain. Big fucking deal. I'm sure Jet orchestrated it as retaliation for that stupid article in the paper. The joke's on me, huh?"

"Jet didn't orchestrate anything."

He gives a short, mocking laugh. "Yeah, right."

His words sting. "Please say you don't mean that."

"Fine. I don't mean it," he says unconvincingly.

I glance at Monika and Trey, who are trying their best to pretend they're not listening to our argument.

I try to swallow, but there's a lump in my throat as I say what's been on my mind ever since Dieter wrote my name on the board this morning. "You . . . you don't think I deserve to be captain, do you?"

He doesn't answer.

CHAPTER 7

Derek

The sun is setting as I jog with Falkor. At the last minute I decided I might as well try to make nice with the beast and give him some exercise. I don't have a destination, but the hot, fresh air hitting my face loosens my tense muscles.

Within minutes, Falkor and I pass the high school and the football field right next to it. Memories of my mom watching me play football fill my head. She was always the loudest parent in the bleachers; I swear her lungs must've been sore by the end of each game. Even after she'd just had chemo and felt nauseous and tired, she'd be there. "Watching you play is my favorite thing to do," she'd say.

I'd do anything to play for her just one more time. Hell, I'd do anything just to talk to my mom again. But that's never gonna happen.

The beast and I jog around the track a couple of times before getting bored and venturing through town. As I stop at a red light and follow signs to the beach, I think about Ashtyn. Man, that tight shirt and short shorts didn't leave much to the imagination. It was a complete transformation from this afternoon, when her body was covered by a big hoodie. Maybe Ashtyn is a chameleon, changing into a new person depending on who she's hanging with. I wonder if her boyfriend likes her wearing sexy clothes so he can show her off like a trophy. When he picked her up, he looked at me like I was an opponent about to intercept one of his passes.

"I don't like her boyfriend," I say to Falkor.

The beast stares up at me with gray eyes and pants, his long tongue hanging out the side of his mouth.

"Next time he comes over you should pee on his leg," I suggest.

I'm talking to a dog. I feel like that movie where the guy is stranded on a desert island and ends up talking to a volleyball as if it's his best friend. I sure as hell hope this isn't a sign that I'm destined to have Falkor as my only friend while I'm living in Chicago. That would suck more than being stuck in Headmaster Crowe's office getting lectured for an hour.

When we get to the beach, I look out over the calm water. The shoreline is tame compared to Cali, where sleeper waves can take your feet out from under you without warning. I stand at the water's edge and look across the moonlit water with Falkor at my side. I wonder how my dad feels being surrounded by nothing but water. He told me once that living in a submarine is like escaping the outside world and living in your own bubble. While some guys enlist for money or education or to find themselves, my dad says being in the military makes him feel useful. *Everyone has a purpose in life,* he once told me. *Finding out yours is crucial to knowing who you are and who you want to be.*

What's my purpose? I haven't told my dad that I'm going to enlist after I graduate, in an attempt to find my purpose in life.

As I jog along the shoreline, I come across a small crowd hanging around a fire listening to music and laughing. I recognize Ashtyn immediately. She's sitting next to her boyfriend, but they both look miserable. The dude's holding a beer in one hand and is leaning on the other. If she were my girlfriend, I'd have one hand tangled in that long blond hair of hers and the other on her waist, pulling her close so our bodies were pressed against each other as I kissed her until she was breathless. But I'm not him.

Falkor barks, attracting the attention of more than a few people. Including Ashtyn. Shit. Her distrusting eyes meet mine before she looks away and pretends I don't exist.

I end up taking a detour and jog the rest of the way back to the house. I wish the workout made me stop thinking too much, but seeing Ashtyn reminds me of all the crap I have to deal with.

"Ashtyn isn't all that," I tell Falkor.

This weird sound, kind of like a groan, comes out of the dog's mouth.

"She's got a boyfriend. And she can't stand me livin' in her house, right?" But she's got full, kissable lips. And these eyes that seem to change colors with her moods. I can't shake her from my mind.

I stop and look down at the dog for confirmation, since he

knows her better than me. He's looking up at me with droopy, clueless eyes.

"I'm talking to a damn dog, and I called *her* crazy." I laugh to myself.

Back at the house I'm trying to find a comfortable position on my air mattress, but it's not easy. On top of that, I keep imagining Ashtyn's lips as if they're some kind of artwork to be admired and analyzed. When I'm finally so beat and bored I can sleep soundly even on this crappy blowup, Falkor jumps onto the bed with me. I'm waiting for the mattress to puncture and explode, but it doesn't. Within seconds, the beast is snoring.

I've been dozing for at least an hour when someone bursts into the room. "Why are you sleeping with my dog?" Ashtyn demands.

"I'm not," I respond in a sleepy moan. "He's sleepin' with me."

"Isn't it enough that my sister and nephew worship the ground you walk on? You want to steal my dog, too? I saw you at the beach with Falkor. I don't want you thinking he's your dog. He's mine."

"Listen, Sugar Pie, Falkor snuck into my room. I didn't invite him. You got issues with your family, keep me out of it." I sit up and note that she's changed into a hockey jersey and baggy flannel pants with skulls and crossbones on them. It's a drastic change from what she wore on her date. "Just take your dog and go to bed." I lie back down and expect her to leave, but I feel her gaze on me. I wish I wasn't tempted to reach out and pull her close, to shut her up with a kiss that would make her forget that boyfriend. "What?"

"If you call me Sugar Pie again, I'm going to knock you out."

I'm tempted to say the word on the tip of my tongue. *Promise?*

CHAPTER 8

Ashtyn

'**ve** been curled up in bed for the past three hours with my eyes closed tight, wishing my life would stop spinning out of control. Landon and I didn't get along last night at all. I don't even know where things stand now.

I look at my phone to see if he's called or texted. He hasn't, although it's Saturday. He's probably still sleeping.

I slowly head for the bathroom. I'm about to sit on the toilet when I'm suddenly off balance and feel like I'm going to fall in. The damn seat is up. I cringe as I set it back down, silently cursing Derek and fully intending to call him out.

First I need to eat. Then I can confront Derek and head to the field to practice. Though Dieter doesn't have official practice on the weekends, we don't want to lose our momentum.

Derek walks in the kitchen a few minutes after I do, wearing shorts and a T-shirt. His long hair is messed up and he looks sweet and innocent. I know guys like Derek, who look innocent but are just the opposite. Falkor, who'd disappeared from my room in the middle of the night, comes prancing in on Derek's heels.

"Did you lure my dog back in your room last night?" I ask in an accusatory tone.

"He kept scratching on my door and whining like a baby until I let him in."

"You're stealing him."

He shrugs. "Maybe he's sick of you and wants new company."

"A dog can't be sick of his owner, Derek, and I'll have you know that I'm *great* company. My dog loves me."

"If you say so." He rummages through the fridge, pulls out some eggs, then grabs a loaf of bread from the pantry. "What happened at the beach between you and Loverboy? Looked like you two were havin' one hell of a night," he says in a lazy drawl as he makes himself scrambled eggs and toast.

"What happened to my rule about not leaving the toilet seat up?" I counter.

The side of his mouth quirks up. "I've got this condition, you see. It prevents me from being ordered around."

"Uh-huh. A condition, you say?"

"Yeah. It's *real* serious."

"Ooh, I feel so bad for you. You poor baby, being told to do something by a female. That must've threatened your masculinity." I pull out a bag of Skittles from the pantry and sort out the purple ones like I always do, then start munching on the rest.

Derek leans close and whispers in my ear, "Nothing threatens my masculinity, Sugar Pie."

A tingly sensation zings up my spine when his warm breath touches my skin. I'm momentarily paralyzed.

He opens the fridge again. "Besides eggs and toast, you got anythin' in here besides junk and processed food?"

I pretend he has no effect on me. "Nope."

Derek sits down with his eggs and toast, but stares at my collection of purple Skittles with those clear blue eyes that belong on someone who doesn't leave the toilet seat up on purpose.

"Nutritious," he says.

"It's comfort food," I tell him.

He quirks his eyebrow, clearly amused. "If you say so."

"Ugh. Don't tell me you're a health nut."

He scoops up a forkful of eggs. "I'm not a health nut."

"Good. Here," I say, pushing my collection of purple Skittles toward him. "You can have the purple ones. I'm allergic to them."

He raises a brow. "You're allergic to purple Skittles?" he asks, skepticism laced in his voice.

"I'm allergic to purple dye." I grab an orange one and pop it into my mouth. "But I'm not allergic to the rest of them. I love Skittles."

"I'm good with my own breakfast, but thanks." Derek takes bite after bite of eggs and toast. When Julian walks in, Derek focuses on my nephew. "Hey, buddy," he says. "Want some breakfast?"

Julian nods.

"I can help," I quickly tell Derek. I need to redeem myself so Julian doesn't think I'm the worst aunt who ever lived. If I have to work hard and long for that hug, I'm gonna do it.

I start to get out of my chair, but Derek holds up a hand. "I got it."

After my mom left, my dad never made home-cooked meals. I had to fend for myself and ate what he brought home from the store: frozen, microwavable food and junk. Obviously Derek's mom spent more time with him than my mom did with me. While it's not his fault, I'm overwhelmingly jealous.

Julian sits in the chair next to where Derek had been sitting. Derek's presence in my house makes me feel insignificant and unneeded. I might as well be invisible.

"Want some Skittles?" I wave the bag in front of my nephew's face in a lame attempt to get him to bond with me. I've never seen a kid who didn't like candy. "It's super good breakfast junk food."

He shakes his head. My nephew wants nothing to do with me.

My nemesis puts a plate of steaming scrambled eggs and toast in front of Julian. My mouth waters from the smell of freshly toasted bread. Julian eats, humming enthusiastically with each bite. The tune reminds me of our school fight song, which is chanted by the fans during halftime at our games.

Thinking of our fight song reminds me that I didn't look outside to make sure my house hasn't been tp'd by Fairfield. It was all clear when I went to bed last night, but Falkor slept in the den and might not have heard anything. I pull back the curtains in the living room. My hand flies to my mouth as I take in the sight of my entire front yard.

No! No, no, no, no, no!

It's *worse* than being tp'd. Worse than I could have ever imagined, and completely humiliating.

Toilet paper isn't hanging down like white flags waving from branches of every tree. Instead, hundreds of maxi pads are stuck to the tree trunks, and tampons are tied to the branches like a bunch of little Christmas ornaments fluttering in the wind.

As if that wasn't sick enough, all of the pads and tampons have fake bright red blood marks on them. Even my mailbox has pads stuck all over it.

I seethe with anger and burn in embarrassment as I rush to clean up the yard, then suck in a breath when my eyes focus on my driveway. In big letters are two words written in a multitude of pads: FREMONT'S BITCH.

CHAPTER 9

Derek

Ashtyn cursed a bunch of times, then rushed out of the house like a zombie was chasing her. I find her in the front yard, staring at the mess littering the lawn and the trees.

Holy shit.

"Go away," she cries as she frantically lifts the pads that are stuck to the driveway spelling FREMONT'S BITCH. She's got what looks like ketchup all over her hands. It gets on her hockey jersey as she piles pads in her arms.

As a guy who appreciates pranks, I'm impressed. This took some serious thought and effort. Retaliation would be fun to plan. But Ashtyn's breathing hard, like a dragon about to spit fire. She's not amused or impressed. She's pissed. I grab a garbage can next to the garage and start untying tampons from the branches.

She yanks the can away from me. "What are you doing?"

"Helping."

She's managed to get ketchup on her face and hair. She pushes stray strands out of her face, but that only makes it worse. "I don't need your help."

I glance at the tampons waving in the air above her. "Come on, Ashtyn. You know it'll take you twice as long to do it yourself." I pull a tampon off a branch and wag it at her. "Let go of that big ego of yours and let me help you."

She grabs the tampon out of my hand and tosses it into the trash. "I don't think you'd find it funny if this happened to you." Turning her back, she drags the can out of my reach. "Why don't you get brownie points by helping my sister or nephew, because you're so good at that? You're not earning any with me, so you might as well go back in the house."

If that's the way she wants it, fine. I hold my hands up in surrender. Let her deal with the mess. I know from past experience that getting mixed up with girls like Ashtyn, who take life way too seriously, is more trouble than it's worth. "You are one bitter girl."

"What's going on out here?" Gus demands, then turns to me. "Did you have anything to do with this?"

"No, sir."

Ashtyn keeps ripping pads off the trees.

Gus huffs and looks at Ashtyn as if this prank is the worst thing that could possibly happen. "I'm calling the police."

"Dad, no!" Ashtyn gives her father a pleading look. "If you call the police, everyone will accuse me of being a weak girl who can't handle being team captain."

"You *are* a girl, Ashtyn," Gus states matter-of-factly. "Why don't you let some boy be captain? Have someone else's family deal with vandalism to their yard."

"Gus, it's not her fault," I say. Maybe they need to hear the voice of an unbiased third party who doesn't think getting pranked is the end of the world. "It's just a prank."

Gus turns on me. "Just a prank, huh? Pranks are not funny."

"It's not a big deal, Gus. Instead of yellin' at her, why don't you—"

"Derek, stay out of this." Ashtyn stands in front of Gus, demanding all his attention. She stands tall, shoulders back and head high. "Dad, I promise I'll clean everything up before you get home from work. Don't call the police. *Please.*"

Gus shakes his head, completely frustrated as he eyes the yard again. "If your mother were here, she'd never allow you to be on the football team. She'd sign you up for cooking classes or dance classes or something like that."

Ashtyn looks like his words are a slap in the face. "I like football, Dad. I'm good at it. If you'd come to a game or practice and just watch me . . ."

Her voice trails to a whisper as Gus dismisses her words and walks to his car. "Make sure the yard is clean before I get home, or I will call the police." He gets in his car and drives off. After he's gone, Ashtyn takes a deep breath to compose herself, then goes back to taking pads off the trees.

I start pulling tampons off branches too high for her to reach.

"You know," I say as I reach around her and toss the tampons in the trash. "Just because you can deal with bullshit on your own doesn't mean you should."

CHAPTER 10

Ashtyn

Yo, yo, anyone home?" Jet's human-bullhorn voice booms through the house. Jet never rings the doorbell. If our door was locked, he'd knock so loud he'd put a dent in the door.

I rush down the stairs, hoping I've washed off all the fake blood. It took Derek and me over an hour to clean the front yard. By the end, we looked like victims in a slasher film.

In the living room, Jet makes himself comfy in my dad's favorite chair while Trey and Monika sit next to each other on the couch. Victor stands in the doorway with his hands crossed on his chest. I know what's bothering him, but I'd never reveal his secret.

I'm still thinking about what I'm going to tell the guys about the prank when Jet says, "We know your house got tamponed and padded last night."

I was hoping the prank happened late enough and I'd cleaned up early enough that word wouldn't spread. This morning, only a few cars passed our house and only one slowed to check out the scene.

"How'd you find out?"

"Every guy on the team got pics e-mailed to them anonymously." Trey holds out his phone, showing me picture after picture of the tampons and pads all over my yard . . . and my driveway with the words that still make me cringe.

"They're also on the Internet," Jet adds as he sweeps his hair to the side. "Time to plan revenge, 'cause I'm not about to sit back and do nothing."

Monika taps Trey on the knee and urges him to tell me something they've obviously been discussing before they came here. "What we're trying to figure out is how they got all our e-mail addresses," Trey says. Monika nods in agreement.

"Sounds like an inside job," she adds.

"You two have been watching too many crime shows," Vic tells them.

"It wouldn't be hard to get our team roster and e-mails. Some people who live on the south side of Fairfield go to Fremont." Jet moans. "I'm fucking starving. What'ja got to eat?"

"Not much," I tell him, but he heads to my kitchen anyway, stating that he can't think without eating first. The guy eats a ton and is the leanest and fastest guy I know, burning off calories with his endless amount of energy. One of his dads is a chef, so why he'd want to eat something from my house is beyond me.

We all follow Jet into the kitchen. Derek is sitting at the table, typing on his laptop.

"Hey." Derek gives a short wave to the guys.

Victor eyes Derek suspiciously while Jet asks, "Who're you?"

"He's Derek . . . my sister's stepson," I explain before rummaging through our pantry and pulling out random crap to feed the guys. My teammates don't care if I feed them healthy food or not . . . anything fuels them.

I can almost hear the wheels turning in Jet's head. I wish I could tape his mouth shut to prevent him from talking, but that would require me having the strength to hold him down long enough. "Wait. Ash, that makes him your step-nephew." Jet laughs, completely amused. "That is *hella* fucked up."

"Tell me about it," Derek mumbles.

Jet grabs a handful of the purple Skittles still in a pile on the table and pops them into his mouth. "We gotta come up with a plan, Ash," he says, munching. "Those motherfuckers at Fairfield gotta know not to screw with us."

My sister walks in with her big hair piled on top of her head in a messy bun. She glances at the guys. "What plan?"

"Retaliation," Jet chimes in before I can give him a signal not to mention anything.

Brandi wags her finger at Derek, something my mom used to do to us. "Don't you even think of getting involved," she tells him. "Remember what happened the last time you pulled a prank?"

"What happened?" Trey asks.

Derek shakes his head as my sister prepares to give us the scoop. "He got expelled for letting pigs loose during the senior graduation."

Expelled? When I saw Derek in his Regents Academy shorts yesterday, the last thing I expected to hear was that he got kicked out.

Jet laughs heartily and gives Derek a fist-pump. "That's *epic*, man."

My sister turns to Jet with her hands on her hips, looking more like a mom than a girl who used to be a pothead and dance around the house in her underwear on a daily basis. "It's not epic. It's, like, not okay at all." She directs her attention to Derek. "Don't do anything stupid with my sister's friends."

Derek gives her a two-fingered mock salute.

"I'll bet that dude Bonk was the mastermind," Vic says after my sister grabs a cup of coffee and leaves the room. He's still eyeing Derek as if he's some superspy who's not to be trusted.

"Just so we're all clear, my man isn't fighting anyone," Monika says. She lovingly cups Trey's cheeks in her hands. "Nobody's gonna mess up this gorgeous face. Right, baby?"

They start to kiss and do some baby talk.

Vic looks away.

Jet rolls his eyes and pretends to gag. "Seriously, guys, get a room."

I nudge Jet. "Leave them alone. When you fall for a girl, you won't be any different."

"Thank goodness that'll never happen. If it does, shoot me and put me out of my misery."

Victor gets a text and swears under his breath. "I gotta go."

Jet holds up his hands. "Am I the only one ready to come up with a plan to kick some Fairfield ass?"

"Maybe we should, you know, *not* retaliate and show we've got more class," I offer.

"Who said we have class?" Jet asks. "Not me. Ash, you're

delusional if you think our teammates voted you captain because they expect or want you to act classy. Let's face it, if we voted for the best-looking guy on the team I would've won."

Monika raises her hand, but keeps her eyes locked on Trey. "I disagree. My baby's the best-lookin' guy on the team."

Jet laughs. "You're biased. Yo, Parker, you really wanna know why *you* were voted captain?"

"Not really." I'm sure Jet'll say I've got the biggest boobs or something crude like that. Or say that he rigged it like Landon claimed, which would make me feel awful and undeserving. I want to know the truth . . . I just hope the truth isn't what Landon thinks it is.

"I want to know," Derek chimes in.

Jet puts his arm around me and pulls me close, squeezing me like a stuffed doll. "She got voted captain 'cause she's the best-lookin' chick on the team."

"I'm the *only* girl, Jet," I say.

"I'm not done. She also got voted captain because she's got major balls for a girl. She doesn't give up or cry every time she gets bruised, cut up, or roughed up on the field. She brings her A game every fucking time. She motivates us, that's for sure." He looks at Derek and says, "This girl here tried out freshman year. There were bets made that she'd quit within a week. I should know because I was one of those people who lost money on that bet. I'm not sayin' some of the guys didn't try to make her quit, yours truly being one of them, but she never gave up. She earned our respect." He eyes my chest. "And she's got the best set of tits on the team."

CHAPTER 11
Derek

At the mention of Ashtyn's chest, I look away and pretend I'm interested in the rest of the purple Skittles. I don't want to notice Ashtyn's chest, or any of her other body parts, for that matter. I'm already too aware of the girl as it is. Paying attention to her female parts is not an option, for more reasons than the obvious.

I close my laptop when the big Latino guy calls out, "Derek, wait. How about helping us out?"

Ashtyn says, "We don't need any help, Vic. Besides, you heard what my sister said. Derek is forbidden to help us."

Yeah, but that just makes me want to break the rules even more. "What kind of help?"

"Retaliation for messing up Ashtyn's yard."

Jet, the self-declared best-looking dude with a big mouth, says, "We gotta come up with a plan so they know not to screw with us. We could use any ideas you've got."

Ashtyn steps between me and the guys. "He doesn't have any ideas. Right, Derek?"

"Right." I burst her short-lived moment of triumph. "But I'll work on it."

"No, you won't," she orders as her teammates say, "Great" and "Let us know if you come up with anything."

Ashtyn shoots me a glare, then pats each of her friends on the shoulder. "We'll talk about this later. It's team business. You guys go do drills. I'll be there in a few minutes."

After they file out, Ashtyn leans on the table, her face close to mine. I wish to hell Jet hadn't mentioned her breasts, because the way she's leanin' I have a good view of her lacy pink bra.

"You seem to think I need a savior." I have a hard time concentrating on her words and not her bra. "I don't. And while I appreciate you helping me clean the mess in my yard, I was more than capable of doing it myself."

I pick up my laptop. "I'm no savior."

"Then what's your agenda, Cowboy?" she continues. "Besides annoying me."

"Don't got one," I say. "Annoying you has taken up so much of my time since I got here, I *reckon* I don't have much time for anythin' else."

I walk out, hoping I'll forget about that lacy pink bra and the girl who's wearing it. Lying on my blow-up bed, I open my laptop again. I intend to watch random videos, but instead I search online for the pictures of Ashtyn's front lawn. It doesn't take long to find them. They're on some bogus profile created this morning, someone claiming to be a Fremont student named Booger McGee. Pictures of the tampons and pads strewn on the lawn were uploaded today. Ashtyn is tagged in the picture marked FREMONT'S BITCH.

One picture is taken from the street to showcase the entire mess. A few others are closer up, showing their artful distribution of the pads and tampons. The pranksters were careful not to out themselves, probably afraid of the consequences of being recognized. Smart, but not that smart. I squint closely at a picture including Ashtyn's car. There's a reflection of the front end of another car in her side window. I easily identify the distinctive shape of a Jeep Wrangler with a custom light bar on top. Wranglers can never be mistaken for any other car.

I tell myself I don't want to be Ashtyn's protector. The girl is more than capable of fighting her own battles, and for the ones she's not capable of fighting . . . well, she's got a boyfriend and teammates for that. I need to remind myself to stay out of her life even when instinct tells me otherwise.

Falkor jumps on my lap and paws me. His breath smells like he's been eating something other than dog food.

Spending the summer at Regents would've been awesome, with parties that would last all night. Now I'm in the suburbs of Chicago living with a stepmother who suddenly wants to make sure I stay out of trouble and a girl with a pink lacy bra who plays football and would like nothing better than for me to fall off the face of the earth.

Because I have nothing better to do and need an adventure, I decide to drive to Fairfield to see if I can spot the Jeep. It's easy to infiltrate enemy territory when nobody recognizes you as the enemy. I wear jeans, boots, and a plaid button-down with my beanie to emphasize that I'm not from around here. When I first met Jack at Regents, he asked me if I lived on a ranch because of the way I talked. I might have talked like a cowboy, but I looked like a California dude who surfs and wears beanies. I've lived so many places, I don't fit into any mold.

Fairfield is the town next to Fremont. I set my GPS for Fairfield High and find their football field empty. It's Saturday, but hard-core players practice on weekends. As I cruise the streets on the alert for a Jeep, it doesn't take long to realize there's a rich side of town and a not-so-rich side. I turn down one block, then another, where buildings are tagged with gang symbols. The guys hanging out on the street corners look more than ready to sell me drugs.

I'm about to give up when I spot a red Jeep with a custom light bar parked in front of a sandwich shop called Rick's Subs. A dude who looks like Ashtyn's boyfriend, accompanied by some chick, pulls out of a spot and drives off. I take it. Once inside, I sit at the end of the long counter and pretend to look at the chalkboard menu above. This is obviously the Fairfield High hangout of choice.

A bunch of guys who look about my age are in a booth, laughing and acting like they're the shit.

"Bonk, upload another close-up," one of the guys says a bit too loudly. Bonk has a shaved head and piercings in his ears and eyebrows. He tells the guys to keep it down and looks around to make sure nobody is eavesdropping.

"What'll ya have?" the waitress asks.

I glance at the menu again. "I'll have a meatball sub to go."

"You got it." She calls out my order to the chef, then pours me a glass of water. "You go to Fairfield? I haven't seen you in here before."

"Nah, I'm visiting from California." I nod toward Bonk and his posse, who now have a crowd around them. "So, um . . . do those guys go to Fairfield?"

"Sure do. Football players. The one with the shaved head is Matthew Bonk," she adds. "He's our star receiver," she says proudly as if he's someone famous. "We won State again this past year. Matthew's our local celebrity."

She goes to take someone else's order.

Bonk walks up to the counter. He notices me sizing him up. "What're you lookin' at?" he asks as if he's some deity unworthy of my gaze. He's obviously taking the local celebrity thing seriously.

Time to have some fun . . .

"I just . . . wow! Matthew Bonk in the flesh." I take his hand and shake it with an overabundance of enthusiasm. "It's a pleasure finally meetin' the famous receiver from Fairfield High."

"Thanks, man." He pulls his hand away. "Who'd you say you were?"

"Payton Walters," I tell him, reversing the name of one of the greatest running backs of all time. The dude is clueless. "I was wonderin' if I could get your autograph for my girlfriend. She's a *huge* fan o' yours, man. You'd earn me some serious brownie points if she knew I met you." I grab my napkin and hold it out as the doting waitress eagerly appears and provides a pen. "Make it out to Sugar Pie." I peer over his arm as he straightens out the napkin. "It's what I call her."

"Whatever floats your boat, dude." Bonk makes the napkin out to Sugar Pie and signs it: *Matthew Bonk, #7.*

"Can I take a picture of you?" I lay on my thickest southern accent. "Sugar Pie'll shit a massive cow pie if I show her a picture of you holdin' up the napkin with her name on it."

Yankees often assume people with southern accents are stupid. What they don't know is that we use our accents to our advantage when we find it useful. Like now, because Bonk is posing with the napkin as I take a picture with my cell.

"Listen, buddy, I got to get back to my friends," he says as he hands back the napkin and asks the waitress for a drink refill.

"No problem." I grab his hand once again and shake it hard. "Thanks, man!"

He walks back to his friends and I hear him tell them what a dork I was. After I pay for my sub, I follow Bonk and his buddies outside. They're standing by the Jeep. One of the guys mentions Ashtyn and suggests they break into the Fremont locker room and hang the leftover tampons on the lockers.

When they realize I've followed them, they look at me like I'm an alien from another planet.

"That picture I took was blurry," I say apologetically. "Can I trouble you for just *one* more? I swear my girlfriend will pee in her Daisy Dukes when she sees I got a picture of you holdin' your signature."

Bonk rolls his eyes and laughs, but doesn't protest as I hand him back the napkin with his signature. He leans on the back of his car as if he's a stud and holds up the napkin. It couldn't be more perfect, except . . . "Can y'all get in the picture with him?"

The guys are all too willing to pose for the camera.

Mission accomplished.

CHAPTER 12

Ashtyn

Monika comes over Sunday morning with Bree, the two cocaptains of the cheer squad. They want my opinion of a new cheer and a dance routine they've made up, as if I possess some insider knowledge of whether my teammates will like it.

On my front lawn, Bree and Monika start clapping and moving their bodies like they're made of some secret flexible material. I have no clue how they're able to move like that. I'm jealous, although neither of them can catch, throw, or kick a football like I can.

Derek walks outside and heads for the shed. He looks masculine, wearing jeans with cowboy boots and a white tank. Falkor follows closely on Derek's heels.

Bree stops her routine. "Who *is* that?" she asks a bit too loudly.

"Derek."

"He's Brandi's stepson," Monika tells her. "He's—"

"*Super* hot," Bree interrupts almost breathlessly. "Oh, my God. You have definitely been holding out on me, Ash. I love his boots, and that knit hat he's wearing is so cute."

"It's a beanie," I correct her. "I don't know anyone who wears one in the summer. It looks stupid."

"I disagree one bazillion percent." Bree is practically drooling over Derek like he's a hunk of meat to be devoured in one sitting. I'm tempted to ask if she needs a bib. "If a guy looks like that, he can wear whatever he wants. Introduce me to him, Ash."

"Trust me, you don't want to meet him."

"Oh, yes, I do." She nods so fast it's a wonder her head doesn't just fly right off. Monika and I give each other a knowing look. We've been friends long enough to know that when Bree's on the prowl, there's no stopping her.

When Derek reappears, I make a weak attempt to wave him over, hoping he'll ignore me. Unfortunately, he doesn't.

"Derek, this is my friend Bree," I say. "You already know Monika."

"Hey, Monika. Nice to meet you, Bree." He tips his head like a perfect southern gentleman. I'm surprised he didn't call her ma'am.

"Want to watch us?" Bree asks. She twirls her hair on her finger and flashes Derek a big smile. Oh, man. She totally bought the southern gentleman act. "We could use another opinion on our new routine. I'm the captain of the cheer squad."

Derek flashes her an appreciative glance. "I don't know much about cheerin'."

Monika eyes his physique. "So, Derek . . . do you play sports?"

"Not anymore."

"Really? With that body?" Bree cocks her head to the side for a better view of Derek's backside. "Well, then, you must work out. A lot."

It sounds like Derek is coughing, but it's obvious he's covering up a laugh. "I jog and lift weights." He shoots me a mocking look. "And I try to stay away from ice cream, Skittles, and cookies for breakfast."

"What's wrong with a little comfort food?" I ask him. "It's good for the soul."

"I'll bet."

"So, Derek," Bree interrupts. "How do you like Chicago so far? I know we don't *technically* live in Chicago, but you'll get used to us suburbanites claiming Chicago as our own."

"It's all right, I guess," he answers. "Let's just say I don't plan on claiming Chicago as my own. I'm fixin' to move back to Cali the first chance I get, then join the Navy after graduation." After glancing at me again he says, "Well, I'm gonna see if I can get the lawn mower started. It was nice chattin' with y'all."

Bree raises an eyebrow after Derek puts his earbuds in his ears and pushes our old, beat-up mower out of the garage.

"What?" I ask.

"Derek is dreamy, Ashtyn. With a body like that he'll probably end up as one of those Navy SEALs. How sexy is that!"

Sexy? Dreamy? Derek is not what dreams are made out of. More like nightmares, where the girl is continually being annoyed by a boy who haunts her. "He's not all that."

My friend looks at me as if I'm nuts. "Umm, did you take a look at those biceps, and that hair . . . and those eyes? Oh, my God, those blue eyes could make any girl melt."

"He needs a haircut and was totally showing off his body," I counter.

"I, for one, am grateful for his body. It's beautiful to look at. I'm going to ask him if he wants to hang out tomorrow night. Maybe I can get a look at those abs up close and personal." Bree practically skips over to Derek in haste, as if another girl will steal him away from her if she doesn't act fast.

Soon she's laughing at something he says.

"Girls are gonna be all over him, huh?"

Monika nods. "Oh, yeah. He's no Trey Matthews, but he's super cute."

"I don't know." I put my hands up when she looks at me like I'm nuts. "Okay, I'll admit Derek's kind of attractive if you're into that California surfer-slash-cowboy look, but he's not my type *at all*."

I look down at my charm bracelet, a reminder of my boy-friend. It doesn't escape my attention that I haven't heard from Landon since Friday night when he dropped me off. I should miss Landon more than I do. I don't know why I don't. The past few days have been a whirlwind of change, and it's like I'm trying to catch up but I'm moving in slow motion.

"What's going on with you and Landon, anyway?" Monika asks. She's got a sympathetic look on her face as if she expects me to break down and cry any second. I feel more like screaming at the top of my lungs. "For a minute I thought you two were breaking up on Friday night."

I ignore the feeling in the pit of my stomach, because I'm not sure what's going on with us. I know he likes his space when he's stressed out, so I've left him alone, but every day we don't talk I feel more distant and disconnected.

"Landon and I will be fine. We've just hit a rough patch."

Monika tilts her head to the side. She gets that look when she's overanalyzing something. "Do you and *Derek* have something going on?"

I can feel my face getting hot just thinking about it. "No way. Why would you say that?"

"I don't know." She shrugs. "I just sense a strange vibe between you two, and it's weird that you're hating on him so much." She looks back at Bree and Derek, talking to each other. "Looks like Bree is staking her claim on him already. Look, did you see that? She touches his arm every time she talks."

"She's perfected the art of flirting," I mumble. "And he's totally falling for it, although maybe she's the one being sucked into his fake charm. I have a feeling that nothing that guy does is sincere."

"Yo, Bree!" Monika yells. "Get back here so we can show Ashtyn the routine."

A car pulls into my driveway and honks, delaying the cheerleading show once again. Monika squeals in delight when Vic parks his big SUV in my driveway and she sees Jet and Trey are in the car with him.

"Epic," Jet says, completely amused as he steps out. He's wearing a baseball cap backward and he's got cutoff sweats he probably cut himself. "That's all I gotta say."

"What's epic?" I ask.

He looks confused as he brushes his perfectly styled hair to the side. "You mean you had nothing to do with it?"

"Do with what?"

"I told you it wasn't her," Vic says. "She doesn't have the balls to do it."

That is so insulting. "I have balls, Vic!"

"I *knew* it!" Jet wags his eyebrows and reaches for my waistband. "Let's see 'em, Ash."

I roll my eyes and slap his arm away.

"You need to stop having a life and go online more." Trey pulls out his phone. "Someone created this bogus profile named Payton Walters and posted pics of Bonk and his teammates holding up signs."

Oh, no. I'm almost afraid to ask. "Pictures of what?"

Jet holds out his phone. "Here, take a look."

In one picture, Bonk and a bunch of his football buddies are leaning on the back of a Jeep. They're holding a napkin that says FAIRFIELD SUCKS in big bold letters and the license plate on the car spells out DMBASS. When I take a look at the second picture, I gasp. Bonk is in Rick's Subs in Fairfield holding up a napkin that reads I WANT TO BE FREMONT'S BITCH. It's signed MATTHEW BONK #7.

"Who did this?" I ask the guys.

None of them fess up. This is crazy. The guys from Fairfield are going to freak when they see the pictures that look professionally Photoshopped. It's impressive. I wish I'd thought of it.

"Maybe it was Landon." After I suggest it, the guys eye each other as if they have big doubts.

"Yeah, right," Jet says. "Your boyfriend's such a hero."

"Have you talked to him?" Vic asks me.

I shake my head.

"Hmm," Trey says. "McKnight's been MIA since Friday night."

I don't tell them that he's been MIA in our relationship, too.

CHAPTER 13

Derek

On Monday morning I wake up late and realize everyone else is already out of the house. As I eat breakfast, I look out at the neglected backyard. This house sits on a big piece of land, but nobody cares enough to make the backyard look decent. It's as if they're making the front look good to put on a facade for everyone who passes by.

The mower I found yesterday is in crap condition, but at least I got the engine to start up. It's not gonna be easy to cut the grass since the entire backyard is a haven for overgrown weeds, but I need to busy myself or I'll go insane.

I turn on the mower and put on my headphones so I can zone out like I did yesterday when the girls were over and Ashtyn's teammates came by. My mom used to tell me that music always helped her escape to another place. She used to make me listen to Ella Fitzgerald and Louis Armstrong, especially when she was in the hospital going through chemo. At first I hated it, but then those singers became a symbol of her.

Moving on is fucking tough.

An hour later I'm sweating my ass off. Little pieces of grass stick to my back, arms, and legs. I look back at my progress, proud that I've made a sizable dent. The shed, the place where Ashtyn and I first met, has seen better days. I spotted some old paint in there and figure it's long overdue for a new paint job.

As I soap my body in the shower, thoughts of Ashtyn invade my mind, and my body starts reacting. I reach down and fantasize for the moment, glad nobody can read my mind. Afterward, I rinse off and am about to just chill in my bedroom, but Falkor bolts to the front door panting like crazy. The poor guy wants to go out. I put the leash on him and jog toward the football field. The place is like a magnet to me.

It doesn't take long to get to the school. The football team is having practice. I watch some players do drills. Immediately I'm thinking like one of them again. I haven't been on a team in almost two years, but those plays and drills are still so familiar I could run them with my eyes closed.

Ashtyn is doing sprints. She doesn't notice me, but when she does I fully expect her to ream me out for taking her dog without permission.

I watch as she grabs a few footballs and jogs to the opposite end of the field. She moves with grace as she sets up a ball and positions herself. A couple of guys on the sidelines watch her and nod, impressed. I can tell she's so focused she isn't aware of anything but the ball and the white goalposts. She kicks the first ball through the posts with ease.

As she gets into position for another kick, she spots me in the stands. She misses her next two attempts, but keeps trying. She makes six out of ten. Not bad, but nothing to write home about.

I size up the team, something I used to do to my rivals. It's easy to spot the head coach—he's sporting a black-and-gold golf shirt and Rebels cap as he calls out plays. The guy has been ripping into the offensive linemen since I've been here, although I'm impressed with their execution. Without solid linemen, the quarterback is vulnerable and the team is weak.

I turn my attention to the current QB, a lanky guy wearing the number three on his jersey. Number three doesn't look confident even though he's got good form. He makes a few plays, but can't connect with his receivers when the defensive line rushes him.

Number three buckles under pressure. The problem is that he knows it. He's stuck in his head. He's got to stop thinking when he's in the game and let instinct take over.

After he repeats the same mistake three plays in a row, the coach grabs the QB's face mask and gives him hell. I'm too far away to hear his exact words, but I know he's getting an earful.

"Yo, Derek!" Ashtyn calls out. She throws a perfect spiral into the stands toward me, but I duck and let it fly past. It bounces onto the benches behind me and Falkor sniffs it. I haven't touched a football since the day my mom died. While instinct tells me to catch it, I'm conflicted.

"Yeah?"

"Who said you could take my dog for a walk?"

"He begged me to take him out. He obviously thinks I'm the alpha. You know dogs have a hierarchy." I shrug. "I'm just sayin'."

"Toss the ball back, will ya?"

I look at the football, lying there waiting to be put back on the field. I never thought I'd pick one up again. It's not like I'm committing to play again. *It's just a football.*

I slowly pick up the ball and toss it underhand to her, the familiar feeling of the smooth leather rolling off my fingers a reminder of the past. Most girls I know would be afraid they'd break a nail when a football comes flying at them, but Ashtyn reaches out and catches it without hesitation.

"You're not the alpha. I am." She tucks the ball under her arm and starts walking back to the field. "I'm just sayin'."

CHAPTER 14

Ashtyn

I told Derek I was the alpha, but right now I don't feel like one. I was totally off my game today. Seeing him sitting in the bleachers watching me practice only made it worse because I was self-conscious and too self-aware.

Fremont's bitch.

It's been two days and those words are still swirling in my head. This morning Dieter called me into his office to tell me he'd heard the rumor about the pictures. He told me to forget about any rivalry and just concentrate on winning.

Landon didn't show up to practice. He hasn't answered my calls or texts, either. Last year he never missed a practice or game. I called him before I left the house this morning, but his phone was off. I assume he received the e-mail showcasing the dreaded pictures of my yard. Why didn't he stop by my house like the other guys, or at least call or text me to see how I was dealing with it?

Brandon Butter, a sophomore and our backup QB, had a hard time filling Landon's shoes. When he got rushed, his passes were all over the place. I didn't want him to be discouraged, though, so I gave him a pat on the back after practice and told him he showed a great effort. I don't think he believed me, but it did make him smile and hopefully boosted his confidence. Even a little bit will help.

Even though early summer practices are optional, I know Dieter is disappointed his star QB hasn't been on the field. Truth is, we don't have a competitive backup QB and we're screwed if Landon gets hurt. He's such a solid player, nobody's been too worried about that. Until now.

After I wash up in the girls' locker room, I call Landon again. Still no answer. I text him for the fourth time today, but he doesn't text back. My heart sinks a little and I get a ping of anxiety. Is he not answering on purpose? Did he call back his old girlfriend Lily instead of me? Ugh, I'm never insecure about our relationship. I refuse to start being insecure now.

In the parking lot, Derek is leaning against my car with his feet crossed at the ankles.

Falkor barks a greeting and drools the second he sees me. "Can I have my dog back?" I ask, annoyed my dog seems to think he has a new owner. I grab the leash from Derek and kneel down to pet Falkor behind his left ear, his favorite spot. "If you want a ride home, my dog's riding shotgun." I open the door and let Falkor in the front seat.

"I don't think so." Derek leans into the car. "Falkor, get in the back."

My usually stubborn dog obediently jumps into the backseat as if Derek is a dog whisperer.

I turn on the radio as I drive home.

"You might be used to bossin' people around, but it ain't workin' for me," Derek says.

"I can't hear you," I lie, then cup a hand over my ear.

He turns the radio off. "Why the attitude? Don't act as if I asked to be here, 'cause I didn't." I wonder if he can turn that accent on and off at will. "Hell, if I didn't get expelled and Brandi wasn't knocked up, I'd have found a way to stay in Cali."

Wait a minute. Did I hear him right?

"My sister's p-pregnant?" I ask. "Pregnant, as in having a baby pregnant?"

"That's what bein' knocked up usually means."

I look at him sideways, then keep driving. When I pull into my driveway, I turn to him. "Be honest for once. You're joking about my sister having a baby, right?"

He sighs and rolls his eyes as he opens his door. Falkor jumps out after him.

I stare at the dashboard. My sister, pregnant again? She hasn't said anything, but I never heard from her once in the last seven years. Since she's been home, I've tried avoiding her like I've avoided Derek.

Brandi is just like Mom. It took me a long time to come to the realization that my mom was never coming back. Brandi's back, but it's no use getting close to her when I know she's leaving again.

It really irks me that Derek knows more about my sister than I do. And that my nephew prefers Derek over me. And that Falkor follows Derek around like he's the alpha.

I glance toward the garage and am shocked to see Landon sitting in his convertible with his sunglasses on. When did he drive up, and how long has he been there?

"Where were you today?" I walk toward him as he steps out of his car. I don't even know what to say after our fight on Friday night. I don't mention our relationship problems or Lily. "You ditched practice."

"My parents made me go to some family brunch thing," he says. "I couldn't get out of it."

"Oh." In the past, Landon's dad would never make him go to a family brunch instead of practice. Landon doesn't seem to want to elaborate. "Did you see the pictures of my house online? And the ones of Bonk?"

He nods slowly. "Yeah, I saw 'em."

"Did you post the ones of Bonk? Nobody else fessed up."

He nods. "Yeah, but keep it on the down low."

"How'd you get them to pose like that? I mean, I can't imagine Bonk posing willingly."

"I got my ways. So how was practice?"

"Butter is doing drills," I inform him. "But the guys are getting frustrated that his throws aren't accurate and his handoffs are sloppy. You know the team needs you."

There's a long, uncomfortable silence. I feel a pang of sadness as he reaches out and fingers the bracelet with a heart and football charm he got me for my birthday last year.

"Sorry about Friday night," he says. "My old man was on my case about being a leader of the team my senior year and wearing the coveted *C* like he did when he played."

I get it. Carter McKnight was a legend in Chicago when he played. He's got super high expectations. Landon always wants to meet or exceed them. Up until I was voted captain, he had.

Coach Dieter made me realize I don't want to give up being captain. I want to lead and motivate my team. I like knowing my place on the team means more than just being on that roster.

"I never wanted to take anything away from you, Landon."

He avoids looking at my eyes. "Sure. Right. I know that, Ash."

There's an awkward silence again. I don't know what to say to fix this . . . fix us. I can't change what happened or turn back time any more than he can.

He touches my charm bracelet again. "Did I mess everything up between us?"

"No." I don't want another person in my life to leave me. At least if I have Landon, I'm not alone. "But . . . you made me feel awful Friday night. The whole Lily thing kind of freaked me out, and you haven't called or texted in days. I don't know what to think anymore."

"Just forget about all that."

He bends his head down to kiss me. For the moment, everything seems to be fixed. I want to believe him, but it's hard. Since my mom left, I haven't fully trusted anyone. Even Landon.

We talk about practice. I ask if he's started packing for our Texas trip at the end of the month. We've both been accepted to

Elite, a football training camp that's practically impossible to get into. Only top high school players in the country are admitted. The plan is to drive there and stay in posh hotels for free by redeeming the frequent traveler points Landon's dad has racked up and said we could use.

"So what's the deal with that Derek dude?" Landon asks. He looks over my shoulder. Derek is mowing the lawn while listening to music with his earbuds. I have no clue why he wants to fix our place up. It's not like my dad cares if the backyard looks nice. Dad mows the front of the house every couple of weeks, so everyone who passes can think that we're doing just fine. The backyard represents us better.

"I have no idea. All I know is that we've agreed to stay out of each other's way and I'm pretending he doesn't exist." It's not exactly true. I'm trying to pretend he doesn't exist, but he's not letting me do a good job of it.

Landon gestures to my house. "Your old man home?"

"I don't know. Probably not, since his car is gone." He prefers to go to work, where he can drown himself in projects at the accounting firm he works at.

Landon pulls me close and whispers into my ear, "How about you and me go up to your room right now? I could use a back rub."

Now? I look back at Derek. "Maybe this isn't a good time."

"Come on, Ash." He takes my hand and leads me into the house. "You always say we don't get enough private time. Let's make use of it while we've got it."

In my room, Landon takes his shirt off and sprawls out on my bed. I sit beside him and start massaging his back, kneading his taut muscles.

"That feels so damn good." He moans as I rub his shoulders. "You totally relax me, Ash."

"Why don't you relax me by rubbing my foot, which is sore from kicking the ball so many times today?"

"Feet gross me out," he says. "The only feet I touch are my own." He turns to face me and slowly slips his hands under my shirt. He unhooks my bra, then rubs his thumbs over my nipples. "I can massage other parts of you, though."

I still his hand, because fooling around with him right now is not going to relax me. "Landon, I need to talk about my crazy life."

His hands are still on my breasts when he puts his lips on my neck. He kisses my pulse, then licks it over and over. It reminds me of Falkor when he slobbers on my face. "So talk. I'm listening."

When he starts sucking on my neck about to give me a hickey, I push him off me. "You're not listening. You're trying to distract me."

"You're right. Can I listen to you later? Now all I want to do is mess around." Within seconds, his pants are unzipped. He glances at his groin, a not-so-subtle cue for me to go down on him.

I look down at the twitching material of his boxers. "I'm just not into it right now."

"You serious? C'mon, Ash," he moans in a frustrated voice. "You know you want it. I want it. Let's do this."

CHAPTER 15

Derek

The bed squeaks above me.

I look at Falkor.

He looks at me.

I took a break from mowing and came inside to cool off, but knowing Ashtyn and her boyfriend are upstairs fooling around is making me nauseous. "Tell me why I have the urge to go up there and kick her boyfriend out of the house?"

Falkor picks his head up as if he's going to answer, but instead starts humping one of his stuffed toys.

"You need a girlfriend," I tell the dog. He looks at me with his droopy gray eyes, then cocks his head to the side. I can imagine him saying "You're just jealous."

When her boyfriend kissed her outside, I didn't miss the silent "fuck you, she's mine" vibe he sent me. Ashtyn is oblivious. The guy obviously thinks he's God's gift to the universe, with his black Corvette convertible and dark sunglasses he doesn't even take off when he's kissing her. That's like keeping your socks on when you're having sex—complete douche move. I'm surprised Ashtyn fell for that kind of guy, whose car is an extension of his dick.

Why I feel protective of Ashtyn is beyond me. The girl can take care of herself and doesn't need me to protect her virtue.

The bed above squeaks again. Shit, I can't listen to this and stay sane.

I head back to the yard, ready for round two. I turn on the mower and listen to music.

Hearing that squeaky bed, knowing that dude is touching her, makes me want to punch him. I've got no right to feel this way, which sucks even more.

After pushing the mower through a patch of overgrown weeds, I look at her bedroom window. I don't know what's up with me. I'm not into girls like Ashtyn. She's not my type. I like girls who just want a good time and don't take life too seriously. So why do I keep thinking about what it would be like to kiss her and feel her hands on me?

After Landon leaves and Ashtyn is about to walk back to the house after kissing him good-bye, I take my earbuds out. "Please tell me you didn't get back together with him," I call out from across the yard.

She eyes me up and down. "Pull your pants up. They're sagging. I can see your underwear."

The girl is a master at avoiding the subject. "I mean, seriously, who wears sunglasses when they kiss a girl?"

"Who I date and how I kiss is really none of your business."

Damn. I shake my head and step closer. "You know when a guy is bullshittin' you, don't ya?"

She gives an impatient eye roll. "You should know, right?"

"Absolutely." I'm standing in front of her now. I lift her chin with my thumb and forefinger until our eyes lock. Damn, she's beautiful. Every time I catch her looking at me, it's hard to look away. Now isn't any different. "A guy is bullshittin' you when he doesn't look you in the eye," I say.

She breaks eye contact. "Stop."

"Stop what?"

"Making me question my relationship with Landon. I can do that without your help, thank you very much." She swats my hand away and storms into the house.

That was interesting. I'm about to go after her when my cell rings. It's Ashtyn's friend Bree.

"Hey," Bree says when I answer. "I was just wondering if you wanted to go out Saturday night?"

"Saturday?"

"I think it would be cool if we got to know each other better. You know, because you'll need someone to show you the ropes at school. Ashtyn's kind of preoccupied with Landon and football. I can fill in the gaps."

The gaps. There's so many fucking gaps in my life it's comical. I've got to start making changes right now, because if I keep going on the same path I'm liable to go insane.

"Yeah," I tell her, knowing I've got to fill in those gaps sooner rather than later. Avoiding Ashtyn is what I need to do to keep me sane. "Sounds great."

CHAPTER 16

Ashtyn

Parties in Fremont are legendary, especially when they're at Jet's house. His dads are out of town for the weekend, so he's throwing the first bash of the summer. Landon picked me up. I'm determined to make things right between us.

Landon takes my hand as we walk through the door. Jet is sitting in the living room playing a drinking game he made up called Fact or BS. I've played it before. One thing about playing Fact or BS—someone is going to be completely wasted by the end of the night.

Jet motions for us to join them. It's obvious they started playing a while ago, because Jet's eyes are bloodshot and Vic is smiling like he doesn't have a care in the world. Vic hardly ever smiles. He's always brooding and pissed that his dad runs his life.

Jet moves over so we can sit next to him. "Yo, Ashtyn. Fact or BS . . ."

"I'm not playing, Jet," I say. The last time we played, Jet got so drunk he started puking all over the place. We thought he had alcohol poisoning.

"C'mon, Capt'n, don't be such a party pooper. Fact or BS . . . Monika and I hooked up in seventh grade."

I look over at Monika and Trey. She's sitting on his lap with her arms wrapped around his neck.

That's an easy one. "That'd be bullshit."

"That's right," Monika says proudly. "I'm not into pasty white guys. I like my men as dark as I like my chocolate. Right, baby?"

Trey kisses her. "That's right."

"That's just because you've never been with a pasty white guy," Jet says jokingly, making Trey roll his eyes and Monika laugh.

Jet takes a shot as a bunch of girls from school walk in. Including Bree, who's wearing a black off-the-shoulder minidress that barely covers her . . .

"Damn! Bree is definitely looking for some action tonight," Jet says under his breath and gives a low whistle.

Derek walks in. Bree looks back at him and smiles, then takes his elbow and leads him to sit with us.

"Hey, guys!" she says, completely excited to have Derek as her date. I don't miss the stares from everyone else interested in finding out more about the new guy on her arm. Derek didn't tell me he was coming here tonight. He was holed up in his room and hadn't given me a clue that he was going out with Bree.

"Derek's a Fact or BS virgin," Landon says. "I think we need to de-virginize him."

Jet nods in agreement.

"I don't think so," I protest.

"We're playing a little drinking game we call Fact or BS. You up for it, Derek?" Landon asks, ignoring me.

I nudge my boyfriend and give him an angry glare. "Landon, don't."

"What?" Landon gestures to Derek. "You want to play, don't you? I mean, if you don't think you can handle it . . ."

"Hit me with it," Derek says without hesitation as if Landon is challenging his manhood.

"Here are the rules," Landon says. "First, you have to take a shot. They're only spiked Jell-O shots. Then you have to answer without thinking."

Derek nods. He has no clue the shot has more vodka than Jell-O.

"I sling a question at you," Landon explains further. "Then you sling a question at me. For every answer you think is a fact, you take another shot. For every answer that you hesitate on, you take another shot. If you think my answer is BS, you say 'BS'—and if you're right, you don't have to take another shot. I can challenge you on the BS call, and the group takes a vote. Majority rules."

"Fair enough," Derek says, not the least bit intimidated. I don't tell him that usually you only have to drink if you hesitate, and you don't have to take a shot beforehand, but Landon seems to be making up his own rules tonight.

Two bucks going head-to-head isn't going to end well. I need to stop this game before it starts. "Landon, don't do this."

"It's cool, Ash," Derek says. "I got this."

Bree weaves her arm through Derek's. "Let them play, Ash. Don't be a party pooper."

I should get up and refuse to watch the disaster about to happen, but Landon has one arm wrapped around my waist and urges me to stay.

Derek and Landon each down a shot. I predict they're both going to have one hell of a hangover in the morning and I'm not happy.

Landon clears his throat. "Fact or BS. You trim your ball sac."

Derek doesn't break eye contact with Landon as he picks up a shot glass and downs it in one gulp.

Derek leans forward. "You hate that Ashtyn got voted captain."

"BS."

Derek shakes his head at Landon's answer. "You're lyin'. I call BS on your BS."

"That's not part of the game. Fact or BS, you hate living in Fremont."

Derek takes another shot, then fires his own question. "Everyone thinks you're a dick."

Landon takes a shot.

"Fact or BS . . . you've jerked off to thoughts of my girlfriend."

"Landon!" I cry.

"What?" Landon puts his hands up, like he's completely innocent. "We're just playing a game."

Derek doesn't answer or look at me.

"I'll bet that's fact," Trey mumbles under his breath.

"You want to go there?" Derek asks Landon, all fired up now. "You really want to get personal like that?"

"Yeah, let's go there."

Derek downs another shot. "You're fucking around with some chick behind Ashtyn's back."

What's going on? This is completely screwed up, and I'm caught in the middle. Landon is pissed and rushes to his feet. Derek did not just say what I think he just said. It's a complete lie but now everyone is looking at us.

"Stop!" I yell, but nobody's listening. I give Jet and Vic pleading looks, but Vic is out of it and Jet is too amused to stop this.

"Take a shot," Derek says, seemingly content with himself. "You hesitated."

Landon narrows his eyes as he picks up the shot glass and downs it, then slams the glass on the table. Landon does not like being bested, and there's about to be a showdown.

"Ashtyn's mine, you know," Landon says.

"That's what you think," Derek shoots back. "You're not the one shackin' up with her every night."

Derek swallows. And glances at me. His lies feel like a hard slap in the face. My face feels hot and the rest of my body feels numb. He didn't just say that.

I push past him and run out of the house.

CHAPTER 17

Derek

A shtyn, wait!" I call out as I leave the house and rush after her. She's walking down the street.

"My life isn't a game, Derek."

"I didn't say it was." I feel the slight slur of my words as the alcohol hits my system. My thoughts are clear for the moment, though. If anyone's not thinking clearly, it's Ashtyn. She'd even left her jacket behind, but I grabbed it. "What are you blamin' me for? Landon made me play the stupid game. It didn't even make sense."

"I'm blaming both of you for coming up with the stupid questions and both of you for making people think about whether or not Landon's cheating on me or if you and I are getting it on. If you can't keep your ego in check, stay home."

I'm not going to let her off that easy. "I already told you I didn't ask to come to Chicago, Sugar Pie. I got suckered into it, just like I got suckered into playin' your boyfriend's stupid little game."

"I told you not to play, but no! Your ego got in the way of your brain and those shaved balls of yours."

"I didn't say I shaved them. I trim."

She looks at me as if I'm nuts. "Same difference. You were supposed to stay out of my life, while I stayed out of yours. That was the deal, but you keep breaking it."

"How the hell was I supposed to know he'd ask me a question about you? What's the problem, anyway? Give me a fuckin' break. Reality check, Ashtyn. I'm a teenage guy with raging hormones who hasn't had a lot of action lately . . . I admit I jerk off. I'm sorry I got caught up in your boyfriend's game of who's got the bigger dick."

"You're insane, Derek Fitzpatrick. Certifiably insane."

Drunk is more like it.

"I can't believe you and Landon have somehow managed to involve me in your little game of one-upping each other," she continues. "You know people are going to gossip now, don't you?"

I rake my hand through my hair and wish I wasn't having this conversation. "I don't really give a shit what the people in this town think."

Landon comes out of the house with a bunch of people following him. "Ashtyn, come here."

Ashtyn looks at me as if I'm the enemy. "Just so you know, you're my least favorite nephew," she says through clenched teeth, then walks over to Monika. "Take me home," she pleads to her friend.

After she gets into Monika's car, music from inside the house reminds me that the party is still going strong. And Bree is probably wondering why I didn't call BS on Landon's stupid comment about me jerking off while thoughts of Ashtyn race through my brain. I walk through the maze of people until I reach Bree.

"Can we talk?"

Bree puts her hand on my cheek. "You're so cute. If you're going to apologize, don't. I know you were just bullshitting to get Landon off your case. I think you succeeded."

"Thanks."

She kisses me on the lips. "My pleasure."

We stay at the party a little while longer, but soon I'm so wasted all I want to do is sleep it off. At some point Bree wants to leave and we get a ride from someone who didn't have one too many Jell-O shots. As I walk in the house, I know I've got to straighten things out with Ashtyn.

She made it clear that she doesn't want to have anything to do with me, so why can't I erase her from my head? What did I think, just because I feel a connection to her that she'd feel the same way or believe that her boyfriend is unfaithful?

That's a joke. It's actually a good thing Ashtyn resents my presence in her life, because if she didn't we could really complicate our already complicated lives. I'm eternally thankful the front door is unlocked, but my luck is short-lived. Brandi's still awake. She's standing in front of the computer, taking a video of herself. It's kind of weird that she's got her shirt pulled up to show off her growing stomach.

"I'm home." I walk past the office, trying to hide any hint that I've been drinking.

"Hey, Derek. I'm recording how big my stomach is every day. I figure when your dad gets home he'll want to see the progress." She rubs her bare belly, which is something I definitely didn't have to see. "I miss him tons. Come record a message for your dad."

I wave into the camera and hope he won't notice I'm wasted when he watches it. "Hey, Dad. Hope you're accomplishing whatever you need to in the middle of the ocean. Peace."

It sucks having my dad so far away, especially knowing I can't talk to him. When he's away I feel like he's an acquaintance, someone on the fringes of my life but not actually in it.

Before I leave the office, Brandi says, "How much did you drink tonight?"

"A lot."

"I smelled it on you the second you stepped close." She pulls down her shirt to cover her belly. "Okay. Well, I guess I should, you know, tell you that it's probably not a good idea to drink when you're underage."

"Did you do it?"

She nods. "Yes. I'm probably not one to preach about the benefits of staying away from high school parties. Just . . . don't go overboard, okay? Or don't do it at all, which is probably what I'm supposed to say. If your dad knew, I'm sure he wouldn't be happy—"

"Tell him if you want." At this point, what's he gonna do? It's not like he can ground me or take my car away. He's not here to enforce any kind of rules. Nobody is.

She shakes her head. "How about if I leave it up to you to tell him?"

"Cool." Life is back to the normal state of abnormality in a matter of seconds. Before I leave I turn back to Brandi. "You know where Ashtyn is?"

"Yeah. She's upstairs sleeping. Is everything okay between you two?"

I rub the back of my neck. "I don't know."

"You want some advice?" Before I can tell her to keep her opinions to herself, she puts her hands up and exclaims, "My sister lives hard and loves hard. It's in her nature, just like me."

I think for a minute, which is pretty tough to do when I'm this buzzed. "Thanks, Brandi."

Brandi smiles proudly. "You're welcome. Good night, Derek."

" 'Night."

When I was younger, my mom used to lie in bed with me and we'd make up stories. She'd start a sentence, and I'd finish it. *"There once was a boy named . . ."* she'd start and I'd insert, *"Derek."* Then she'd continue, *"One day, Derek wanted to go to . . ."* and I'd insert whatever place I wanted and together we'd come up with a wild adventure. Every night she came into my room, and every night we'd continue the ritual. When I got too old for those stories, she'd give me advice about girls, school, football, and anything else that I wanted to talk about.

Brandi is totally unlike my mom, so I miss her all the more. I just want to be able to talk to my mom one more time, see her smile at me one more time, create one of our mom-son stories one more time. I'd do anything to ask her what to do about Ashtyn, because she'd probably have the answer.

I guess I'm on my own to figure it all out.

I strip down to my boxers, curse my trimmed balls, and go upstairs to brush my teeth. On my way out of the bathroom, I remember that I forgot to give Ashtyn the jacket she'd left at the party. After going downstairs and grabbing it from my room, I stand in front of her door. I'd knock softly, but I'm afraid Falkor will start barking like a mad dog and wake Julian in the room next to hers.

"Ashtyn," I say quietly. The door is slightly ajar. I push the door open further and peek inside.

Falkor is sleeping at the foot of her bed, a guardian to his princess. I walk in with the sole purpose of putting her jacket on her desk chair, but when I glance at Ashtyn lying in bed with her eyes open just staring at me, I freeze.

"Go away," she says bitterly.

I hold up the jacket. "You left this at the party. You could pretend to be grateful and say thank you."

"Sorry. *Thank you so very much* for bringing back my jacket," she says sarcastically. "Now *please* put it down, then *please* go away."

I drape her jacket over the chair. She wants to hate me so much, but why? Suddenly it dawns on me. "I think you like me." The words are out before I can take them back.

"Really?"

"Yep. When you're ready to admit it, let me know."

CHAPTER 18

Ashtyn

The greatest part about having close friends is that they know everything about your life.

The worst part about having close friends is that they know everything about your life.

Monika comes over in the morning with two lattes in hand. She hands me one while she sits on the edge of my bed and takes small sips from the other.

"Want to talk about it?"

I take a sip of the hot liquid and sigh. "Talk about what? The fact that Landon and I aren't getting along, or the fact that Derek Fitzpatrick is the bane of my existence?"

"Bane of your existence? That's harsh, especially for you. Normally you're the one supporting the guys. You're like the go-to BFF for guys, Ashtyn. You get guys. What's the problem with Derek?"

I slide the covers off. "He brings out the worst in me."

"Why is that?"

I shrug. "I don't know. He doesn't take anything seriously. Oh, except what he eats. Did I tell you he's obsessed with eating healthy?" I throw my hands up. "He won't even touch a Skittle. And he leaves the toilet seat up on purpose—just to annoy me. I almost fell in the other day." I'm getting fired up just thinking about how much Derek has infused his way into my life. I pace while I drink the latte.

"He's gotten to you."

"Tell me about it." I look at Monika sideways and know what's going on in her head. My best friend thinks she's got a knack for interpreting people and situations. "Don't overanalyze this."

Monika downs the rest of her latte. "I won't. If you don't over-analyze what I'm about to tell you."

"What?"

"It's about me and Trey."

I sit next to Monika. I've been such a shitty friend, so self-absorbed that I've neglected asking how my best friend is doing. I guess I just think Monika has this perfect life and perfect rela-tionship with Trey that I don't expect her to have any issues. "What's wrong?"

"Nothing's wrong. It's just . . ." She lies back on my bed and moans. "So Trey and I . . ."

I motion for her to continue. "You're not breaking up, are you?" I ask when she hesitates. I've never revealed to her that Vic-tor has had the biggest crush on her since freshman year. I've been sworn to secrecy and would never betray Vic's trust.

"No! Nothing like that. Promise me you won't tell anyone."

"You have my word."

She sighs heavily. "We haven't done it." She grabs my pillow and covers her face, completely embarrassed.

I lift up the corner of the pillow. "What do you mean? Like sex?"

"Yeah."

"Wait. I thought you guys did it on Valentine's Day." Trey saved for months and planned this super romantic evening. He rented a hotel room and took her to dinner. I helped him plan the night, because he wanted to make sure it was perfect for her. "When I asked how it went, you said it was the best night of your life. In fact, I happen to remember you saying it was *magical*."

"I lied."

"Why?"

Monika used to tell me that losing her virginity was no big deal, and if Trey wanted to do it she was all for it. I know they fool around. Most of the time they can't keep their hands off each other.

"We had dinner, then went to the hotel and we were fooling around. It just felt weird and forced, you know. I wasn't into it." She starts peeling off her nail polish. "Trey said it was fine and we'd do it when we were both ready, but I know he was disappointed."

It's so weird to hear the truth from her, because the way Trey talks when she's not around, you'd think they were doing it every chance they got. I've heard him say they did it three times one night. And they did it at Ravinia under blankets during a concert. And in the back of his car on several occasions; he'd said one time the condom broke. He makes it sound like they have a crazy active sex life, which secretly drives Vic nuts.

How do I balance the relationship I have with Monika and the friendship I have with Trey and Vic? The guys aren't just my teammates. They confide in me. Obviously Trey didn't want to reveal the truth about his sex life. It's such a guy thing.

I pat Monika's hand. "Your secret is safe with me."

"I love him, Ashtyn. Seriously, I know this sounds stupid but I totally fantasize about marrying Trey and having kids with him one day. I swear he's my soul mate. I want to make love with him and he's always so slow and patient with me. I'm just . . . I don't know. Maybe something's wrong with me."

"Nothing's wrong with you, Monika. You're just not ready."

"I wish my parents didn't hate him. They can't even look past the fact that he lives in The Shores."

The Shores is the apartment complex on the south side of town. It's not the safest place to live in Fremont, and there are definitely some gang members living there, but Trey has stayed away from all the crap. His parents might not be the richest family in town, but they're super close and Trey's dad is the funniest guy I've ever met.

Monika seems more relaxed now that I know the truth. She pops off my bed like she's propelled by a spring, then looks out my window. "So what's Derek's story?"

"I don't know. He's from California, his dad's in the Navy, he doesn't eat junk food, and he got kicked out of some academy for letting pigs loose. That's it."

"Does he have a girlfriend?"

I shrug.

"Does he like Bree, or does he have the hots for you like Landon suggested?"

I laugh. "I assure you he doesn't have the hots for me. He just likes to piss me off."

"That's foreplay."

"You're crazy. Listen, I know you want to be some sort of superspy or FBI investigator one day, but Derek is off-limits as a subject."

"Why?"

"Just . . . because. I don't want him interfering in my life, and I promised not to interfere in his. It's that simple."

My best friend laughs. "Doesn't sound like a good enough reason to me." She puts her hand on my shoulder. "Listen, my friend. I think we need to do a reconnaissance mission and find out more about the guy living in your den." She heads downstairs with purpose and determination.

I hurry after her. "We're not going to spy on him."

"Why not?"

"Because it's not cool and probably illegal."

The door to the den is open. Monika walks inside without hesitating. "Keep a lookout and let me know if he's coming," she instructs.

"For the record, I'm against spying."

"For the record, you're curious about what I'm going to find."

I can't argue with her there.

My heart is racing as I peek through one of the windows in the den and watch Derek push our lawn mower through the tall grass. He's got his shirt tucked into his back pocket and his muscled back is glistening with sweat. I duck so he can't see me watching him if he happens to look in this direction.

"He sure does like boots." Monika holds up a brown leather boot. When she puts it back down, a bunch of hundred-dollar bills fall out. "Whoa. He's loaded. Where did he get the money from?" she asks as she shoves the bills back in the boot.

"I have no clue. Let's get out of here."

"Wait. Well, well . . . lookie here!" Monika says as she lifts the top of Derek's suitcase. "Seems like your boy wears boxer briefs, wears Calvin Klein cologne, and plays poker. Maybe he won all that money playing poker."

"Poker?"

Monika reaches in his suitcase and pulls out a bunch of poker chips. "Yep. He's obviously a gambler."

She abandons the suitcase while I glance back at the window. Derek is now gathering the cut grass and shoving it into bags. She peeks into some boxes, but doesn't find anything.

"Ooh, his wallet!"

I rush over to Monika as she opens his brown leather wallet. "You can't look in his wallet."

"Why not?"

I grab it out of her hand. "Because that's, like, super personal."

"Exactly. What better way to find out about someone? Besides his phone, a boy's wallet is a window to his soul."

"Really?" I hear Derek's voice behind us. "I've never heard that before."

Oh, crap!

I whip around and wish I wasn't the one holding the evidence of us snooping. Derek eyes the wallet, then me. My heart skips a beat. I feel like a kid who just got caught with her hand in the cookie jar. I quickly toss the wallet on his bed and step back, as if that will somehow erase my involvement in this scheme.

"Hi, Derek," I manage to croak out. "We were just . . ." I look to Monika for help.

Monika walks over to Derek with an innocent smile on her face. "Ashtyn and I were having a disagreement, and we *had* to come in your room to settle it."

"What was the disagreement?" he asks.

"That's a good question," I mutter under my breath.

"Yes, that *is* a good question," Monika agrees. Derek looks mighty amused right now as we struggle to come up with something that doesn't sound like the truth—that we were snooping around his room to get intel on him. He doesn't look mad or nervous that we might have found out that he plays poker and is stashing a bunch of cash in his boot.

I might as well try to get us out of this. "We wanted to know if you . . ."

"Carry a condom in your wallet!" Monika points to his wallet. "Yes. That's it! Ashtyn bet that guys carry condoms in their wallets, and I said that's, like, something guys did in the '80s."

Condoms? Couldn't Monika come up with something less . . . embarrassing?

The side of his mouth quirks up. "So what's the verdict, ladies?"

I glance at his wallet. "We didn't have a chance to find out, but that's okay."

Derek picks the wallet up and hands it to me. "Here. Open it. You came all the way down here to find out, why stop now?"

I clear my throat as I stare at it. Monika gestures for me to just get it over with. I clear my throat again, then unfold the thing and peek inside. There's a bunch of bills. I check the side pocket and slide out a picture of a pretty woman wearing a bright blue dress standing next to a guy in Navy whites. It must be his parents, because the woman has Derek's eyes and the man has Derek's chiseled bone structure. I check the other side pocket, which is empty.

"No condom," I say.

He takes the wallet from me. "I guess you lose."

CHAPTER 19

Derek

A week after Ashtyn and Landon made up, she walks into the kitchen and tosses a FedEx envelope on the table. "This is addressed to you." She turns and opens the pantry.

A FedEx letter? At first a pang of dread settles inside me, thinking that it might be bad news about my dad. But bad news to families of military personnel doesn't come by FedEx. The time to panic is when a couple of guys in uniform show up on your doorstep.

I wince when I look at the return address. It's from my grand-mother in Texas, my mom's mom. How the hell did she know where I was? She used to send the obligatory birthday gift, but I haven't personally heard from her in years.

My grandmother Elizabeth Worthington hated that my par-ents married. My dad wasn't from upper-crust Texas society like my mom. When they got married, my mom's parents cut her off. My grandmother didn't even come to my mom's funeral. Instead, she sent a truckload of flowers. What did she think, that flowers were bandages that would replace all the years lost? Fat chance of that.

I don't give a shit what *Elizabeth Worthington* has to say to me. I toss the unopened envelope in the trash.

"What did it say?" Ashtyn asks, turning around with a stack of cookies in her hand. Obviously she's clueless to the fact that I never opened the thing.

"I thought we weren't supposed to pry into each other's business."

"I'm just curious. Besides, you owe me one."

"For what?"

She opens her mouth wide in shock. "Come on, Cowboy. You said you weren't going to interfere in my life, and all of a sudden you're fist-pumping my guy friends, playing stupid drinking games with my boyfriend, and flirting with my girlfriends."

"Flirting? With who?"

"Duh. Bree."

I hold a hand up. "Listen, the girl asked if the gas and the oil go in the same hole in the mower or separate ones. Then she called and asked if I'd go out with her Saturday night. What'd you want me to do, ignore her?"

"If you really think she was interested in gas and oil, you're an idiot. She wants to get into your pants."

"What's wrong with that?" When she doesn't answer, I say, "If you must know what's in the FedEx envelope, it's a letter of acceptance from the US Olympic team," I lie.

Her eyebrows go up. "For what?"

"Men's synchronized trampolining." I brush imaginary dust off my shoulders. "I don't like to brag, but I won gold at the national championships last year."

"There's no such thing as synchronized trampolining, Derek."

I pat the top of her head like she's a kid. "Yes, there is."

She rolls those sparkling, bright eyes that draw me in. I tell myself I like annoying the crap out of her, but the truth is that I like being around her when she's all riled up. "You're such a liar."

Ashtyn is wrong. What's worse is that she thinks she's not. "Wanna bet on it, Sugar Pie?"

She puts her hands on her hips. "Yeah, I wanna bet on it. And then we'll go to the computer so I can prove it to you."

This is getting interesting. "What's the bet, then?"

She thinks for a minute, then rubs her hands together as if she's come up with the most brilliant idea. "If I win, you have to eat an *entire* bag of Skittles."

"The purple ones, too?" I laugh. The girl doesn't know how to play in the big leagues. "Done. And if I win, you gotta go out with me some night."

She swallows, hard. "Wh . . . what? I don't think I heard you right because I thought you just said 'go out with you.'"

"Only if I win," I clarify.

"Whoa, like, on a *date*? Umm . . . I have a boyfriend, remember?"

"Don't get too excited, Sugar Pie. Did I say anythin' about a date? I just said you had to go out with me some night. If I win, that is."

"Landon won't like it."

"Ask me if I give a shit."

"Do you give a shit about *anything*?" she asks me.

"Not really."

"That's pathetic," she says, then disappears. Soon she's back carrying her laptop and wearing a cocky grin. "I've got an entire bag of Skittles with your name on it in the pantry, Cowboy. Jumbo size," she adds.

My mouth curves in a mischevious grin. "And I've got an entire night planned. Just for you."

She doesn't look the least bit worried as she searches "Olympic synchronized trampoline." It doesn't take long for her expression to change and the cockiness to vanish. She leans forward with furrowed eyebrows while a huge grin forms on my face. Usually her every move is calculated, but not now. As she scans various websites that prove I'm right, she sits back and wrinkles her cute little nose, defeated. "It's a real sport," she mumbles.

"I told you. Next time you should trust me."

She focuses those gray eyes on me as she slumps in the chair. "I don't trust anyone."

"That sucks."

She nods. "Sure does."

"Well, call me an optimist, but I for one believe trust can be earned. Maybe I'll surprise you and change your mind."

"Doubt it."

I give her a gentle chuck on the chin. "Ah, a challenge. I like those."

I leave Ashtyn to stew about going out with me and find Julian in his room, looking at a picture book about sandcastles. Julian points to a huge, detailed creation with moats and bridges. "Daddy made a sandcastle with me the last time we were at the beach." He puts the book down. "That was before he went on the big submarine."

Daddy. That's what I used to call my dad when I was Julian's age. The kid never met his own father, so it shouldn't surprise me that he considers my dad his dad, too. But it does. It's like every time I turn around, I'm reminded I'm part of a new family and my old one is fading fast. I want to reject it all, but when I look at the kid . . . I don't know. I feel connected to him, like a big brother would.

I kneel next to my stepbrother and say, "Well, how about you ask your mom if you can get into a bathing suit and you and I can go to the beach to build a sandcastle."

"Really?" He tosses the book on his bed and pops up with a huge grin. "Yeah!"

At the beach, Julian gets all excited once we start digging in the sand. A couple of other kids watch us and start building their own creations nearby. Julian sits a little taller knowing he's got the biggest, best castle by far.

"That's my big brother," he tells one of the kids who admires the impressive moat we created.

"Want to help us?" I ask the kid. "We could use a couple more hands."

Once that kid joins us, others crowd around. Soon we've amassed a small army of mini soldiers who gaze up at me as if

I'm some kind of sandcastle god, and they're talking to Julian as if he's twelve instead of five. Our creation looks like an entire kingdom now, with multiple castles and moats and tunnels.

When I'm ready to call it quits on the castle making, I race Julian into Lake Michigan to wash off the sand. I show him how to float, supporting his back. We splash and play until the little guy starts getting sunburned, so he climbs on my shoulders as I carry him back to shore.

He leans down and hugs my neck. "I'm glad you're my brother, Derek."

I glance up at his little face, looking at me as if I'm his hero. "I'm glad, too."

The fact that Julian's own father abandoned him, and now my dad is away, makes me the only male in his life. I wish his grandfather took an interest in him, but I haven't seen Gus have an interest in anything except disappearing and being grumpy.

After we dry off and are ready to leave, Julian agrees to go grocery shopping with me. I stock up on yogurt and kale and fruits and vegetables I bet have never graced the Parker household before.

Back at home, the FedEx envelope from my grandmother has magically resurfaced from the trash. It's on my pillow. And it's open. Shit. Ashtyn had something to do with this, no doubt.

I find Ashtyn in the living room, intently watching some reality show while munching on potato chips. Her hair is in a braid again and she's wearing cutoff sweats and a T-shirt with the words FREMONT ATHLETICS on it.

I wave the envelope in front of her face. "Why did you take this out of the trash?"

"Why did you lie about it? It's not an invitation to be on the synchronized trampoline team." She tosses a chip to Falkor and sits up. "It's from your grandmother."

"So?"

"You didn't even read it, Derek."

"And it's your business because . . ."

"It's not my business," she says. "It's yours, so read it."

I don't want to know what's in the letter. It's in the category of things I don't care about. "Are you aware it's illegal to open someone else's mail? Does violation of privacy mean anythin' to you?"

Ashtyn doesn't look guilty at all as she pulls another chip from the bag and pops it into her mouth. "It wasn't yours anymore. You threw it out. Legally speaking, it's not a violation of privacy."

"What are you, a lawyer now? How about the next time you get a letter I open it? That cool with you?"

"If I toss it out, it's fair game. You're more than welcome to have at it." She points at the envelope in my hand with her greasy fingers. "You *need* to read that letter, Derek. It's important."

"When I want your advice, I'll ask for it. In the meantime, stay out of my personal stuff." I walk in the kitchen and toss the letter in the garbage for a second time, then take out a blender.

"Why are you and Auntie Ashtyn fighting again?" Julian asks as he walks in and watches as I pull stuff from the fridge.

"We're not fightin'. We're arguin'. Want a snack?"

He nods. "Did you know it takes more muscles to frown than smile?"

"At least I'm giving my face muscles a workout." I make Julian a banana yogurt and spinach smoothie in the blender, then hand him a tall glass. "Here you go. Enjoy."

"It's *green*." He stares at the liquid as if it's poison. "I . . . I don't like green drinks."

My mom would get up every Sunday morning and make us both smoothies. We had a ritual of clinking our glasses together before downing them. "Try it." I pour a glass for myself and hold up my glass. "Cheers."

"Derek, no kid wants to drink that healthy crap." Ashtyn pulls out a box of cookies and a bag of marshmallows from the pantry. "Julian, I'll make you something that doesn't look like liquid grass."

I watch as she excitedly makes little cookie sandwiches with marshmallows and nukes them in the microwave.

"You have to be careful not to cook them too long," she says. She peeks into the little microwave window that's probably nuking her brain cells along with her cookie sandwiches. "Otherwise you'll burn the marshmallows."

She takes the plate out and displays it for Julian, proud of her creation. Julian looks at the cookie sandwiches, then the smoothie, then at me, and finally Ashtyn. Julian is the final judge of our little competition.

"I think I'll just have string cheese." Julian pulls some out of the fridge and waves it at us as he walks out. "Bye!"

Ashtyn makes a big deal out of eating her rejected sandwiches while I attempt to ignore her blissful moaning as she takes bite after bite. Those moans make me think about things I have no right thinking about. When she's done, she pulls the FedEx letter out of the trash again.

"Just let it go."

"No." She holds it out to me and practically shoves it in my hand. "Read it."

"Why?"

"Because your grandmother is sick and wants to see you. I think she's dying."

"I don't give a shit." At least I don't want to give a shit. I put down my glass and stare at the envelope.

"Come on. You're not that heartless. Take something in life seriously besides those gross smoothies of yours."

She leaves the tattered envelope on the counter. It belongs in the garbage. Oh, hell. If she hadn't taken it out and read it, I could pretend it didn't exist. I wouldn't know my grandmother is dying. Not that I should care. I don't even know the woman. She wasn't there for my mom, even when she got sick and needed her. Why should I be there for her? The simple answer is, I won't.

I grab the envelope and toss it back in the trash.

Later in the evening, Julian runs outside when he sees fireflies in the front yard. I bring a glass jar I found in the kitchen so he can catch them.

"Why do you always fight with Auntie Ashtyn?" he asks as he waits for the fireflies' butts to light up.

Leave it to the little kid to mention it again. "It's entertainin', I guess."

"My mom says that sometimes girls fight with boys because they like them."

"Yeah, well, your aunt Ashtyn doesn't like me very much."

"Do you like her?"

"Of course I like her. She's your mom's sister."

He doesn't look convinced. "If she wasn't my mom's sister, would you *still* like her?"

I decide to put it in little kid terms, so he'll understand. "Julian, sometimes girls are like junk food. They look good, and they sure taste good . . . but you know they're not healthy for you and cause cavities, so it's better to just leave 'em alone. Got me?"

He looks up at me with big, bright eyes. "So Auntie Ashtyn is like Skittles?"

I nod. "Yep. One big, jumbo bag of 'em."

"I hate going to the dentist," he says, then goes back to catching the bugs. After putting them in the jar, Julian sits on the grass and studies them. He keeps intense focus on the random flickering lights. "I wanna let them out."

"Good idea."

He unscrews the top and empties the entire jar. "Now you're free," he tells the bugs in an enthusiastic voice that resembles his mom's.

I hear the screen door open. Ashtyn walks toward us, her eyes outlined and shadowed with smoky, dark makeup. Her lips glisten with shiny lipstick. She's changed into a tight pink sundress that shows off her tan and toned curves. The way she looks could get her in trouble if the wrong guy took one look at her. Which is the real Ashtyn, the one who wears the black hoodies and T-shirts, or the one who wears the low-cut, tight clothes meant to turn guys on?

"What are you guys doing?" she asks.

"Catchin' fireflies," Julian responds, doing a pretty decent imitation of my Texas drawl.

"Can I help?"

I hold up the empty jar. "You're too late. We're done." Her faint smile fades. "Sorry 'bout that."

Julian touches a charm on her bracelet. "Cool."

"My boyfriend bought this for me," she tells him.

Her boyfriend drives up in his Vette, which explains the sexy dress.

Landon gets out of his car and pulls Ashtyn close after admiring her outfit. They kiss, but I've seen more passion when Falkor licks his nuts.

CHAPTER 20

Ashtyn

Landon takes me to dinner at a Japanese steak house. We share a table with six other people who are there to celebrate one of their birthdays. They're a rowdy group and completely wasted.

"Aren't you Carter McKnight's kid?" one of the men asks.

Landon puffs out his chest. "Sure am."

Suddenly Landon is the center of attention. He ends up talking to them about football the entire two-hour meal. They question him about the upcoming season and ask if Landon is going to follow in his father's footsteps. He nods and says, "My plan is to have a bigger career than my dad had." His statement is met with praise from the group, as if they're seeing a pro in the making. He doesn't mention that I play, too. It's all been about him tonight.

As the waitress clears our plates, Landon excuses himself to go to the bathroom. "Be right back."

A minute later his phone vibrates. He'd left his cell on the table, so I glance at the screen. It's Lily again . . . but this time she texts a picture of herself standing in front of a mirror wearing nothing but panties. She shields her breasts with one arm, her cell obviously in her other hand as she smiles into the camera. I look away, telling myself I'm not jealous of her flawless olive skin, her shiny, long black hair, or her dark, exotic eyes. I want to think she's ugly, but she's not.

Remember this? her text reads.

When Landon gets back to the table, I hand him his cell. "You got a text."

He glances at his phone, then slowly sits down. "It's not what you think, Ash."

"I think it's a naked picture of your ex-girlfriend."

The other people at the table are listening to our conversation. Landon is starting to squirm. "Can we talk about this later?" he murmurs through clenched teeth.

I don't care if he's embarrassed. "Take me home," I demand after we pay the bill. I don't wait for an answer; I head for the door.

"Let me explain," he says once we're in his car.

"Have at it. I'm sure there's a perfectly logical reason why Lily is sending you naked pictures of herself."

"It's not my fault. She wants to get back together, I guess." When he senses I'm not satisfied with his explanation, he sighs in frustration. "You know I hate the girl drama jealousy thing, Ash. There's nothing going on between me and Lily. I love you. Trust me." He avoids my gaze as he starts the car.

I remember my conversation with Derek. *A guy is bullshittin' you when he doesn't look you in the eye.* That he might be right only makes me angrier.

I'm so busy fuming that I don't realize Landon isn't driving me home until we pull up in front of Club Mystique. On the border between Fremont and Fairfield, it's our suburb's most popular club that allows entry if you're seventeen and older. Landon loves it here.

"Landon, I'm not in the mood to dance."

"If you don't want to dance, don't dance," he says, putting his hand on my knee. "We'll go to the VIP section and just chill. I'll prove to you that you're my one and only. Cool?"

I nod reluctantly. "Cool."

He squeezes my knee. "That's my girl. Trust me."

He parks out front and hands the valet his keys and a twenty-dollar tip. It's Monday night, but the place is packed because supposedly some famous DJ from LA is spinning. And it's summer, when college and high school students treat every day like it's a weekend.

Landon's arm is wrapped around me as we bypass the line and walk to the door designated for VIPs. The bouncer immediately recognizes Landon and waves us through. Most kids have to show an ID to prove they're at least seventeen. Not Landon.

I feel the floor vibrate with the beat of the music. The place is so crowded it's hard to move. It's dark except for the flashing lights on the dance floor. Landon takes my hand and leads me up the stairs to the roped-off VIP section, where anybody with either money or status is assured a seat and alcohol. We end up sitting on a red velvet couch overlooking the dance area. When a waitress comes by in a skimpy thong bikini with white ruffles to ask if he wants a shot, without checking for an "over 21" mark on his hand, Landon opens a tab and seems all too happy to be served by her. She lifts a bottle of tequila above his head and he tilts his head back, waiting for her to pour the shot straight into his waiting mouth. He shakes his head and quickly downs the liquid.

"Want to try one?" he asks me as he swipes the back of his hand across his mouth.

"No."

He slips the girl a twenty, an overly generous tip. She gives him a big thanks with a practiced wink and a smile. He eyes her butt as she heads off to serve other customers.

"What's wrong with you, Landon?" He's showing off. This isn't the Landon I know, the Landon I fell for and have been dating for months.

"Nothing. Loosen up for once, Ash. See, even Derek knows how to have a good time." He points below, where lights are flashing and the dance floor is packed.

I scan the crowd and see Derek dancing with Bree. She's got her back to him, grinding against him. Monika and Trey are dancing next to them. They're all smiling and laughing. I can't help but feel left out and annoyed. I don't own Derek and stake no claim to him, but for some stupid reason it's hard to watch him with someone else. To top off my annoyance, Derek is a great dancer and isn't afraid to tear it up on the dance floor. I would've thought if he knew any kind of dancing it'd be line dancing to country music. I never expected him to be impressive in a club with house music.

Since when do my best friend and her boyfriend double-date with Derek and Bree? I just wish they hadn't gone to the same place as us tonight. Seeing Derek here stirs something in me that I don't want to feel.

Bree turns and wraps her arms around Derek's neck. His hands are now on her waist as they move together to the music. I just want to leave so I don't have to watch them. When the song ends, he glances up. I look away so he doesn't catch me staring and somehow realize that I can get lost in those eyes of his that give a glimpse into his soul.

Landon moves closer and licks my neck. "You smell good, Ash," he whispers in my ear before sucking on my lobe and resting his hand on my inner thigh. "And you look sexy as hell." Normally I don't mind when Landon tries to turn me on, but I'm used to it being in private. This seems like a big show and completely unemotional.

"I have to go to the bathroom. I'll be right back." I grab my purse and head for the nearest restroom. I lock myself in one of the stalls and lean my head against the door as I try to force my confused emotions into order.

Seeing Derek with Bree ripped open a wound I never knew existed. I bang the back of my head against the stall door in frustration. This can't be happening. Not now, when everything was starting to fall back into place. I'm captain of the football team. My sister and nephew are back home, at least for the moment.

Derek is ruining everything, because the reality of it all hits me like an oncoming lineman in a blitz. Not only did Derek invade my house and my friends and my life . . . he's wormed his way into my heart.

I have a crush on Derek that's not about to go away anytime soon. And I have to break up with Landon.

My life is a complete mess.

I walk back to Landon and am shocked to see him talking to Matthew Bonk as if they're old buddies. It's like I'm in another dimension. Bonk and Landon hate each other. They're rivals on and off the field, so why are they smiling and giving each other high fives? Wouldn't Bonk be furious that Landon was behind posting those humiliating pictures online?

"Catch you later, man." Bonk gives Landon a pat on the back like they're teammates. The guy gives me a private, evil laugh as he passes me, reminding me of a predator about to strike.

"Why were you talking to Bonk?" I ask Landon. I have an uneasy feeling in the pit of my stomach. Landon and Bonk are from rival teams. Fairfield plays dirty on and off the field. Landon knows this. He also knows that Bonk instigates things. I don't trust him at all. Nobody on my team does.

"Sit down, Ashtyn," Landon orders.

I shake my head and step back when he reaches for my wrist. "Not until you explain why you and Bonk are suddenly acting like besties."

He reaches out again and catches my elbow this time, wrapping his fingers around my arm and forcing me to sit next to him. "Don't cause a scene."

I try to wrest free, but his grip is like a vise. He's never been like this. It's scaring me. I wince when his fingers dig into my skin.

"I'm dropping out of Fremont and transferring to Fairfield. Since I live on the borderline between the two districts, I had my pick of schools. So when they offered me their captain position, I took it," he admits.

The pain in my arm is nothing compared to the betrayal crashing down on me. "You're quitting?" Suddenly it all sinks in. "You missed practice because you were being recruited by Fairfield, not because your parents had you busy with family stuff." I narrow my eyes. "You lied!"

"I didn't lie. I took what was offered." He acts like it's no big deal to change teams. "If Fremont wants you as their captain, that's cool."

I'm trying to breathe normally even though I'm getting dizzy from shock. "If you leave, all we have is Brandon Butter. There's no way we'll make it to State."

"Listen, I gotta do what's good for me, not what's going to please everyone."

"Why take me out tonight? Why make me think everything is cool between us when all along you were going to ditch me and your teammates? You told me you loved me. Was that a lie, too?"

He shrugs.

CHAPTER 21

Derek

I try to focus on Bree so I don't look at the balcony where Landon is all over Ashtyn. This inner battle to leave her alone is being lost, because I'd like nothing better than to switch places with the guy.

The night was going just fine until Ashtyn showed up with her boyfriend.

Bree rubs against me again as if I'm her personal stripper pole. She's a good dancer. When Bree asked me to come out with her and Monika and Trey, I thought it would be a relief to have one night without Ashtyn acting like I'm ruining her life.

Hell, in reality it's the other way around. I glance up at the balcony, unable to stop myself. I expect to see Ashtyn snuggled up all cozy with Landon on that red couch.

But Ashtyn doesn't look happy to be sitting next to her boyfriend. Landon's got his fingers tightly wrapped around Ashtyn's arm. It looks like she's trying to pull away, but he's got a solid hold and won't release her. She looks alarmed and upset and . . . she winces in pain.

Fuck!

With rage firing an adrenaline rush, I shove through the crowd and rush to the stairs. There's no way I'm about to let him hurt her on my watch. I don't give a shit if she wants me to stay out of her business.

I eye the big bouncer blocking the roped-off VIP section leading to the second story. "Two chicks are fightin' over there." I point to the center of the room. "You better get there quick, 'cause I think one of 'em is gettin' her dress ripped off her."

The bouncer abandons his post. I jump the VIP rope. As I take the stairs two at a time, I see Ashtyn rake her nails clear down her boyfriend's cheek.

Landon drops her arm as he touches his face and realizes she's cut him. She stands proud and tall, eyeing him in disgust. His gaze darts left and right, taking notice of everyone staring. He's pissed now and has his hand raised as if he's about to hit her.

I rush toward Ashtyn and plant myself between her and Landon before he has a chance to touch her. "Lay a hand on her and I'll kick the everlovin' shit out of you," I say with a vengeance, my hands in fists at my sides ready to fight.

"You want a piece of me?" Landon challenges, shoving me. He looks me up and down as if I'm insignificant.

I shove back. "Man, I've wanted a piece of you since I first met you," I say. This is the point of no return. McKnight isn't about to back down, and there's no way in hell I'm letting him get away with hurting Ashtyn.

"Get your hands off me!" Ashtyn screams from behind me. Her frantic voice jerks my attention to her.

Panic jolts through me as I see her being held by one of Bonk's friends. She's trying to claw and kick her way out of his grip, but the dude is twice her size.

When my head is turned, McKnight lands a solid right hook to my jaw. Shit, that hurt. I lost focus and made myself vulnerable. If there's one thing I learned fighting in Regents' boxing club, it's never take your eyes off your opponent.

Time to get back in the game.

I punch Landon and make sure he's on the floor before I glance back at Ashtyn. Bonk is barreling toward me with fury written all over his face and five guys backing him. I lunge for the guy holding Ashtyn, but Bonk and his posse cut me off.

"That's the guy who took the picture," Bonk announces to his friends. He aims a punch at me, but I'm too fast and dodge his fist.

I land a solid one to his side, but his friends pull me away. They restrain me while I struggle and Bonk pummels me. I fight to get loose, but there's like six guys holding me. I can't get free. Bonk is having a field day. I taste my own blood from my busted lip, and even though I get a good kick in and Bonk flies backward, it doesn't matter because another one of his friends is right there to pick up where he left off.

I know how to dodge punches, but not with four guys holding me back. I'm breathing hard and starting to get dizzy. Then Trey and a bunch of guys on the Fremont football team join the fight. They rip the guys off me and start pummeling their rivals. The entire balcony is in chaos, with fists flying and security trying to break it up.

I scan the crowd desperately for Ashtyn. She's managed to break free of the guy who'd been holding her, so I get between her and the fighting and lead her to an alcove. "Stay here," I tell her, then turn to help Trey and the guys.

I should know better than to trust that Ashtyn will listen to me, because I see her clutch at Bonk's arm as he's about to fight Victor. I grab Bonk and pull him back, hoping that Ashtyn will be scared enough to go back to the alcove.

"Are you ever gonna listen to me?" I ask her.

She shakes her head and says simply, "No."

CHAPTER 22

Ashtyn

'm devastated. And shocked. And mad and hurt. But I'm not some diva who needs to be rescued by Derek. I'm about to jump onto the back of a Fairfield player when someone comes up behind me and throws me to the ground.

Before I can get up, Derek is there to pull me to my feet. His mouth is a bloody mess and his face is bruised. "Shit, Ashtyn. Why didn't you hide off to the side where you'd be safe?"

By now huge bouncers are flocking up the stairs.

"Leave me alone." I shove him away.

"Like hell I will. I'm gettin' you out of here." He slings me over his shoulder and muscles through the crowd.

"Let me go, you jerk," I say, attempting to squirm out of his grasp. "I don't need your help."

He doesn't answer. Instead, he takes me outside and puts me down in front of his car. "Get in the car. Now." I open my mouth to protest, but he puts a hand up. "Don't argue with me."

I sit in the car stewing about everything that happened, while Derek goes to talk to the guys just now coming out of the club. Vic looks all too happy that he arrived just in time for the brawl. Bree's fingers gently trail down Derek's bruised face as her perfectly shaped eyebrows furrow with compassion.

"Bree, you're laying it on thick," I mumble to myself.

Trey and Monika leave in Trey's car while Derek opens the backseat for his date.

"Thanks." Bree slides in the car. "Oh, my God, Ashtyn! Can you believe what just happened? Those guys from Fairfield are just awful. I feel *so* sorry for Derek. I mean, did you see how many of those Fairfield guys it took to hold him down?"

"I wasn't counting."

"It was four, or maybe five!"

Derek is in the car now. He's holding his side and moving slowly.

"You okay to drive?" I ask.

"I'm fine."

"You sure? Because your face looks like a piece of raw meat."

"Uh-huh." He pulls out of the parking lot as if the fight never happened and he doesn't have bloodstains on his clothes or a busted-up lip. I watch as Bree reaches through the headrest and caresses Derek's shoulders, occasionally slipping her fingers under his collar in a not-so-subtle flirty way. When he glances at me, I pretend to look at something super interesting out the window.

It isn't long before he pulls into Bree's driveway and he's walking her to her front door.

"Don't kiss her," I mumble. "Your mouth is bleeding, and it's unsanitary and gross." And I don't want you to like her. Please don't kiss her. And don't have any physical contact with her, either. Just walk away. Walk. Away. Like now would be a great time.

I want to avert my eyes from the two silhouettes, but I can't. Bree is an experienced flirter and isn't subtle. She's a girl who's used to getting whatever guy she wants. She has the perfect body, perfect face, perfect hair. She's feminine, is a cheerleader, and laughs a lot. Bree wraps her arms around Derek's neck and he pulls her in for a short hug. Then he must've said something funny, because she laughs and puts her hand on his chest. Does she have to touch him every two seconds?

I'm tempted to honk the horn, but it's late and I'm not sure Bree's neighbors will be happy if I wake them up. Finally Bree walks in her house and Derek comes back to the car.

"Took you long enough," I say in a huff as he slowly slides in the driver's seat, wincing in pain.

"You're kiddin' me, right?"

I don't answer, because my feelings are as raw as his face. I'm aware I'm acting immature and irrational. Truth is, I don't want him to be with Bree. I'm jealous and vulnerable and dealing with Landon's betrayal and the knowledge that I've got feelings for Derek and he's probably got the hots for Bree.

"Bree's really pretty," I mumble.

"Yep."

"Do you like her?"

"She's cool."

He doesn't get it.

When he pulls into our driveway, I want to tell him what I'm feeling. The problem is I have no clue what to say—my mind is a jumble of emotions that don't make sense. He'd probably laugh at me and run in the opposite direction if I told him I didn't want him going out with Bree.

I open my mouth to express something more than animosity toward him, but all that comes out is, "I could've handled Landon myself."

He swipes his bloody mouth with the back of his hand. "You keep tellin' yourself that and you might actually start believin' it."

Ashtyn, tell him you're developing feelings for him. Tell Derek that seeing him beat up scares you. Tell him you want to hold him. Tell him that you need him.

I slowly step out of the car and ignore all the inner voices telling me what to do. Because expressing any or all of those things will make me vulnerable, will set me up to be emotionally wounded once again.

I'm almost at the door when Derek says, "Ashtyn, wait."

I keep my back to him, but hear gravel crunch beneath his shoes as he steps closer. It's dark, except for the small yellow light on our front porch giving off a soft glow.

"You're a girl, you know," he says. "And you can't fight all your battles alone. You might be a football player, but you can't fend off a two-hundred-pound linebacker." He urges me to turn around, then glances at the nasty red marks on my arm from Landon's tight grip. "Or your boyfriend."

"He's not my boyfriend anymore." Landon lied to me. And

manipulated me. And he's transferring to Fairfield in the fall. It's over. We're completely screwed. I don't know . . . maybe I can convince him to come back if I give him the captain spot. Our division is tough. We need a good quarterback to get any attention from scouts. I rub my eyes and wish someone would tell me everything will be okay. But it won't.

Derek lets out a slow breath as my words sink in. "You broke up?"

I nod.

We're standing a few feet away from each other. It would be so easy to close the distance between us, but neither of us is moving. I have the urge to reach up and lightly touch the side of his cut, bruised face. For a moment, I feel his pain as if it were my own. But no matter what's going on beneath the surface, I have to remember that Derek and I are never going to happen. He's the guy who'll love you, then leave you without a backward glance. I can't do that . . . it could destroy the thin thread of hope that I can have feelings for someone who won't turn their back on me and leave. I'm dealing with more than enough betrayal tonight. I don't need to add to it.

Derek walks inside the house and heads to his bedroom. I prepare a washcloth, raid our medicine cabinet, and find an ice pack in the freezer. I find Derek sitting on his bed looking at his cell phone.

He glances up at me. "If you came here to mess around, I'm not really in great shape, but if you want to do all the work while I sit back I'm game—"

"Put that ego to rest. I only came to help disinfect those wounds. Shut up or I'm out of here."

"Yes, ma'am," he says, then moves to the center of the bed to give me room. I'm surprised he tosses his ever-present phone aside.

I kneel on the bed and gently swipe the washcloth over his cut eyebrow. I'm too aware of the fact that we're on the same bed and if things were different . . .

No. I can't let my mind wander to the "what if" because reality is what it is. Derek has made it clear that fooling around is a game to him. I don't play those kind of games.

How can I hide the fact that I have a crush on him when I have a major case of nerves right now? I'm trying to stop my hand from shaking, but there's still a slight tremor in my fingertips. The only time I get this jittery is during a game where whether we win or lose depends on me making a field goal. Normally I shrug the feeling off and focus on the task at hand.

"Why are you doin' this?" Derek asks, his deep voice sending electricity through my veins.

If I look into his mesmerizing clear blue eyes, will he immediately know what I'm feeling? He'd laugh at me if he could read my mind and my body. I avoid eye contact and instead concentrate on wiping dried blood off his lip now.

"Because I don't want to see you get an infection," I say. "Don't flatter yourself, Cowboy. This is for my benefit more than yours."

I wash away the blood, careful not to make him wince in pain.

I'd never tend to a wound with the guys on my team. When one of us gets hurt or cut up, we either take care of it ourselves or let one of the trainers do it. Right here, right now, my female instincts to protect and heal have kicked in. When all the dried blood is off, I dab some antibacterial ointment on his wounds. It feels too personal and intimate.

"Your hands are shakin'."

"No, they're not," I lie as I dab the ointment on his warm, smooth skin. "I'm annoyed and tired and pissed off." And frustrated with myself for wanting Derek to pull me close and hold me all night. Fantasies are never as good as reality.

I sit back on my heels and regard my work. I'm suddenly tired and feeling emotionally and physically weak. If Derek reached out for me, I'd snuggle into his chest. Right now if he asked me how I felt, I'd be tempted to tell him.

He leans back on the bed and holds his breath, an indication that his face isn't the only thing bruised. "Thanks, Ashtyn."

"I'm not done. Take your shirt off and I'll check your ribs."

"If I get undressed, you're gonna want to do more than check my ribs."

Acting like I don't care has become the new normal for me. I point to my stoic expression. "This is my 'not impressed' look."

The side of his mouth quirks up as he lifts his shirt over his head and tosses it aside. He flexes his pecs.

I yawn in response, refusing to show any sign of admiration. I zone in on the red marks that are starting to form on his side and ribs. It's going to take more than a few days for him to heal.

"Want me to take my pants off, too?" he jokes as he wags his brows suggestively. "I might have some swelling down there."

Everything is a game to him. I look him right in the eye as I slip a finger under the waistband of his pants and shove the ice pack underneath. "There," I say as I get up to leave. "That should help."

CHAPTER 23

Derek

What the hell happened to you?" Gus barks when I pass him on my way to the bathroom in the morning.

"I got in a fight."

"I don't need a delinquent or troublemaker in my house. Brandi!" he yells, his gravelly voice bouncing off the walls of the house.

Brandi has a big muffin in her hand as she walks out of the kitchen. "Yeah, Dad?"

Gus throws his hands up. "Your stepson got himself in a fight. Look at him, all beat up and looking like a thug."

The Parkers sure like to use that word.

One look at my face and Brandi sucks in a breath. "Oh, my God! Derek, what happened?"

"It's nothin'," I say. "I just got in a fight, that's all."

"About what? With who? Were the police called? How did you

drive home like that?" Brandi asks, bombarding me with questions when all I want to do is take a piss and a painkiller.

"It's not a big deal."

"Sure, it's not a big deal to you," Gus argues, "because I'll be the one having to foot the bill if whoever you fought decides to press charges and sue you."

"Sue me?" That's a joke, considering I'm the one who got my ass kicked. You'd think he'd ask if I'm the one who wants to press charges. "You won't have to foot any bill, Gus."

"That's what you think."

I think the guy just wants to be miserable. I don't want to get caught up in the Parker family drama. If I did, I'd tell Gus he should be more concerned about his family than whether or not he'll be sued for a fight.

In the bathroom, I look in the mirror. Damn. Ashtyn was right. I look like a piece of meat that's been through the grinder one too many times. Dried blood is on my lip, my cheek is black and blue, and the side of my rib is bruised.

Ashtyn came in my room last night to nurse my wounds. She had no clue I was tempted to mess around with her in an attempt to make me forget the searing pain in my body. Just the thought of it made my body excited. The girl has power over me. When she looks at me, I feel like a fucking virgin again. Not that she looks at me often. She avoids eye contact most of the time. The sight of me obviously makes her sick. She practically told me as much last night.

She said she wasn't impressed. I made fun of her comment

and pretended to mock her, but in reality I wanted her to admit that she had a reaction to being so close to me. Hell, I had a reaction. Little did she know I actually needed that ice pack in my shorts.

"What are you doin'?" I ask myself.

I'm not supposed to get caught up in someone else's messy life. I've got my own to deal with. Up until now I've gotten along just fine, cruising through without getting too involved or too interested in anyone else.

Ashtyn Parker is dangerous. She's got this tough exterior, talks like a guy, and dresses like one half the time. Then there's the other half, the half that's vulnerable and insecure and wears sexy clothes to make sure people know she's all woman underneath that harsh facade. I thought I was pushing her buttons in an attempt to push her away. But maybe it's to break down that wall she's got up.

This morning I saw her leave the house. Her head was down as she took Falkor for a walk. Ugh, if she keeps moping around, I'm gonna be annoyed. Is she pining after that dick of a boyfriend? She said they broke up. I'll bet the guy comes back and tries to lure her into his life again.

"Derek, are you in there?" Julian's voice echoes from the other side of the door.

I open the door and let the little guy in. His eyes go wide and his jaw drops when he takes one look at my face. He steps back in fear.

"It looks worse than it is," I tell him. "I promise."

"Did you get in a fight?"

"Yep."

"I think you lost."

I laugh. "Looks that way, huh?"

He nods. "You look tough with bruises on your face. Did Daddy teach you how to fight?"

"Nah."

"Will you teach me?"

"Buddy, you don't want to learn to fight. Just use your words like your mama says."

"But what if someone hits me first?"

"Tell a teacher or your mama."

"Then all the kids will call me a tattletale and I'll have no friends." He puts his hands on his hips. "You don't want me to be a friendless tattletaler, do you?"

The kid should be a lawyer, because he's already got negotiating skills. Just to ease his curiosity, I kneel down and hold my palms up. "All right, show me what you got."

The little guy puts his fists up and strikes my palm. "How's that?"

"Not bad," I say. "Again."

He does it a few more times. I can tell his confidence is building because his punches are getting harder and he's starting to loosen up. "I was watching professional wrestling on TV when my mom wasn't in the room," he says. "Randy the Raider gave this guy the F.U. move."

"The F.U. move?"

"What are you doing, Derek?" Brandi asks, suddenly appearing behind Julian. "Are you teaching my son how to fight and use profanity?"

Umm . . .

Julian turns around excitedly. "Mom, Derek was just showing me—"

"Julian, go to your room. I need to talk to Derek alone." Julian is about to protest, but Brandi urges him out of the bathroom. When he's out of sight, Brandi pushes back her long hair. "Julian was excited when I told him you were coming to live with us. He calls you his big brother and looks up to you." She sighs slowly, a clue that a well-thought-out revelation will come out of her mouth next. Wait for it . . . wait for it . . . "I thought of making you and Julian real brothers."

What is she talking about? Does she expect us to do a ritual thing like cut ourselves and rub blood together so we're blood brothers? "Brandi, I hate to break the news to you, but no matter what, Julian and I didn't come from the same mother."

"I know." She tilts her head to the side. "But I thought it would be nice if I, you know, made it official by adopting you."

"I'm not an orphan."

"I know. I just thought you and Julian . . . you know, if something happens to me and your father . . ."

I get it. She doesn't want to be my mother any more than I want her to be mine. It's all for Julian's sake. Time to put her wayward thoughts to rest. "Julian's my little brother, Brandi. Period."

"Good. We need to be on the same page. And regarding you and my sister . . ."

Oh, man. Maybe Brandi's more with it than I give her credit for. That's not good. "Nothin's goin' on between us," I tell her. "Your sister drives me insane. I could never date a girl like her even if we—"

Brandi suddenly bursts into fits of laughter, cutting me off. "You're kidding, right?" she says as she tries to catch her breath. She holds her stomach like she's trying to stop the baby from being violently jiggled around while she laughs. "Oh, my God! That's *hilarious*! No offense, but you are *so* not my sister's type. I just . . ." She bursts out laughing again, letting out a couple of snorts in the process. "I just . . . Wait, did you actually believe I thought something was going on between you and Ashtyn?"

Umm . . . "No. What's your sister's type?"

She wipes her eyes and holds in her giggles. "She likes guys who are serious and dedicated and driven. That's not you *at all*."

Nope, that's not me. And no girl is going to turn me around, especially one who likes guys who are serious and dedicated and driven. Ashtyn and I would never work.

Even if I did want to get tangled up in the sheets with her last night.

CHAPTER 24

Ashtyn

After my run with Falkor this morning, I go into Derek's room to check up on him. Bree is there, sitting next to him on the bed. If that vision wasn't enough to make me feel ill, Bree is feeding him cookies. She's got her hand poised over his mouth as he opens it like a baby bird about to be fed by its mother.

"Hey, Ash," Bree says when she notices me. "I just came to make sure Derek was going to survive. I made him carob and wheat germ cookies because you told me he likes to eat healthy."

"That's so . . . cute."

"I know, right?" She feeds him another cookie. He's all too happy to munch on it while she reaches into the container for another one. "Have fun at practice today."

I wave bye, knowing that I have no right to be upset that Bree has taken my place at his bedside and wants to stay there permanently. The thing with Bree is that she'll be happy with whatever attention Derek gives her. If he suddenly gets tired of the relation-ship, she won't be devastated. She'll start crushing on someone else right away.

My emotions don't work that way, which makes me realize that Landon and I were over long before it ended.

Landon. I have to break the news about him to my teammates sooner rather than later. I'm not looking forward to it, but it has to be done. During practice, I pull Trey, Jet, and Victor aside when Dieter orders a water break.

These guys are my friends and teammates, guys I never want to let down. But they deserve to know the truth.

"What's up, Capt'n?" Jet holds up a water bottle and squirts water into his mouth.

If they only knew beforehand that voting me captain would make Landon quit the team, they'd have changed their votes. All the guys would've made sure Landon got to be captain. I'm find-ing it hard to ask how they'd feel if I turned down the captain position and offered it to Landon to lure him back to Fremont.

"You know Landon lives on the dividing line between Fre-mont and Fairfield, right?"

Victor pats me on the back. "We know he's transferring, Ash."

What? "You knew?"

They all acknowledge that they know about it, too.

"Since when?"

Jet and Trey both look at Victor. "My dad found out over the weekend," Vic says. "One of the assistant coaches does business with my dad, and he told him the news. Dieter knows, too. We were kind of waiting for him to break the news to you so we didn't have to."

I don't know if that makes them good friends or bad ones. At this point, I don't trust anything that comes out of anyone's mouth.

When I get home, my dad is watching television in the living room. "Dad, I need to talk to you about football camp."

He lowers the volume. "What about it?"

"You know Landon and I were supposed to drive together in his car, but plans changed. He's going on his own. I don't have anyone else to go with and I know my car won't make it, so I was thinking that maybe you could drive me in your car or let me borrow it." I'm hoping he'll feel sympathetic enough to help me out.

"I can't. I've got to work. Find some other friends to go with, or don't go." He turns the volume back up. "It's already costing me a fortune for the tuition, and it's only one damn week. I'll be more than happy to get my money back."

"I want to go." I *need* to go.

He holds his hands up. "Then figure it out. You know I think heading off to Texas in an attempt to get noticed by scouts is a waste of time. If you think you're going to be scouted and get a scholarship, think again. They don't recruit girls."

"Katie Calhoun got recruited. She's a girl."

"Katie Calhoun is probably going to be cut or hurt her first season. Mark my words," he says.

I call Monika, but she's taking summer school and can't make it. I call Bree, but her acting agent just booked her for a short film they're filming in Chicago this summer, so she's out. Trey has to work to save money for college, Jet has to stay home to help his dad open a new restaurant, and Victor's dad threatened to cut him off if he left town.

Everything right now seems hopeless.

Four days later I'm still trying to figure out how I'm going to get to football camp when someone knocks on my bedroom door. "It's Derek. Open up."

I open the door and stand there looking at a very annoyed teenage boy. "What's wrong?" I ask him.

"You."

"What about me?"

He throws his hands up in the air. "You're no fun to live with anymore. What happened to the girl who used to make fun of my smoothies and called me a thug? What happened with the girl who yawned when I took my shirt off when she was in bed with me?"

"I wasn't in bed with you. I was cleaning your wounds."

"I mean, c'mon, we set up a routine and now you're breakin' the rules. What's *up* with that?"

"You're mad because we're not arguing or butting heads?" I ask, completely confused at why he'd care if I paid him a lick of attention or not. We argue most of the time, so what's the big deal? Bree's been hanging around him all week while I've walked around completely depressed.

"Did you even realize that I've been takin' your damn dog for walks all week and he's been sleepin' in my room every night? Seriously, Ashtyn, I bet my left nut you wouldn't even notice if I changed his name to Duke."

"Your left nut?" I ask. "Why not your right one? Guys never say they'll bet their right nut, only their left. Why is that?"

"Because all guys know their right nut is the dominant one, so bettin' the left one is a safe choice. Now don't change the subject and answer my question."

That is the most ridiculous thing I've ever heard. I try to contain my amusement, but a laugh escapes my mouth. "You really believe your right nut is dominant? You're kidding me, right?"

He doesn't look amused. "Answer the question."

I throw my hands up. "Give me a break, Derek. Can't I be depressed?"

"About what?"

You. Football. Everything. I want to tell him the truth, but instead say, "None of your business."

"Well, fine. You've had a few days since you and Landon broke up," he says, agitation and annoyance in his voice. "Snap out of it already, it's annoyin'."

"How about if I snap out of it when you read that letter from your grandmother." There, that should get him off my back and divert his attention for the moment. Derek makes an about-face, heading back down the stairs. I follow him. "You're not about to get off that easy, Derek. You just want me to entertain you so you don't have to think about that letter. But not reading it is eating you inside, isn't it?"

"Nope, not even one little bit," he says. "I haven't thought about that letter *or* my grandmother at all."

"Liar. You want a challenge, I just gave you one."

Derek almost trips over Falkor on the way to his room. "Talkin' about my grandmother or that letter is off-limits. Seriously, Ashtyn, I'm not goin' there. You have no clue what that woman is capable of."

"Why are you afraid of an old lady?"

"I'm not afraid." He tries to laugh it off, but I don't buy it for a second.

"You're acting like you are. She wants you to come see her before she dies, Derek. You need to go. She knows she made mistakes."

"You're talkin' like you know the old hag," he says as he opens the container of carob cookies that Bree made him. He takes one bite of Bree's cookies and winces as if they're made from dirt. "You know nothin' about her. You read that letter and think she's a poor, dyin' old lady that deserves to have her last wish granted. Fuck that."

"So you're saying you have no problem denying an old lady her last dying wish? Really, Derek, you *are* heartless."

He holds out the cookie container. "Want one? I warn you, they taste like a mixture between cardboard and mud."

"Stop trying to change the subject, Derek." His grandmother's letter made me cry. I wish I had a family member want to spend time with me as much as Derek's grandmother wants to spend time with him.

We're in the den now. Boxes line one side of the room. Derek's suitcases and belongings are on the other. Derek's doing his best not to pay attention to that envelope now sitting on top of one of the boxes. I put it there because he needs to read it.

"When I told you I wanted you back the way you were, I didn't mean the annoyin' Ashtyn. I meant the Ashtyn who separated her Skittles, shoved an ice pack in my shorts, and didn't pine after her douche bag of a boyfriend just because he left her—"

"For your information, I'm not pining for Landon."

Derek rolls his eyes. "Whatever you say, Ashtyn."

"If talking about your grandmother is off-limits to me, talking about Landon is off-limits to you." I don't want to tell him that Landon is playing for Fairfield as a revenge move on my teammates.

"Fine."

"Fine. But you still need to read that letter." I leave his room.

"And Landon is still a douche bag," he exclaims.

CHAPTER 25

Derek

I close the door and look at the envelope. Yesterday morning I was tempted to read it, burn it, and never think about it again.

But I didn't.

Instead, I stared at the damn thing for what seemed like forever.

While Ashtyn wants me to read the letter, Falkor doesn't seem to mind watching me do nothing except stare at it.

"Falkor, catch!" I toss the envelope to him like a Frisbee.

The dog watches the envelope land a few inches from his outstretched paws. He might actually be the most useless dog on the planet.

Ashtyn called me out for being afraid of reading the letter.

I'm not afraid.

I was afraid of losing my mom. The day she sat me down and told me she had cancer, I was scared. Not one day went by after that when I wasn't afraid. When her blood counts were low, I thought it was the end. When she got dizzy and sick after chemo, it freaked me out. When her hair fell out and she looked fragile, I felt helpless. When I held her frail hand in the hospital when she looked like a shell of her former self, I was destroyed.

I'm definitely not afraid of reading a letter from a grandmother who's a complete stranger.

Just do it already.

I pick the envelope up and sit on my bed as I open it. The letter is written on heavy pink cardstock with my grandmother's initials embossed on the top in shiny gold lettering. I think the paper was sprayed with some sort of perfume, because it smells like a woman.

Just so I don't have to listen to Ashtyn nag me about it anymore, I unfold the letter and read it.

My dearest Derek,

I'm writing this letter to you with a heavy heart. I have just been diagnosed and have been reflecting upon the mistakes I've made in my life. There are things I need to make right before my imminent death. Since you are my one and only grandchild, it is imperative we meet after my treatment on June twentieth. It's my last, dying wish. There are things that you don't know—that you need to know—that you MUST know.

With Eternal Love,

Elizabeth Worthington (your grandmother)

Ashtyn was right . . . my grandmother is dying. She didn't specify what she's been diagnosed with. My mind is swirling with the possibilities. It's got to be bad since she didn't mention it. I wonder if it's lung cancer, like my mom had. My mom was one of those few unlucky souls who got lung cancer even though she didn't smoke a day in her life. Heredity and the environment were to blame, I guess.

Or maybe my grandmother has pancreatic cancer, which is a death sentence to anyone diagnosed with it.

Or some horrible, debilitating disease that's too painful to mention.

Shit, now I can't stop thinking about it.

Most teenagers would have probably been on a plane by now, rushing to their ailing granny's side. But most teenagers don't have Elizabeth Worthington as their grandmother, famous for thinking her social status is something to admire and aspire to. I'm sure she's realized by now that her blood isn't blue and no amount of money can buy health.

I read the letter two more times before placing it back in the envelope and telling myself to forget about it. I almost wish I hadn't read the thing. It's all Ashtyn's fault. If it weren't for her, I wouldn't have to carry around guilt. I need to get my mind off it, or I'll be thinking about it all night.

One person has the ability to keep my mind off that letter.

Ashtyn is in her bedroom on her laptop. Her room is pink with painted flowers running up and down the walls. She's even got little hummingbird stuffed animals on her bed. Above her desk are posters of the Chicago Bears and an eight-by-ten picture of someone named Katie Calhoun wearing a Texas football uniform.

"This is the girliest room I've ever been in. Just being in here makes my testosterone levels plunge."

She jerks her head up from the computer. "That's a joke, right?"

"Kind of." I clear my throat and lean back on her dresser. "I just wanted to tell you to be ready at seven tonight."

"For what?"

"You lost the bet, remember?"

"Yeah, well, I don't have to honor that bet because you said that the letter was an invitation to join the Olympic synchronized trampoline team. You lied."

"That doesn't make any difference. You said there was no Olympic synchronized trampoline team, and I bet you that there was. It's cut and dried, Ashtyn. You lost. It's time to pay up, and tonight's the night."

CHAPTER 26

Ashtyn

'm sitting in my room, watching the clock. It's six thirty. I wasn't going to humor Derek and actually go on this nondate, but I don't want him thinking I'm backing out of my end of the deal. Derek probably expects me to dress up, but he'll realize pretty quickly that's not the case.

I'm sure I've got bags under my eyes and look like crap because I didn't sleep much last night, perfect for my nondate with Derek. Determined to go through with this, I stumble into the bathroom to get a hair tie so I can put my hair up . . . and come face-to-face with Derek. He's leaning over the sink shaving . . . with a towel wrapped low around his waist.

"You didn't lock the door." I cover my eyes with my hand so I don't have to look at his ridiculously hot half-naked body.

"Is that what you're wearin' tonight, Sugar Pie? Sweats and a T-shirt?"

I keep my hand over my eyes. "Yes."

I hear him rinse his razor in the sink. "Sexy."

"I'm not trying to be sexy."

"Ashtyn, look at me."

"Why?" I get a tingly sensation in the middle of my stomach because we're so close and he's only dressed in a towel that shows off his "V" and I'm trying to keep my distance even though I don't want to. "You might want to pull up your towel. It's falling off."

"It's not falling off unless you pull it off."

"You wish." I take my hand from my eyes. "I think you have a self-esteem problem."

"Self-esteem problem?" He looks at me sideways, then chuckles. "Yeah, okay."

"Derek," I say in the most soft, feminine voice. "Admitting it is the first step to recovery."

"I'm not sayin' I don't got problems, but self-esteem probably isn't one of 'em. I'm glad you're back to your old self. You wanna stand here and watch me shave, I'm cool with that. It'll boost whatever self-esteem you seem to think I'm lacking."

"I don't want to watch you, Derek. I want a hair tie." I reach around him and pull one out of the drawer. The smell of his freshly washed skin mixed with whatever cologne he's wearing envelops my senses. I wish he hadn't taken a shower as if he was getting ready for a real date. This isn't a real date. It's payment for losing a bet.

"Want to give me a hint where we're going?" I ask him so I can prepare myself for the worst.

"Nope. Don't you like surprises?"

I was surprised when my parents announced they were getting divorced. I was surprised when my mom packed up and left. I was surprised when Brandi disappeared with Nick. I look at him with a completely serious expression. "Not. At. All."

"That's too bad." He raises a brow and smiles mischievously. "I love surprises."

I close the door and walk back to my room to wait until exactly seven before going downstairs for the nondate.

My sister and Julian are playing some card game in the living room when I walk downstairs ten minutes later. Derek is probably in his room, contemplating the best way to make my life miserable. He doesn't know how I feel about him . . . he can't know how I feel about him. Hiding my true feelings will be so hard. I'm going to have to sabotage our night together as much as I can.

"Derek said you guys were going out," Brandi says. "That's *so* nice you two are getting along. It looks like you're turning over a new leaf. I like that."

I nod. "Uh-huh."

My sister claps excitedly. "What are you gonna wear?"

I gesture to my sweats. "This."

"Oh," she says, confused that I'd pick something so casual. "Umm . . . do you want to wear something of mine?"

"Nope. This is perfectly fine. I'm comfy."

Clearly she doesn't agree that comfy is the best attire for going out on a Saturday night. "Try something else on. Maybe comfy isn't the best idea, especially when a boy is taking you out."

"It's not a boy. It's Derek," I tell her.

"You ready?" a clean-shaven Derek says from behind me. He's wearing jeans and a button-down shirt that I've never seen him wear before. And a pair of cowboy boots. His hair is still wet. He looks like he's about to go on a real date. Time to make sure he knows that I'm not about to make this thing official.

I glance at my cell phone. "Okay, it's five past seven. Where are we going and when are we going to be back?" I slip into my fuzzy UGG slippers, getting a chuckle from Derek and a gasp from my sister.

"I told you it's a surprise." He holds up the keys to his SUV. "Let's roll."

"I better be back by ten," I tell him when we're on the road to who-knows-where.

"You're damn sexy with those sweats on," he says sarcastically as he eyes my outfit.

"Thank you. Where are we going?"

"And your hair. It must've taken you forever to get it just right."

It did take me a while to get my hair up in a messy bun, with strands sticking out every which way. "Where did you say we were going?"

"I didn't." He pulls onto the highway, following signs to Chicago. "Why do you play football?" he asks me after a while. "I know a bunch of girls who like it, but they either become groupies or cheerleaders. They don't play it."

"You don't play anymore, so you won't understand."

"Try me."

At first I'm not going to tell him. But then when I look at his face all serious, I let him know the truth. "I always watched football with my dad. I'm sure you know by now he's kinda . . . rough around the edges. He wasn't always like that. We used to bond over football. He was the kicker for Fremont."

"So you wanted to play to get his attention."

I shrug. "It didn't work, but that didn't matter. It was something I was good at, something that could take my mind off whatever crap was happening in my real life. I bet you think that's stupid."

"I don't think it's stupid, Ashtyn. Not by a long shot." After a while he adds, "Your dad's missin' out."

He's the first person to tell me that. I don't answer, because my eyes well up and I can't talk. I wanted my dad to watch me play and be proud that I was following in his footsteps. But I might as well be invisible.

Derek ends up parking the car at this place called Jumpin' Jack.

"What are we doing here, Derek?"

We walk in the place. It's a big gymnasium full of trampolines. A guy and girl wearing matching red leotards greet us at the entrance.

"Welcome to Jumpin' Jack. I'm Jack and this is my partner, Gretchen. You two must be Derek and Ashtyn."

Derek shakes Jumpin' Jack's hand. "Yep. Thanks for takin' us on short notice."

"Our pleasure. Ashtyn will follow Gretchen to the women's locker room, while you'll follow me to the men's."

I tap Derek's back. I watched videos of synchronized trampolining. I have a dreaded feeling I'm not about to be a spectator. "Derek, please tell me we're not doing what I think we're doing."

He winks at me. "My mother always said to be unpredictable and you'll never get bored."

I don't want to be unpredictable. Unpredictable is reckless and dangerous. Unpredictable brings out the unknown. I thought Landon was predictable and he wasn't. I know Derek is unpredictable. I don't want to fall into his web, because it'll only end in disaster.

Against my better judgment, I follow Gretchen and find myself face-to-face with a shiny blue leotard hanging in one of the cubbies in the locker room. Gretchen, who can probably fit into a keyhole she's so petite, says in a heavy Russian accent, "Put it on, then meet me in the gym."

When she walks out of the room, I stare at the blue spandex and think . . . what horrible thing did I do in my life to deserve this?

CHAPTER 27

Derek

I look ridiculous and stupid. As I check myself in the bathroom mirror, I want to back out. I'm wearing a skintight leotard/bodysuit obviously designed by women who have no clue about men's plumbing, because the outline of my dick is obscene. Don't dudes who do this sport wear a cup or something? I've been on a trampoline, but I've never done synchronized trampolining. Looking at myself in the mirror, I can see why. I thought having a private trampoline session with two pros would be funny, something completely off the wall. This idea has completely backfired.

I hear a loud knock. "Derek, come out!" Jumpin' Jack bellows through the men's dressing room door.

I adjust and hope I can avoid further embarrassment by not getting a hard-on during this training session. When I walk into the gym, Ashtyn's standing atop the center trampoline wearing a matching skintight leotard that leaves nothing to the imagination.

Her gaze moves downward and her hand flies to her mouth as she giggles. "Oh my . . . Derek, your, umm . . ."

"Huge, I know. Stop staring at it or soon you'll be seein' how impressive it really gets." I gesture to her chest. "You cold, Sugar Pie?"

She crosses her arms on her chest when she realizes that I'm not the only one with body parts sticking out.

"Hold hands," Gretchen instructs.

Ashtyn stares at my hands as if she's not about to touch them anytime soon.

"Don't we jump on separate trampolines?" I ask. This wasn't supposed to be an intimate holding-hands session. I've seen the videos online. We're supposed to be jumping on two different trampolines.

"You need to find and feel each other's rhythm first."

Sounds like screwing, not trampolining, but I'm game. I hold out my hands. Ashtyn takes a deep breath, then slides her hands on top of mine. Her touch sends a jolt of electricity through me. I look for a sign to see if she feels it, too. She obviously doesn't, because her eyes are averted and she looks like she'd like to be anywhere but here.

"Start jumping!" Jumpin' Jack orders.

We do. Ashtyn tries to stay upright, but falls backward. Since our hands are still attached, I almost fall on top of her.

"Sorry," I mumble. This is way closer than I thought we'd be, and it's throwing me off my game. Tonight was supposed to make me stop thinking about my grandmother. It was supposed to be entertaining, mocking her and the nondate I manipulated her to go on in the first place.

Ashtyn stands and holds out her hands so we can try again. "This is ridiculous. You know that, don't you?"

"Feel my rhythm," I say, then wink at her in an attempt to make light of the situation.

She tilts her head and smiles sweetly. "Fuck you."

She tries to pull her hands away, but I hold tight and keep jumping.

"Feel your partner's energy," Jack instructs. "Don't fight it. Match it, imitate it, until you're of one mind."

"Next time we go out, remind me to wear a sports bra," Ashtyn mumbles. "And you'd be better off wearing a jockstrap."

I try to hide a smile. "You're already looking forward to the next time?"

"No. I just meant . . . Forget what I meant and concentrate," she says, flustered.

"You're cute when you're nervous, Sugar Pie."

"I'm not nervous."

"Sure you are. Your palms are sweaty and—"

"Stop talking and focus!" Gretchen yells.

It takes us fifteen minutes before Jumpin' Jack announces that we're ready to separate and try side-by-side trampolines. With each jump, Ashtyn seems to relax. We've finally gotten the hang of it and she even starts smiling and letting out little laughs when we mess up. Jumpin' Jack and Gretchen both take this jumping stuff way more seriously than it needs to be, which is comedy.

Gretchen scolds us every time Ashtyn and I talk or laugh, which makes us laugh even more.

"When you jump in sync," Gretchen says after Jumpin' Jack teaches us a few tricks, "your bodies and souls become one entity. It's like making love."

I look over at Ashtyn and our eyes lock. I imagine what it would be like to be intimate with her, with her looking up at me with those expressive eyes and full lips. At first I'd take it slow, savoring each moment . . . then I'd let her set the pace. Would she let down her fierce protective shell, or would it always be there, a reminder that she'll never fully let go of her inhibitions?

Shit, I better stop those wayward thoughts before everyone in the room knows what I'm thinking. If Ashtyn knew what was on my mind, she'd probably punch me in the groin—which she'd have no problem finding in this leotard. I tell myself I'm sexually frustrated because I haven't hooked up with a girl in a few months. I need to fix that, and not with a girl like Ashtyn. She's made for guys who want a commitment. I'm made for girls who want a good time. While we might be jumping in sync, our personalities when it comes to dating clash like oil and water.

At the end of the hour, and a picture that Gretchen insists we take in our leotards, we've mastered how to jump and do a few tricks in sync. Gretchen and Jumpin' Jack are impressed with our progress and invite us back anytime for another lesson.

In the car, Ashtyn and I are silent as I drive to dinner. I'm still trying to convince myself I'm not attracted to her. We're not in sync at all, in anything. Except trampolining. We rocked it tonight.

"Trampolining was a really stupid idea," Ashtyn says. She's back in her sweats, looking like she's ready for an intense workout at the gym instead of a night out on the town.

"You liked it. Admit it."

She shifts in the seat and looks out my car window. "I won't admit anything. Now take me home so I can pig out. I'm starving."

"I'm takin' you to dinner." I pull into the parking lot of White Fence Farm in a town called Romeoville.

"White Fence Farm?"

"Supposedly they have the world's best chicken, made from real chickens. Admit that you have no clue what's in that frozen crap your sister heats up every night."

"I happen to like frozen crap, thank you very much."

We have to wait over an hour for a table, so Ashtyn walks around the little antique museum inside the restaurant. She looks appreciatively at one of the vintage cars in the museum case. A slimy guy sagging his pants and looking like he's on the prowl walks up next to her. He says something I can't hear, then smiles when she answers him.

"What's up, man?" I say to the dude as I put my arm around Ashtyn's shoulder. He takes the hint and walks away.

Ashtyn brushes my hand off. "What are you doing?"

"Makin' sure that guy knows you're not available. Didn't anyone tell you not to talk to guys who are just lookin' for a piece of ass?"

"Takes one to know one, huh?"

"Somethin' like that."

"Maybe the guy was just trying to be nice."

"I don't think so."

She winds through the crowded museum back to the front of the restaurant. When we're finally seated across from a bunch of guys wearing T-shirts that say ROMEOVILLE HIGH SCHOOL FOOTBALL on them, Ashtyn is silent.

"You gonna talk?"

She doesn't look up from the cartoon picture of a chicken on her plate. "I don't feel like it."

"Well, it's a good thing this isn't a date. If this was, you'd definitely be a dud." She opens her mouth to protest, but the waitress comes. She's a big woman with red curly hair who introduces herself as Tracie. She does her welcome greeting, then takes our order.

"Our sides are bottomless, so feel free to ask for more," Tracie says with a smile, then leans in to whisper something important. "Our corn fritters are legendary and addictive."

"Thank goodness," I tell Tracie, who looks like she's eaten one too many fritters in her lifetime. "Because my girlfriend here is legendary and addictive. Right, Sugar Pie?"

Ashtyn shakes her head, then kicks me under the table. Poor Tracie. Her smile fades as she doesn't know how to respond, so she excuses herself and says the food will be out shortly.

"Thank goodness this isn't a real date," Ashtyn says. "Because if it were, I'd already have called a cab and been on my way back to Fremont."

"If this were a real date, we'd already be in the backseat of my car with our clothes off."

"Eww. Wanna bet?" Ashtyn says.

I grin wide.

She holds up a hand. "Forget I said that."

CHAPTER 28

Ashtyn

I'm glad those guys from Romeoville don't recognize me. We played them this year and beat them 21–20 in the first round of the playoffs. A fight broke out between our players after I'd kicked the field goal to win the game. Police were called in to break it up.

Derek waves a hand in front of my face. "Stop lookin' at other guys when you're with me."

"I'm not looking at other guys."

"I'm not an idiot, Ashtyn. Every two seconds you're checkin' out the football players at that table behind me. Obviously you've got a thing for jocks."

"I do not. They're . . . rivals. I just hope they don't recognize me."

"Then stop lookin' at 'em and pay attention to your date."

"This isn't a date."

"Humor me and pretend it is."

"What would Bree say if she knew you and I were out on a date?"

"Bree?" He laughs. "She just wanted to hook up. Nothin' more than that."

I don't want to know how much he hooked up with Bree. I don't like guys who think they're God's gift to girls and have no goals except to get with as many girls as possible, which is the definition of Derek Fitzpatrick. So why do I like being here with him, trying to one-up him on the witty comment scale? The guy makes stupid jokes and doesn't take anything seriously—especially his relationships with girls. I mean, who thinks of taking a girl on a date to learn synchronized trampolining?

Not that this is a date. It's not. It's paying for a lost bet, nothing more. Sure, Derek's pretending it's a real date, but that's only because he likes playing games. Taking me out is just another game to him, another way for him to amuse himself.

When Tracie brings the corn fritters piled up in a little white ceramic bowl, I sample one. I swear the fritter practically melts in my mouth, perfectly warm and sweet. It's everything Tracie said it would be and more.

I pop one after another into my mouth while Derek watches me with those electric blue eyes.

"You have to try one," I tell him. Tracie brings a second helping after I've devoured the first.

"No, thanks."

"They're *amazing*, Derek. Seriously addictive."

"Obviously."

I lean across the table and hold up a fritter. "Try it. It's fresh, and has corn in it. Consider it a vegetable, surrounded by tasty goodness."

He looks at the fritter, then at me. "*You* eat it."

When I see it's useless, I pop it into my mouth. No need to waste a good fritter on someone who won't appreciate it.

Tracie brings the rest of our meal. Derek takes a bite of chicken and moans. "This is the way chicken should taste."

I'm surprised Derek enjoys the chicken as much as he does. He even reaches over and grabs the wing off my plate when I mention that I'm stuffed and can't eat another bite. It makes me think of Trey and Monika, who share food all the time. Landon and I never shared food.

Okay. I admit it. This night does feel like a date. When we were on the trampoline holding hands, I couldn't look him in the eye. Derek has strong, capable hands that mow lawns and fix old sheds with rusty hammers. My heart skipped a beat when he almost fell on top of me on the trampoline and I could feel his body close to mine. When we jumped in sync, I felt a connection. I know it sounds ridiculous, and I'm sure Derek would laugh if I mentioned it, but I could sense when he was going to jump without even having to look at him.

After dinner, he drives back home.

I don't make eye contact when he parks in our driveway, because I might be tempted to lean in and kiss him. "I had a really . . . interesting time tonight." I don't want to tell him the truth . . .

that tonight was the first night in a long time I forgot to be depressed.

I'm super confused and emotional. I don't want to do anything I'll regret. I open the door, but Derek reaches over to stop me from getting out.

"Wait!" he says. "I wanted to give you somethin' . . ." He reaches into the backseat and grabs a football. "Here. It's signed by the '92 Dallas Cowboys. It's even got Aikman's signature."

My fingers trace the signatures. I'm holding a piece of Texas history. "How'd you get this?"

He shrugs. "My grandmother sent it for my birthday a while back."

"This is really cool, Derek. You should keep it."

"I want you to have it."

I give him a big hug. "Thanks, Cowboy."

I intend to pull away immediately, but when he hugs me back I find myself closing my eyes and lingering in his warm embrace. I've wanted this. I've waited for this. My heart is beating fast and I feel out of breath with his strong hands on my back.

I lean back slowly. Our gazes lock. His eyes practically shine in the dark.

His gaze moves down to my lips. "I want to kiss you so bad right now."

"Do you usually ask a girl, or do you just do it?"

"Usually I just do it."

The words come out without my brain contemplating the consequences. "So what are you waiting for?"

The side of his mouth quirks up, but it's not from cockiness. I think he's shocked that I haven't punched him in the face or left the car. I'm challenging him. His hand cups the back of my neck, his thumb slightly caressing my sensitive skin. Oh, I am in so much trouble right now because I want this so bad.

My breath hitches when Derek leans forward. I wet my lips with the tip of my tongue, eager to see what it feels like to have his lips pressed against mine.

His breathing is ragged. "Damn, that's sexy."

I smile wide. "You know we shouldn't play games like this." My teasing lips are a whisper away from his.

"I know. This is a really bad idea," he agrees, but doesn't seem to want to retreat.

"You better be as good at this as you think you are."

"I'm good, Sugar Pie."

I move back just the slightest bit, knowing I should protect myself and run into the house, but I want to continue to play the game. He wants this to be a game, so I'm playing it the only way I know how. I know guys like Derek. They like challenges and the cat and mouse game.

Time to play the mouse.

"Wait." I place a hand on his chest. I feel the muscles beneath his shirt and the fast pounding of his heart. "Our kissing styles probably aren't compatible."

"Try me," he whispers, then moves in and places slow, thoughtful little kisses on my lips. I fight the urge to moan. Those little kisses are meant to drive me insane. And they are. Damn him!

"How's that?" he asks.

"Umm. . . ."

His tongue traces the line between my lips.

"And that?"

That's it. I'm definitely going all in for this now. I grab the back of his neck and pull him closer so we're full-on kissing and my lips are crushing against his and he feels so different and good and my body is starting to turn into liquid fire . . .

His lips urge mine open. His hot slippery tongue searches for mine. Our tongues mingle in a sexy dance. I like this way too much.

"I think we're compatible," he groans against my mouth.

"You think?" I'm panting and wanting this to last longer.

"Maybe we should keep doing it, just to make sure." His hand reaches up and he slowly slides the ponytail holder out of my hair, which falls around my shoulders. "Hey," he says. "Why are your eyes closed?"

I shrug.

"Look at me, Ashtyn. I don't want to be some faceless guy."

I open my eyes. His lips glisten in the faint light from the porch.

"You're like a warrior princess, you know that?" He gently swipes my hair out of my face. "So beautiful." The moment is too intense and feels so real. It doesn't feel like a game, even though I know it is. It's confusing my already raw emotions, which is exactly what he wants.

"Are you being serious?"

My question has lots of implications, because if he's serious, that means the game-playing is over.

He hesitates, then leans back in the driver's seat. "You should know me by now. I don't take anything seriously."

"That's what I thought."

"In fact," he adds, "I was hopin' you'd let me take a pic of you and me makin' out so I can post it on the Internet and piss off your ex-boyfriend. How about it?"

A picture to post on the Internet? I almost got sucked into spilling all my feelings to Derek, when all along this was just a joke to him. I'm the punch line.

"How about this nondate being officially over." I push him away and rush out of the car as I vow never to play kissing games with Derek Fitzpatrick again.

CHAPTER 29

Derek

Well, I'm a certified asshole. I didn't mean to hook up with Ashtyn. Kissing her felt damn good . . . and made me want to lose control with her. Which is why I made up that idiotic story about posting a picture of us kissing online. I didn't know any other way to push her far enough away so she'd hate me.

Ashtyn isn't just any random girl. She's Brandi's sister and a girl who'd never hook up with a guy without thinking that she'd end up in a serious relationship. Her mom left her, her sister left her, her dad might as well have left her. I need her to think I'm an asshole, because no matter what happens between us, I'm leaving soon and I'm not coming back.

I set the football in front of her bedroom door, knowing it's a lame peace offering but not knowing what else to do or say. I knew she liked it by the way she studied the Dallas Cowboys' signatures as if they held some secret football code.

In the morning, Brandi comes in my room while I'm still half-asleep. She's wearing shorts and a T-shirt that hugs her pregnant belly. Falkor trots in behind her with a chewed-up football in his mouth. He sits next to my bed and drops the drool-covered, deflated ball. Aikman's signature is torn in half . . . some of it is missing, probably been swallowed by the beast.

"He ate it," I mumble in shock.

"I know, isn't that *so* cute! Ashtyn was tossing it to him this morning in the front yard, teaching him how to play fetch."

Shit. Ashtyn really knows how to say *fuck you* without uttering a word.

"I have an appointment for an ultrasound next week," my stepmother says in an excited tone. "I want you to come with me."

"No, thanks."

"Oh, come on. Since your dad's not here, I really *really* want you and Julian to be there." The woman doesn't realize that it might be weird for me to go to her ultrasound. "I can take you and Julian out afterward, like . . ." I can practically hear the rusty wheels in her brain turning. "I'll take you guys, like, apple picking afterward. You'll love it!"

"Apple-picking season isn't until the fall," I inform her.

"Oh. Right. We can do something else, then. Something *super* fun. *Super.*"

"How about we just go to lunch." At least I can be spared having to eat another one of her home-cooked meals. I sit up and try not to stare at her growing belly.

"Does that mean you'll go?"

I look at her pleading face and feel sorry for her. I guess if she were my wife, I'd want someone to go with her. "Yeah, I'll go."

"Thank you, Derek! You're The Best!" She attempts to sit on the edge of my bed, but loses her balance and almost tumbles off until I reach out to steady her. Giving up on sitting, she stands next to my bed and rests her hands atop her stomach. "So . . . I hear from a little birdie that you got a letter from your grandmother. That's nice."

"Right." If she knew my grandmother only cared about herself and would probably insult Brandi on sight, I don't think she'd think it was nice.

"What did she say?"

"That she's joinin' the circus as the bearded lady."

"Really?"

"No, not really. She's dyin' and wants me to visit her in Texas." She cocks her head. "Is that another joke?"

"No joke. I'm gonna visit her." After last night, I realized Ashtyn is my kryptonite. I feel myself getting too close and need to back off.

I hear the front door slam. Ashtyn must've left for practice and she's obviously still mad. Two hours later, when she pulls into the driveway in her beat-up car and I'm fixing the broken slats on the shed, I still don't know what I'm going to say to her.

She limps into the house. Her hair is in a low ponytail and she's got grass stains on her pants. She definitely had a rough practice. I tell myself to leave her alone, but I can't get her off my mind. I find her in the living room soaking her foot in a bucket of ice. Brandi is painting her nails and Julian is sitting next to Ashtyn watching TV.

"Ashtyn, can we talk?" I ask.

"No." She gestures to the bucket with her foot inside it. "I'm kind of indisposed and am sick of playing games. Call Bree."

"Don't give me crap. I didn't plan last night to play out the way it did."

Julian taps me on the leg. "Derek, you said 'crap.'"

"So?"

He leans in close and whispers, "It's a bad word."

Brandi nods. "It's written on our no-no word list. You can't say it."

Only Brandi could have a no-no word list.

"'Crap' is not a bad word." I look to Ashtyn for confirmation, but she shrugs like she has no opinion whatsoever. The girl can think of an argument for any little thing, but when it comes to backing me up, she's at a loss for words. "I can think of a ton of other words that are way worse than 'crap.'"

"Stop saying it." Ashtyn joins the no-no list brigade. "You're corrupting my nephew."

"You're just pissed at me 'cause of last night."

"You're *so* wrong," Ashtyn says. "You couldn't be more wrong."

"Wait, did I miss something? What happened last night?" Brandi asks.

Ashtyn gives me a level stare. "*Nothing* happened. Right, Derek?"

"Right."

"Where did you two go?"

"Trampolining, then White Fence Farm," Ashtyn says.

Brandi puts down her polish and furrows her brows. "Then why are you pissed at him? It sounds like fun."

"I don't want to talk about it, Brandi. Okay? You just keep thinking that Derek's perfect just like everyone else."

"Nobody's perfect," I tell her. "Not even you, Ashtyn."

"I never once said I was perfect. In fact, I'm an idiot."

"Join the club."

When Gus arrives home a few minutes later, he takes one look at Ashtyn with her foot in the ice bucket and mumbles something about canceling football camp and getting his money back.

"What football camp?" Brandi asks.

"Your sister wants to drive to some football camp in Texas. By herself," Gus announces. "It's not happening."

"Wait, I have an idea!" Brandi, my scatterbrained stepmother, whirls around and looks at me as if I will save the day. She claps her hands, careful not to ruin her freshly manicured nails and says excitedly, "Derek is going to Texas to visit his grandmother. Derek can drop Ashtyn at football camp, then go see his grandmother. Then he can pick Ashtyn back up and come home. It's the *perfect* solution!"

Everyone's eyes are on me. What, does Brandi think that putting us in a car together will miraculously fix whatever's wrong in her sister's life? Not gonna happen. "I don't think so."

Ashtyn nods. "I agree. That's the worst idea."

Gus nods. "Then it's settled, Ashtyn. You're *not* going."

CHAPTER 30

Ashtyn

I spend the next two hours calling everyone I know outside of my core group of friends. Nobody can make the trip to Texas with me. I'm out of options . . . almost.

Derek.

I'd rather eat nothing but green smoothies for an entire week than be stuck with him on a road trip. I made a complete fool out of myself on our nondate, and feel like an idiot because every time I think of his hands on my body or the way his tongue slid against mine, my knees go weak and I get a tingling sensation in my stomach. I hate myself for falling into Derek's trap.

I close my eyes and take a deep breath, then try to come up with a plan on how to get to Texas without Derek. Ugh, it's impossible.

Derek is the only person who can help me. I find him outside, on top of the shed, shirtless. He's hammering a nail, but all I can think about is getting carried away feeling those tight abs last night. I wish I could wipe that memory from my brain, but it's obvious that's not about to happen.

"I need to talk to you," I say.

He continues to pound away. "Why? You ready to talk about why you're so pissed?"

"Not really, but I don't have a choice." I sigh. "I shouldn't have kissed you last night. Or let you kiss me. It was a *huge* mistake that I'll regret *forever*. I'm pissed at you for tempting me and I'm mad at myself for letting it happen. You got me at a weak moment and it sucks knowing I can't turn back time and erase it. There, I said it."

"Forever's a long time, you know," he says.

"I'm well aware of that, thank you," I say. "I didn't want to ask you this, but I need your help with the whole driving-to-Texas thing so I can go to football camp. I've called everyone I know and even some people I don't really know. Nobody can do it."

"I'm your last choice, huh?"

"Yep."

He jumps off the roof of the shed and walks up to me. "You made the rule that we weren't supposed to get into each other's business. Last night we did and look what happened. I'd say drivin' you out of state and sleepin' at campgrounds in a tent together definitely counts as gettin' into each other's business."

Wait. I think I heard him right, but I'm not sure. "Campgrounds?"

"I like to rough it."

Roughing it isn't my thing, but I'm desperate, so I lie and put on a big, fake smile. "I love camping!"

He shakes his head. "I don't think so."

I shield my eyes as I look up at him. "You wanted me to challenge you and argue with you. I'm willing to keep playing this game if you are, minus the kissing and touching part. Think of all the time we'll have to argue and annoy each other driving to Texas."

"Sounds temptin', but after last night, that's probably the worst idea. Ever." He points to the chewed-up football. "Oh, yeah. And thanks for feedin' the football I gave you to your dog. I'll bet it's sacrilegious to destroy Troy Aikman's signature, but don't worry. I won't out you."

He heads for the house. I can't let him walk away from me, not now. I catch up and stand in his way.

He gently nudges me aside. "Sorry, Ashtyn. I can't help ya."

Time to let it all out, no matter if my ego is bruised. "Wait! Derek, football means *everything* to me. I need to go to Texas. I need to prove to everyone else and myself that I deserve to be there as much as any guy. I didn't tell you before, but Landon left our team to play for our rivals. I refuse to give up, even though everything seems useless now." I look away because my eyes are starting to tear up. "You don't understand. I don't have anything else besides football." I gesture to Falkor, whose head is resting on Derek's feet. "I don't even have my dog anymore because he likes you better. I don't have much, and I don't ask for much. You're my last hope."

I take a deep, shaky breath, knowing full well that my tears are on the brink of overflowing. Derek rubs the back of his neck, deep in thought.

"Sorry, can't do it."

"Name your price," I offer in desperation.

"My price?"

"Yeah. Just throw out a number."

"A million dollars," he says.

Yeah, right. "Obviously I don't have a million dollars." I calculate how much money I've saved up from babysitting, holidays, and birthdays. My dad gave me cash for special occasions—his consolation prize for my crappy home life. "I'll pay you a hundred bucks and I'll split the cost of gas."

"Just a hundred?" he asks, unimpressed. "That's less than minimum wage."

"This is a cash job, remember?"

"You're not takin' the stress factor into consideration. Dealin' with you, Sugar Pie, ain't a piece of cake."

"I'll throw in two boxes of granola bars for the car ride." I hold out my hand. "Deal?"

He looks at my hand for a long time. Then he shakes his head. "Listen, Ashtyn. I don't—"

"Come *on,* Derek. This isn't a joke. I don't have anyone I can count on anymore. My boyfriend ditched me, we don't have a decent quarterback. My life is a complete mess. I'm, like, drowning here. Prove to me that it's not all hopeless."

He rubs his neck again, then sighs a few times as he looks across the yard. Finally he says, "All right. Deal."

CHAPTER 31

Derek

I got suckered into coming to Illinois.

I got suckered into going to Texas.

I got suckered into going on a road trip with a girl who makes me want to kiss her and stay far away from her at the same time.

How the hell does this stuff happen to me? I couldn't say no to Ashtyn when she talked about how much football and this trip meant to her. Once upon a time football meant that much to me.

Ashtyn has that spark I used to have. I see it in her eyes. I don't know what she thinks she'll accomplish by going to football camp, but I have no doubt she's going to use everything in her arsenal to get noticed by scouts.

Four days later, we load up my SUV. Ashtyn made a big deal out of raiding the pantry for junk food to chow on during the drive. I stuck some granola bars Ashtyn bought in my backpack, but decide to bring stuff to make my own food.

"What is that?" Ashtyn asks as I walk out of the house.

"A blender."

"You're bringing a *blender* on a road trip?"

"Yep." Give me some bananas and spinach and I'll have a good breakfast. If Ashtyn thinks I'm going to eat candy or cookies for breakfast, lunch, and dinner, she better think again.

After saying our good-byes to Brandi, Julian, and Gus, we're ready to get out of town.

Falkor jumps in the backseat when I open the door.

"You're not invited." He looks at me with droopy eyes and doesn't move. Ashtyn tries to get him out, but he doesn't move until I say, "Out!"

Suddenly Julian is at my side, hugging my legs with his little kid arms. "You'll come back, right?"

I kneel down to him. "Of course I'll come back."

Ashtyn peeks out of the window. "Hey, Julian. You want to give me a hug, too?"

Julian nods.

Ashtyn gets out of the car and kneels down. She pulls him toward her and hugs him. That hug is full of warmth and emotion . . . she doesn't want to let him go. It's like she's craving the unconditional love Julian's giving her right now. It's something I could never give her.

Ashtyn kicks her shoes off and makes herself comfortable after we pull onto the highway. Soon, we're out of the city and see nothing but farms and a lone hawk flying overhead.

"You hungry?" She reaches into her backpack and pulls out some crackers and a can of cheese spread. "Want some?"

"Nah."

"It's not gonna kill you, Derek." She holds a cracker, piled high with semiliquefied cheese, in front of my mouth. "Try it."

I open my mouth and she shoves the cracker in, her fingertips touching my lips and almost lingering there until I close my mouth. It feels like an intimate moment, but that's nuts. She was just feeding me a cracker, not trying to flirt.

Tell my body that. It's been reacting since she touched me with those feminine fingertips that totally betray her football-tough-girl image.

She holds out another cracker. I'm tempted to take it, but I don't want those fingertips anywhere near my lips again. Her rule of no kissing or touching is cemented into my brain.

"I'm good."

"Suit yourself." She opens her mouth wide and squirts cheese directly into her mouth.

Keeping Ashtyn at a distance is what I need to do, even though I sense an undercurrent of something I can't put my finger on . . . and don't really want to. *No kissing or touching.* I glance over at Ashtyn. She's licking some cheese off her top lip and has no clue she's driving me insane.

She shrieks and braces both her hands on the dashboard. "Derek, you're about to hit a squirrel!"

Shit! I quickly swerve to avoid the thing, the tires screeching as the car jolts us sideways.

"Did you hit it?" she asks in a panic, looking in the rearview mirror.

"No."

She shakes her finger at me, the same one that was on my lips a few minutes ago. "Pay attention to the road. You could've killed us."

I'm not the one who tested the no-touching rule. I grab the can and toss it in the back. There, now I won't be distracted.

She lets out a frustrated cry. "What was that for?"

"So I can concentrate on the road."

She shakes her head in confusion, but if she thinks I'm about to explain why I tossed the can of cheese in the back, she'll be waiting forever. Some things need to be left unsaid. With nothing to put on her crackers, she shoves the rest in her backpack, which I've got no doubt is filled with more crap.

I stop for gas and hand the keys to Ashtyn. She drives while I knock out in the passenger seat. I wish I was back in my dorm, where all I worried about was how I was gonna make it through the summer without being summoned into Crowe's office. When I was a freshman, I had it all planned out. I'd go to college and play ball.

Everything changed after my mom died.

My brain reaches into the flood of memories locked up like a safe inside my head. I can still hear the familiar sound of my mom laughing in the kitchen with a stained towel around her head after she dyed the ends of her hair blue. It was my dad's favorite color and she wanted to be reminded of him every time she looked in the mirror. He was deployed and she was bored and lonely.

A few months later she got diagnosed with cancer and lost all that hair.

All those times my mom had go to her chemo treatments when I was at school sucked. When her hair started falling out, I found her crying in the bathroom as she looked into the mirror at the massive bald spots and clumps of hair in her brush.

Two days later she held up my dad's clippers and told me to finish the job. I shaved my own head right along with hers, but it didn't prevent her from tearing up the entire time. If I could have fought that cancer for her, I would have.

But there is no negotiating with cancer.

I took care of my mom, but it wasn't good enough. I couldn't save her and I wasn't there when she took her last breath. I know she would've wanted me to be there. I was the only family member around, and she died alone because I was at football practice and got to the hospital too late.

I should've been there, but I wasn't.

There's a long stretch of silence as we drive for hours. After we stop for lunch, I take over the wheel and head for the campground. Ashtyn is leaning against the window, looking out at the farmhouses we're passing. Ashtyn points out a guy pushing a girl on a tire swing outside one of the houses. "That's romantic," she says, sighing loudly. "Derek, have you ever had a girlfriend?"

"Yeah."

"What happened?"

I haven't thought about Stephanie in a long time. We'd gone to homecoming together sophomore year, and afterward she gave me her garter and her virginity. She said we'd be together forever, and at the time I believed it. "I moved to California and she lived in Tennessee. We tried to make the long-distance thing work, but that didn't last long." Forever ended up to be seven months.

"When did you know it was over?"

"When I found out she was screwin' my best friend."

CHAPTER 32

Ashtyn

Ashtyn, wake up. We're here."

I'm not really awake, and just want to go back to sleep. That's not going to happen, because Derek pats me soundly on the shoulder.

"I'm up," I say groggily.

He keeps patting me on the shoulder until I sit up and look out the window. In front of us is a big sign that reads:

HAPPY CAMPER CAMPGROUND
Where nature nurtures you!

Oh, goodie. Nature. Should I mention that I'm not fond of spiders, and just hearing the sound of crickets creeps me out? "Umm . . . why don't we ditch the camping idea and go to a hotel? Between your gambling money and my meager savings, I'm sure we can scrape up enough to stay at a decent place."

"Gambling money?"

"Don't act all innocent. Monika found a bunch of money stashed in your boot and poker chips in your suitcase."

"So that makes me a gambler?"

"Yep."

"Listen, Sugar Pie. Don't be a diva and be quick to judge other people." He steps out of the car and heads toward a sign that reads REGISTRATION AND GENERAL STORE.

A guy at the front desk greets us with a crooked, toothy grin as he produces a site registration form. Soon we're assigned a small campsite with running water and electricity.

While Derek buys a bundle of wood and matches, I buy hot dogs and buns. In the end, I splurge and buy stuff to make s'mores. As long as I'm stuck here, I might as well make the best of it.

Outside, Derek leans against the car while checking the map for our campsite location. He has no clue that two girls sitting on top of the picnic bench a few feet away are staring at him like he's some sort of conquest.

He peeks into my bag. "What'd you buy for dinner?"

"If you're thinking I got organic turkey burgers or flax seeds, you've got another thing coming."

"What about apple cider vinegar?"

"For what?"

"A detox."

I look him up and down. "You don't need a detox, Derek. You need hot dogs."

His response is a laugh. "Let's pitch the tent and make a fire so I can fill up with those nitrates. Yum."

"You're seriously getting on my nerves."

"That's the point, Sugar Pie." Derek drives down the winding gravel road until we reach campsite number 431. It's got a few trees, but mostly it's an open, flat grassy area. "Home sweet home!" he announces.

A couple of our neighbors are playing football, a family is cooking over a fire, and a few girls are sunbathing in bikinis.

Derek practically jumps out of the car and pulls our tent out of the back.

I read the description on the side of the box. "This is for three people."

"Right. We're two people, with a tent for three. We'll have plenty of room to stretch out."

I'm not convinced. "This looks small, Derek. I don't think my blow-up bed will fit very well in this thing."

"Blow-up bed?"

"Yep. I need to be comfortable."

Being around guys in close quarters is second nature to me. I've had to sleep on the bus with the guys when we've traveled long distances for games, and I've been in the locker room when most of them were half-dressed. But this is different. I have to be in a tent with a boy I have a crush on who I don't want to have a crush on.

Derek pulls out the tent and spreads it on the ground.

"Need help?" I ask.

"Nope. I got it."

I sit on a tree stump and watch Derek expertly pitch the tent.

It's hot, even though the sun is going down. He takes off his shirt and wipes sweat from his face with it. When he shoves part of his shirt into the waistband of his jeans, his deep blue eyes meet mine and I feel butterflies in my stomach.

I look away, not wanting him to know I was admiring his naked, bronzed chest and perfect physique. I feel guilty for looking.

The domed tent is green with a purple racing stripe going down the side like a sports car. Most sports cars are bigger than our tent. Most closets are bigger than our tent. All the tents around us are bigger. When Derek refuses to put the blow-up bed I brought in the tent, I lug it in there and inflate it myself. It takes up most of the space, but at least I'll be comfortable.

In the woods, I gather little sticks to kindle the fire as Derek places firewood in the pit. One of the guys in the campsite next to ours tosses a football near me. On instinct, I drop the sticks and catch the ball.

"Whoa," a boy with curly blond hair says. "Nice catch."

I throw it back in a perfect spiral. Curly's friend, who's got a tattoo of a skull on his forearm, says, "Good throw. What's your name?"

"Ashtyn."

"I'm Ben. Where you from, Ashtyn?" the guy with the tattoo asks.

"Chicago."

Curly waves me over. "Want to hang with us?"

Derek looks ready to intervene, as if I need some hero to rescue me if I get myself into trouble. I don't need his help. These are just a few guys having fun. "Maybe I'll meet up with you guys later."

When I come back to our site, Derek shakes his head.

"What?" I ask.

"You fell for it."

"Fell for what?"

He nods in the direction of Ben and his friends. "Those guys were checkin' you out way before that ball was thrown your way, Ashtyn. It wasn't an accident."

I arrange the sticks in the fire pit along with the wood Derek bought. "So?"

He kneels down and starts to light the kindling with a lighter. "So I'm gettin' paid to drive you, not to babysit you."

"I don't need a babysitter. I don't need anyone."

He shakes his head and sits back on his heels. "That's what you think."

CHAPTER 33

Derek

Ashtyn really got pissed at my babysitting comment, like it was some huge insult. Now she won't talk to me. After we ate the hot dogs, she climbed into the tent and hasn't peeked her head out since. Will she still ignore me when we have to sleep next to each other?

"Can we join you?" comes a female voice from the campsite next to ours. "Our fire went out and we're out of wood."

Three girls, all wearing St. Louis Cardinals T-shirts and bikini bottoms, walk up to me. They've all got super long straight hair. One has a stripe of her hair dyed pink.

"Sure." I help bring their chairs around our fire.

The girls introduce themselves and we start talking. Ashtyn steps out of the tent. She doesn't talk much until the guys who'd been playing ball earlier gather around our campfire. They bring a cooler full of beer. Before long, we're hosting an all-out bash with music blaring from speakers in someone's van.

Ashtyn's suddenly chatting it up with a bunch of the guys. She's got all their attention as she relays some story about playing football in the middle of a downpour last season. Ashtyn has power over guys . . . power that has nothing to do with being a football player. She doesn't flip her hair back or giggle or stick out her breasts to get their attention like normal girls. She's just . . . Ashtyn.

"Is Ashtyn your girlfriend?" a girl who introduced herself as Carrie asks.

I glance across the fire at the girl who drives me nuts, then tell myself to look away and stop caring about what she does.

"Nope, Ashtyn's not my girlfriend." I glance around like I'm about to tell Carrie something super secretive. "She's actually royalty from Fregolia, a small country in Europe. She wanted to know what it was like to live with the locals in America, so she's here undercover. I'm her bodyguard."

"Ooh." Carrie glances at my biceps appreciatively, then licks her lips. She leans closer. "You have the most *amazing* eyes. Where are you from?"

I bet my left nut that if I say Fregolia, she might very well believe me. "The answer's kinda complicated."

"What do you mean?"

"I'm from a lot of places."

"Ooh, mysterious." She straightens, seemingly excited to learn about all the places I've lived. "Let me guess, then. You must have gotten that sexy drawl from somewhere."

I nod. "Alabama. Tennessee. Texas."

Carrie touches my bicep and cries out, "Oh, my God! You're from Texas? What a coincidence! I love Texasians!"

CHAPTER 34

Ashtyn

After talking and laughing with the guys from the other campsite until my voice is raw, I'm suddenly exhausted. They ask me to play strip poker at their site. I'm not about to play strip poker with anyone, let alone a bunch of guys I just met. I don't tell them that Derek plays poker, because I don't want him to play strip poker or any kind of stripping game with those girls he met tonight.

Derek is talking to some girl by the campfire. He's been talking to her all night. She's flirting, giggling, and touching his arm. Derek is definitely interested; I can tell by the way he's focusing all his attention on her.

I gather my hockey jersey and toiletries, then walk down the little pathway to take a shower and get ready for bed. I pass Derek and the giggler on the way back to our tent, ignoring them as I unzip the entrance and crawl inside.

I'm lying on the mattress and hear more giggles. And Derek's laughter. Ugh, why do I care if Derek wants to hook up with someone else? Because the truth is that I want to be with him. I find myself craving it. I squeeze my eyes shut and try to wipe out the image of Derek and the girl outside. I wish that girl was me.

What am I thinking? I don't want a guy who cringes at the thought of having a real relationship instead of a one-night stand. I don't want a gambler or womanizer. Just like I told him before dinner, I don't want or need anyone.

I try to sleep, but I can't. As if hearing their low whispers isn't bad enough, through the nylon I see their shadows. Her giggles grate on my nerves because they're so fake.

I turn over, put my earbuds in, and listen to music. The light from my iPod gives the tent a dim glow. I take a deep, calming breath . . . but out of the corner of my eye I catch sight of something crawling on the tent—a big spider is right next to my head!

I scramble to get away from the creepy thing.

Is it on me?

Oh, no. I don't like creepy, crawly spiders with fangs and a bunch of legs and gross, sticky webs. They freak me out.

It moves closer.

"Don't come near me!" I cry out, then whimper for help.

Within seconds, the front of the tent zips open and Derek appears. "What's wrong?" he asks, his voice full of concern.

I point to the offending creature. "There it is!" I moan when it climbs to the top of the tent. "Ewww. Get it away. Smash it. Kill it!"

"You're brutal. It's a spider, Ashtyn. Not a scorpion."

He captures it, then sets it free outside.

"Make sure you put it far away," I tell him.

He appears again. "It's gone. You're a tough football player. Surely you can handle a little spider."

"Surely being a football player has nothing to do with a fear of those eight-legged creepy crawlers, Derek. And that thing wasn't little. I saw its fangs."

"Yeah, right." He shakes his head. "What did you think, that there'd be no spiders at a campground? We're in the middle of nature."

"I didn't expect one to be *inside* my tent," I tell him. "I read on the Internet that it's not uncommon for a person to eat a spider while they're sleeping. I couldn't go to sleep thinking that thing was about to crawl on my face and stick its fangs into me. This is my space."

"Well, it's gone, so you're fine now. I'm surprised we haven't heard from the Happy Camper police. It's quiet hours after ten, you know." He grabs his toiletries from his duffel. "Your bed is takin' up eighty percent of the tent. Where do you suppose I'm gonna sleep?"

I point to a sliver of space, big enough if he doesn't move much. "Right there."

"You're kiddin' me, right?"

"No."

He shakes his head. "We'll figure it out when I get back."

"What about that ugly girl you were talking to?" I ask, trying to hide any trace of jealousy in my voice. "Isn't she still out there waiting for you?"

"She wasn't ugly. And no, she's not waitin' for me."

"Did you see her pink hair? I mean, seriously. It's painfully obvious she's begging for attention."

"She's hot."

"Yeah, well, what do you know? I think bacteria from those algae smoothies have invaded your brain."

He turns to me. "You jealous I was talkin' to her?"

"I'm *not* jealous. I'm just concerned, but I won't look out for you anymore if you don't want me to."

"You need to look out for yourself, Ashtyn. Not me."

Derek leaves to wash up. My stomach has butterflies knowing that he'll be sleeping in the tent with me. I don't want to admit that I want him to want me. But I do. I want him to say that the girl he was talking to tonight was boring and stupid and . . . not me.

He's back. The blow-up bed moves as he sits on it. I roll toward the middle . . . toward him.

"Don't think you're sleeping on my bed," I mumble, scootching back to the edge of the bed and hoping he doesn't sense that I'm totally aware of the electricity between us. If he's feeling it, too, he's masking it.

"Listen, Sugar Pie, you didn't leave me any room. We're sharin' a bed. You don't like it," he says in an annoyed tone, "I have a pocketknife that I'll be happy to plunge into the mattress."

I sit up. "You wouldn't dare."

He reaches into his bag and holds up the knife. "Try me."

Unfortunately, I don't think Derek is the kind of guy to make empty threats. "Fine. You can sleep in the bed, but make sure you stay on your side. Remember our no-touching rule."

"Just move over."

It's completely dark. And it's silent except for our breathing.

My back is to Derek. I hear him slide his jeans off before he lies down next to me. It's strangely intimate with just the two of us alone in the tent. Has he slept all night with a girl before? Did he sleep with that girlfriend from Tennessee who cheated on him?

There's hardly enough room for both of us on the bed. I keep my body totally straight so we don't accidentally touch our legs or hands or arms or . . . anything. I have nothing to worry about. While Derek might want to be with me physically because he's a male, he doesn't have any desire to hold me and tell me everything in my life will turn out okay.

That's what I want from a guy.

That's what I need from a guy.

Suddenly it's super silent in the tent. Even the crickets are quiet. I'm restless. Silence to me is as annoying as nails on a chalkboard, because when it's too quiet my mind goes in overdrive. When my mom and Brandi left all those years ago, our house was too silent. All I did was think about what they were doing, why they left, and how awfully lonely I'd become. I filled that void with music, the pounding kind that doesn't let you think.

Derek is listening to music with his headphones on. It's so

quiet I can hear the songs. Old music from the '50s and '60s softly fills the tent. The songs soothe me. I drift off trying not to think about Derek saving me from the spider. Or sleeping next to me. I remind myself that he's attracted to girls like the one with the pink-striped hair—someone who knows she'll never see him again.

He'd been my hero tonight without realizing it. He's being my hero now, by driving me to Texas and staying with me tonight instead of going off and hooking up with that girl.

"Thanks," I mumble as I drift off, knowing he can't hear me with his headphones on. It's nice knowing that at least for tonight I'm protected . . . Derek is here to make sure I'm not attacked by spiders . . . or hounded by thoughts of being abandoned.

I'm dreaming about Alaska. All I know is that I'm cold and I can't get warm. I'm stuck in the middle of an iceberg and can't get loose. I'd do anything to stop shaking. The wind is as cold as a snowstorm. Somehow I magically get off the iceberg. Now I'm walking in the snow, naked, about to freeze to death.

I'm half-asleep as I turn to find a more comfortable position, barely aware that I'm not in Alaska but sleeping in a tent. I'm cold . . . the temperature has dropped and I'm shaking. My hand rests on something warm. An island of some sort. I move closer to the warmth, cuddling into it.

"Ashtyn, what're you doin'?" a deep, masculine voice says.

Derek. I don't open my eyes, but I know it's him. His drawl is unique and undeniable, like warm hot chocolate. I want him to be my protector, just for tonight. If he leaves me, I'll be all alone.

I don't want to be cold and alone. Not tonight.

In my sleepy state I tell myself I'll do anything to keep him here with me.

"Don't leave me," I mumble into his chest as I shiver uncontrollably.

"I won't." His arms wrap around me and I feel safe . . . away from the iceberg in my dream and the loneliness in my heart and the pain of losing everyone I ever loved.

CHAPTER 35

Derek

I wake up with a hard-on. And my arm around Ashtyn. We're spooning like a married couple and her long hair is in my face. The flowery smell of her perfume reminds me that while Ashtyn talks tough and is a football player, she's 100 percent female. I did my best to stay on my side of the bed, but she kept moving closer. And closer. Then she told me she was cold and asked me to hold her, so I did.

That was my first mistake.

I quickly take my arm off her and manage to get some space between us. I need to cool off. She was half-asleep when she asked me to hold her, so hopefully she won't remember. I'm not about to play her temporary boyfriend until we get to Texas.

Pink-haired Carrie is my type. She pouted after I turned her down when she'd asked if I wanted to spend the night in her tent. I'd told her I had a job to do as Her Highness's bodyguard.

Carrie was looking for a good time.

Ashtyn is looking for someone who won't abandon her.

When she turned to me, was it just because I was a warm body? Or was it because it was *me*? Doesn't matter. I unzip the tent and go make a fire. How did I get here? It's because of that damn pig prank. Fucking pigs are the reason I'm here and not in my dorm room at Regents.

This trip is only a few days. I can do anything for a couple of days, even try to stay as far away from Ashtyn as possible. I hear movement in the tent before she peeks her head out.

"Hey," she says.

"Hey." I point to a Pop-Tarts box on the hood of my car, but I don't make eye contact with her. Instead, I stare into the flames of the fire I just built. "I got you some breakfast."

She opens the box. "Thanks," she mumbles as she takes a bite.

I lean forward on my elbows and wonder what I'm gonna say to her. "We should pack up and head out soon," I say stoically. "We've got a lot of drivin' to do."

We spend the next twenty minutes packing up. She doesn't look my way when we pull out of the campground and head to our next destination.

"Want to talk about last night?" she asks.

"The part where you were flirtin' with those guys, or the part when you asked me to hold you?"

"I was not flirting with those guys. We were talking football."

"Oh, that's right. You only like guys who play football."

"What's that supposed to mean?" When I don't answer, she

says, "Maybe we should start with the fact that you were getting all chummy with that girl with the pink hair. She just wanted to hook up."

"That's what makes it all the better. No emotional involvement. No strings attached. That's what I call a perfect relationship."

"That's what I call skanky." She curls her upper lip in disgust. "I feel sorry for your future wife. She's destined to be a very lonely woman."

"And I feel sorry for your future husband, who's destined to disappoint you and your high expectations."

"High expectations? My expectations aren't high."

"Really? Then don't expect me to be your heater every night."

"I won't."

Ashtyn insists she needs to practice every day while we're on the road. The girl is dedicated, I'll give her that much. She searches for nearby parks on her phone, but nothing comes up, so I end up driving around looking for an open area.

We come upon a high school with a football field out back. "What about there? It's better than a park because you can actually kick through real goalposts and not imaginary ones."

Ashtyn shakes her head. "I can't practice there. That's private school property. Besides, there's a fence around it and it's locked."

I look at her sideways. "So?"

"You're not thinking about breaking in," she says.

"Yeah, I am."

She keeps protesting while I park in the lot next to the field.

"Come on," I say. "It's summer and nobody's here. Trust me, it's not a big deal. Nobody's gonna care."

I walk toward the gate. Ashtyn stays in the car for a few seconds, then follows after grabbing a football and ball holder from the backseat.

"This is a bad idea, Derek," she says in a panicked voice. "I don't do illegal things. I *can't* do illegal things. If we get caught—"

"Keep your panties on, Sugar Pie. We're not gonna get caught." I examine the lock and know it won't take me long to get it open. At Regents my friend Sam and I spent weeks practicing how to jimmy locks so we could get into the cafeteria and snatch food from the refrigerators at night.

"You *are* a thug," Ashtyn says when the lock clicks open and I lead her onto the grassy field.

Thug or not, she's now got a place to practice.

I lean against the post and watch her set up. "I don't suppose you want me to show you how to hold the ball so I can kick it from a live person?" she asks.

"Nah," I say. "I'm good."

She shrugs, then kicks the ball effortlessly from the one yard line. It sails through the posts.

"Want to get the ball for me after I kick it?" she asks. "So I don't have to run after it after every kick? It'll go much faster."

"Nah," I say again. "I'm good."

"You're a lazy ass," she mumbles as she fetches the ball and sets it up, this time on the five yard line.

She spends over an hour setting up the ball, kicking it, then retrieving it. Each time she kicks, the ball sails through the posts. I see the concentration on her face as she takes a calming breath and calculates how far she's got to kick it before her foot touches the ball.

The girl is impressive.

After her practice, we're back on the road. She's leaning back with her eyes closed, nodding as she gets lost in the music through her earbuds, oblivious to everything else around her.

I drive to the next campground, a small private campground near Oklahoma City. There are only four campsites on the property, and two are vacant. Ashtyn is quiet as we set up our tent in our assigned spot before it gets dark and wash up in the bathrooms at the front of the property.

Our site is surrounded by trees. An old couple in a pop-up tent who introduced themselves as Irving and Sylvia are in the campsite next to us. We met the old couple on the way back from the bathrooms, while they were sitting next to their pop-up tent at their fold-out table.

It's still light as Ashtyn takes footballs out of the car and practices kicking again. She stretches first, and I find myself watching her as if she's the star of an exercise show and it's the most entertaining thing on television. She looks back at me. "You watching me?"

"No."

"Come here."

"Why?"

"Just . . . come here."

I walk over to her. She picks up one of the footballs by her feet and hands it to me. "You remember how to throw one?"

Yeah. I look at the ball as if I've never held one in my hand before. "Not really."

"Didn't your dad throw a football around with you when you were a little kid, Derek?"

"He was kind of busy protectin' our country," I say, although that's only half-true. He was busy protecting our country most of the time, but he did teach me how to throw a football. I must've been three when he first taught me how to throw a football. By the time I was eight, I begged my parents to constantly play football with me so I could practice my perfect spiral. I never stopped throwing the ball after that, and would recruit anyone who was around to go to the field with me so I could practice.

I hand the football back to her, but she pushes it in my hands. "Are you a righty or lefty?"

"Righty."

She takes my fingers and places them on the ball, then proceeds to tell me how to throw it. "The key is to let it roll off your fingers. I swear it'll come back to you once you try it."

I pretend like this is the first time holding a football and try not to crack a smile when she gives overly detailed instructions.

"If you're such an expert at throwin'," I tell her, "why aren't you the quarterback?"

She laughs. "I can't throw as far or as accurately as Landon." She shrugs. "Some guys are just born to throw footballs. Landon is a natural."

"I'm sure there's a slew of dudes who're better."

"I haven't seen anyone, especially in our division. His dad played professionally."

The way Ashtyn talks about Landon's talent, you'd think he was some superhuman quarterback. It almost makes me want to show off my skills. Almost.

She jogs away from me. "Okay, throw it!"

It's not easy for me to toss a football awkwardly, like I'm rusty, but I manage to do it. The ball tumbles through the air, then bounces on the ground with a thud. It's not even close to the target.

"That was pathetic, Derek."

"I know. I was an average ball player."

"Try again," she says encouragingly. "Remember to let the ball roll off your fingers as you throw it."

I throw it again, this time managing to get it within ten yards of her but still out of reach.

"You sure you were born in America? You sure don't throw a football like you were."

"Not everyone can be as good as Landon, the 'God of All Quarterbacks,' I guess."

She tucks the balls under her arm. "Lesson over for today. And if you're jealous of Landon, there's no shame in admitting it."

"I'm not jealous of him." With a little practice I bet I could outthrow him.

Ashtyn holds in a chuckle. "Yeah, right."

"What do you love about the game?"

"I'll explain it to you. To me it's more than a game." She touches her chest and says, "When you love something as much as I love football, you just feel it inside. Did you ever love doing something so bad that it consumed you?"

"A long time ago."

"That's what football is to me. It's my passion, my life . . . my escape. When I play, I forget everything that sucks in my life. And when we win . . ." She looks down, like she's embarrassed to admit what she's about to reveal. "I know this is going to sound stupid, but when we win, I think miracles can happen."

"Miracles, huh?"

She nods. "I told you it was stupid."

"It's not stupid. I guess havin' hope is better than givin' up and thinking life will suck forever."

We start walking back to our campsite when Sylvia waves us over. "Come join us! We've got plenty of food. Irv, go get them chairs."

Ashtyn and I walk to their small table while Irv does what he's told and Sylvia dishes out food.

"We don't want to interrupt your dinner," Ashtyn says, although she's eyeing the chicken and rice as if it were a gourmet meal. She looks exhausted, but that chicken sure does bring a light to her eyes.

"Thank you, ma'am." I take a seat.

Sylvia does most of the talking while we eat. She tells us how she and Irv met when they were young and have four children. One is a doctor, one is a lawyer, and one is a pharmacist.

"I don't know what the hell our son Jerry does," Irv says.

Sylvia taps Irv on the shoulder. "Don't say 'hell' in front of these nice kids, Irv." Irv mumbles a quick apology before chowing down.

Ashtyn and I are chowing down, too. The chicken is tender and the seasoning makes my mouth water. The rice tastes damn good, too. I haven't had a good home-cooked meal in forever. Ashtyn must feel the same way, because she's done with her chicken and is chowing down on the rice.

"How long have you two been dating?" Sylvia asks.

"We're not datin'," I answer.

"Why not?"

Ashtyn looks up from her plate. "Because he only likes stupid girls who want one-night stands."

"And she only likes jocks who play football," I say, challenging her.

Sylvia tilts her head as if she's scrutinizing my choice of girls while Irv looks at me appreciatively.

"You don't want to let the girl of your dreams get away," Sylvia tells me. "Tell him why, Irv." Irv is busy eating and doesn't seem to want to stop. "Irv!"

He finally puts his fork down. "What?"

"Do you have your hearing aids on?" Sylvia asks him. After he nods, she repeats in a louder tone, "Tell Derek here why he shouldn't let the girl of his dreams get away!"

Irving brings Sylvia's hand to his lips, kissing it softly. "When I saw Sylvia for the first time, I was hired to paint her house. She had a boyfriend who she was expected to marry, but I knew from the moment I laid eyes on her that she was the one. She probably wasn't supposed to talk to the help, but she'd watch me paint and chat with me while I worked. I'd fallen madly in love with the girl and knew she was the girl of my dreams." He stops to look into Sylvia's eyes longingly. "So when it was time to paint Sylvia's room, I painted MARRY ME on her wall." He laughs. "She wrote her answer on the wall so I'd find it the next day."

"What happened?" Ashtyn asks, completely into the story as if it's a fairy tale.

"Obviously she said yes, because they're married," I tell her.

"Actually, Irving never saw what I'd written because my parents found out what he'd done and fired him," Sylvia says. "They didn't want me marrying a painter."

"But I never gave up. I came to her house every day, asking for her hand."

"Eventually my parents gave in." Sylvia pats Irving's hand. "And we were married six months later. That was sixty years ago."

Ashtyn sits back and sighs. "That's a wonderful story. So romantic."

"That's why you don't let the girl of your dreams get away, Derek." Sylvia wags her finger at me.

I think about what Ashtyn would look like sixty years from now sitting across the table from me. I bet she'd still have that same sparkle in her eyes and those kissable lips. She'd be grateful someone finally stuck by her all those years when everyone else failed her.

But I can't be that guy.

I might not make it past thirty-five, the age my mom was when she died. Right now, as I look across the table at the girl who could very well be the girl of my dreams, I know I won't marry her. I'm going to let someone else be her Irving, someone who'll be able to sit across from her sixty years from now and look into her eyes as if his would have been a horrible existence if not for her.

"Yeah, well, Ashtyn here is bossy and controlling." My food threatens to come up as I add, "Since I don't like bossy and controlling girls, she ain't the girl of my dreams."

"Derek is actually the most annoying boy I've ever met," Ashtyn chimes in with a fake smile. "So if he painted MARRY ME on my wall, I'd put a circle around it and slash a line right through it."

CHAPTER 36

Ashtyn

'm not going to let Derek think his comments weigh heavily on my mind or my heart. Back at our campsite, I announce that I'm tired and want to go to bed.

Tonight I won't freeze my ass off, because I put on two pairs of socks, two pairs of sweats, and two jerseys. I must look like a puffed-up marshmallow, but I don't care. I don't want to be weak in the middle of the night and ask him to hold me.

The entire time Irving was telling his story, I thought about the boy of my dreams. I imagined Derek looking at me across a dinner table sixty years from now.

But Derek doesn't want to be my boyfriend. He says he couldn't be with me because I'm controlling and bossy. But could I be someone else for him? If I change, will he want to love me?

The problem is that last night, knowing he was near and wouldn't let go of me, made me feel something I haven't felt in a long time. When he told me he wouldn't leave me, I believed him. I found myself wanting to fall in love with him.

Truth is, I think I already have.

It hurts, because I have to either give up on ever having my feelings reciprocated or become the kind of girl Derek wants. Ugh, I don't know what to do.

I hear wood crackling and leaves crunching underneath his footsteps as I lie in the tent. A few minutes later Derek peeks inside.

"You sure you don't want to sit outside for a bit?" he asks in that deep voice that penetrates the cool night air. "It's warm by the fire."

If I look at him, my heart will skip a beat and I might be tempted to tell him how I feel. I can't do that. "I'm fine. Just go to the fire and leave me alone," I bark, trying to push him away so I can be alone in my misery. I'm so conflicted.

"What're you wearin'?" he asks.

"Practically everything in my entire duffel." I fluff my pillow and turn away from him. "I won't be cold tonight, so you don't have to worry. You can rest easy knowing I won't ask you to keep me warm."

"I don't . . ."

"You don't what?"

There's a long silence. "Forget it," he finally says. "Good night, Ashtyn. See you in the mornin'."

Tears form in my eyes. This isn't the way it's supposed to be when you fall in love. As controlling as he says I am, I wish I could control the way he feels about me. But I can't. I know there's more between us than just a game, but how do I make him see it?

I wish I could control my emotions as I squeeze my eyes shut and will them to stay dry. But I can't. Silent tears start streaming down my face and fall onto my pillow.

One-sided love sucks.

CHAPTER 37

Derek

'm sitting alone in front of the fire. Irving walks up, holding a can of beer.

"You've got a nice fire going there," he says.

I gesture to Ashtyn's empty chair. "Want to join me? Ashtyn went to sleep a while ago and I could use some company."

He settles into the chair and takes a swig of beer. "Ashtyn seems like a nice girl. Spunky."

"She's trouble. For me, at least." I toss a stick into the fire. "My dad married her sister, so we're kind of stuck together . . . at least for a while."

"You could do a lot worse than being stuck with a pretty girl on a road trip."

"She drives me nuts."

Irving chuckles as if sincerely amused. "Every worthwhile girl drives a man nuts, Derek. Just think what a boring world it would be without girls who keep us on our toes. My Sylvia is a feisty ol' gal, but we complement each other. For richer or poorer, in sickness and in health . . . we've been through it all, which just made us stronger."

I think about all the shit that's happened in the short time I've known Ashtyn. "We made a rule that we're not supposed to, you know . . ."

"Did you agree to it?"

"Well . . . yeah."

He shrugs. "Seems to me that might've been your first mistake."

"I don't know. Maybe it was." And maybe it was an excuse to stay far away from her so I wouldn't have to deal with the consequences.

We spend the next twenty minutes staring into the fire. Irving was in the military, so I tell him that my dad is deployed. He tells me that he's an Army veteran. When I ask if it was hard for Sylvia when he was in the military, he said it was, but they kept in touch with letters and the rare phone call. When he was deployed, you couldn't communicate through e-mail or Skype.

He finishes his beer and stretches his legs out. "Well, I'm gonna get some shut-eye. Have a nice evening." He gestures to our tent. "Keep an eye on her, because if you don't, I'll bet you some young buck is gonna snatch her up."

"Yes, sir."

When he leaves, I stay in front of the fire. Do I sleep next to Ashtyn? Fuck, I'm so aware of her I can't go in there and be next to her.

I sit in the chair by the fire, cross my arms on my chest, and close my eyes. It'll probably be the most uncomfortable night I've ever had, but that's okay. Today I'm not doing anything to shake up my life.

But tomorrow . . . well, tomorrow's another day.

CHAPTER 38

Ashtyn

I wake up in the middle of the night, burning up and drenched in sweat. Derek isn't in the tent. I strip off one of the jerseys and kick off my sweatpants and socks, then go back to sleep. A little later I wake up to the sound of rain tapping on the tent. Derek still isn't here and it doesn't look like he's been here all night. I figure he went to the bathroom, but after fifteen minutes there's still no sign of him. Worry settles in my chest.

What if he got attacked by a bear?

Or slipped in the mud on the way to the bathroom and hit his head on a rock?

Rain is coming down steadily as I grab a flashlight from my bag and walk outside. Derek's sitting with his arms crossed on his chest and a baseball cap perched on his head.

"Are you crazy? It's pouring," I say.

"I know."

"Then why aren't you in the tent, where it's dry and warm?"

"Because I was too tempted to break our no-touching-or-kissing rule." He looks me up and down. "Bein' here with you . . . you've really got under my skin."

"You want to break the rule?"

He nods slowly. "Yeah."

"Why?"

"Because I'm tryin' to push you away when all I want to do is hold you. I know you say you don't want a hero, but damn I'd like to be that guy who'll save you from spiders and whatever and whoever else hurts you."

His words seep deep into the core of my heart. With our eyes locked, I straddle him on the chair. "I want to break the rule, too."

My heart pounds rapidly and I grab his shoulders so he can steady me. I'm dizzy with wanting him to love me as much as I love him. He's soaking wet and now I'm soaking and rain falls on us and around us. I don't feel hot or cold . . . I'm too caught up in being with Derek, here in the dark in the middle of the night.

I've dropped the flashlight, so I can't see much. But I can feel. I can feel Derek's strong thighs beneath mine and his large hands circling my waist. I want to feel more, much more. The road to this moment was full of arguments and misunderstandings, but now we're in perfect sync.

He cups the back of my head and urges me to kiss him. When our lips meet, my insides get all tingly. He places little teasing kisses across my lips until I moan and want more . . . I want him to let go and stop trying to protect me from himself.

I open my mouth for a more intimate kiss in an attempt to

make him lose control. Our wet lips and tongues tangle around each other's.

I break the kiss and lean back. "I don't want to pretend I don't want this, Derek. Not tonight."

"Me neither," he admits.

Ever since I touched his muscular chest, I've wanted to run my hands over it again and again until I've memorized each ripple. I slide his shirt over his head and lightly brush my fingertips over his shoulders, then move down and feel the rapid rhythm of his heart beating against my palm. I trace the muscles on his stomach, and lightly rub his nipples until I hear him groan.

I like hearing his voice change. It means I've broken through that macho facade and his true emotions are exposed.

Through the darkness, I feel his eyes on me. He lifts my jersey over my head. I close my eyes as I let the rain drip on me and enjoy the sensation of Derek gently and slowly tracing the droplets traveling across my body with his fingertips. He replaces his fingers with his tongue. I start moving against him because it feels amazing and I don't want to stop. I want to keep going, to show Derek what it means to have a connection that'll last more than one night.

"You're beautiful, you know that?" he whispers.

I look away. "No, I'm not."

"I can't imagine a more beautiful girl," he says, then adds, "Even if you are controllin' and bossy."

I lick the crook of his neck and he moans. "Maybe you'll learn to like controlling and bossy."

"I think you're right." He laces my hand through his, but stills as my charm bracelet brushes his wrist. He feels for the clasp and unhooks it, then tosses it across the campsite. It hits the ground with a clatter.

"That was expensive. London bought it for me."

"I know. I'll buy you a new one." He laces his fingers through mine again.

We kiss for what seems like forever. When he licks the rain off my neck, I swear my body is on fire. I need something to put out the flame. I need Derek to touch me, to hold me.

I look in his eyes and without saying a word he knows what I'm asking. *Love me.*

"You're cold," he says.

"No, I'm not."

"Then why are you shivering?"

I wrap my arms around his neck and hug him tight. He takes me into his arms and carries me to the tent. The tent is cold, too, but at least it's dry. He kicks off his wet jeans. Soon we're both under the covers completely naked, skin to skin. His strong, capable arms wrap around me. My heart stops racing and the heat of his body makes me stop shivering.

He wipes the wet hair away from my eyes with slow, gentle fingers. "I can't promise you everythin' you want."

"Just promise me tonight, Derek."

CHAPTER 39

Derek

Ashtyn has no clue the effect she has on me. When I opened my eyes and saw her standing in front of me in the rain, I thought I was dreaming. Now she's lying next to me, her body pressed against mine, and I'm defenseless. I want to make love to her. I want to tell her about my past, that football used to be my life. It defined who I was and who I wanted to be. I want to make this night last forever.

But it can't.

Dammit, I know I'm getting in too deep. I should run away from this, from her, but that's not about to happen. Our connection is too powerful and impossible to ignore. She traces my jaw and lips, looking at me as if I'm the answer to everything. I'm not, and I shouldn't pretend I am.

"Stop analyzing this," she says.

"I can't." There's too much that's unsaid between us.

"I know how much you hurt inside," she tells me. "I see it in your face, your eyes." She places her hand over my heart. "Right now I see the real you, Derek. The one you try to hide."

She doesn't know the half of it. Her words sink in. I've never felt this way, but then again, I've never been with a girl like Ashtyn.

I kiss her, the soft fullness of her lips sending bolts of electricity throughout my entire body. Her leg wraps around me and I trace the contour of her hip with the tips of my fingers. When she purrs at my touch and arches her body against mine, I feel myself losing control.

"You make me feel so amazing," she says in a breathless whisper against my chest. Her words seep into my heart.

Shit, this isn't the way it's supposed to go. I'm supposed to keep my emotions in check and only hook up with girls who want a good time, not girls who are desperate to make this something more than it could ever be.

But she's not asking for forever or asking for me to play football again, two things I'd never be able to promise. She's asking me to be with her tonight, nothing more. I need to just take what she's offering. I grasp her wrist and bring it to my lips, kissing it gently and feeling her pulse pounding against her warm, soft skin.

I trace the contours of her body with my fingers and follow with my tongue. Her heart races, matching mine, as she moans and pulls me closer with urgency. Ashtyn is amazing and hot and sexy. My fingers play with her body and I kiss her sweet lips as she moves against my hand.

I place her hand on me and she brings my body to a new, heightened frenzy. Now I'm the one moaning. I feel like I'm about to burst.

"You ready to do this?" she asks me.

"Hell, yeah. You?"

She nods. "Yeah."

I tell myself to calm down. This is just sex with a girl. There are no commitments or expectations beyond tonight, so why is my body reacting like this'll change the course of my life forever? That's insane. We'll have fun tonight and move on tomorrow.

She leans down and kisses me tenderly as her hair falls like a curtain around us. The rain taps on the tent and thunder barks in the distance.

"We're really gonna do this," she whispers against my lips. Something suspiciously like a teardrop falls on my chest. It's dark and I can't see much, but my sense of touch is super alert.

"Are you cryin'?" I ask.

She doesn't answer.

I swipe my thumb against her cheek. More tears.

Damn. I can't do this.

"This isn't gonna work, Ashtyn." I sit up and run a hand through my hair in frustration. I was an idiot to think we could hook up for one night and forget it happened in the morning. She might pretend she can be that girl, but she's not. "I'm fixin' to leave in January and move back to Cali when my dad gets back. I can't . . . I can't be that guy you want me to be."

She doesn't say anything.

"Ashtyn, say somethin'."

"I don't want to say anything. Just leave me alone." She sits up and reaches into her duffel for dry clothes.

"Sorry," I say dumbly. Fuck. I want to say more, but what? I'll be there for her *forever*? I'll be the one she can *always* count on? It'll be bullshit, empty words she's heard before.

She turns her back to me and gets dressed. "Go to sleep, Derek."

I lie back and sigh. When sunlight streams through the tent, Ashtyn is sleeping soundly with her back still to me.

CHAPTER 40

Ashtyn

When I wake up, Derek looks like he hasn't slept at all. His hair is mussed and he's sitting up and rubbing his eyes with his palms. I feel weird and awkward about last night. I went through every emotion, ending with sadness that he couldn't even pretend to love me for one night.

"Hey," he says in a scratchy morning voice.

"Hey." I try to hold in my emotions before they overflow and give me away. Before he says anything else, I hold up a hand. "Don't ask me if I want to talk about last night, because the answer is no. I *never* want to talk about it, so just do me a favor and keep whatever you want to say to yourself."

He nods and leaves the tent without answering.

I wanted to tell him so many times last night how I feel about him. The words almost spilled from my lips outside in the rain, and then in the tent. I teared up because I knew if I told him the truth, he'd run away physically and emotionally as fast as he could.

He wanted to have sex without consequences or commitments, and that's what I offered him. I guess deep down I expected him to be so overcome with emotion he'd admit his undying love for me. What a fool I was. I was the one so overcome with emotion that I couldn't stop the tears from running down my cheeks.

Last night was nothing but my stupid fantasy being crushed by reality.

I hug my knees and tell myself not to cry, that in time my heart will stop hurting so much.

I gather my stuff and go outside to wash up. It's hard to keep my head held high and my emotions in check, so I put on my sunglasses.

Derek isn't anywhere in sight. When I come out of the bathroom, Derek has already packed up the car and is in the driver's seat.

We don't say another word as we drive past Sylvia and Irving sitting at their folding table playing cards. I wave at them and they wave back. It's bittersweet seeing a couple who've beaten the odds and stayed together for so long. My parents couldn't do it, my sister and Nick couldn't do it . . . Derek and I couldn't even last one night.

I look out the window until Derek pulls into a drive-through and asks what I want for breakfast.

"I don't want anything," I say without glancing in his direction.

"You have to eat."

I push my glasses up. "I'm not hungry."

He orders two glasses of orange juice and two bagel-and-egg combos, then parks the car. "Here," he says, placing one of the wrapped bagels on my lap. "Eat."

I toss it back at him and step out of the car.

"Ashtyn!" Derek calls after me.

I walk down the street, ignoring him.

"Ashtyn!"

He catches up with me. My sunglasses can't hide the tears streaming down my face.

"What do you want me to say?" He blocks my path. He's got a tense, frustrated look as he rakes his fingers through his hair. "I'm sorry you and I have this attraction that won't go away. I'm sorry you want someone who'll be there for you when nobody else is. I'm sorry I couldn't just have a one-night stand when I knew you were cryin' about it. I'm sorry I'm not the guy you want me to be."

"I don't want you to be sorry!" I wipe my tears away. *I want you to tell me that I mean something to you.* But the words won't come out of my mouth. I'm a coward, afraid of what he'll say if I tell him how I truly feel. "And I don't want a stupid bagel as a consolation prize."

"The bagel wasn't a consolation prize, Ashtyn," he argues. He shoves his hands into his pockets. "It was breakfast. I was *trying* to get things back to normal."

"Normal? *Nothing* in my life is normal, Derek. But if you want me to fake it, then fine. I'm good at faking shit." I hold my hands over my heart. "Thank you *so* much for the bagel," I say in a fake sweet voice. "I'll go choke it down right now so you can feel like everything is normal."

I turn on my heel and walk back to the car. I have nowhere else to go and can't escape, so I might as well resign myself to the fact that I'm stuck with Derek until we get to Texas.

After we eat in tense silence and I'm done with the bagel, I hold up the empty wrapper. "Satisfied?"

"Not even close," he says stoically.

He drives me to a field when I tell him I need to get some practice time in. I stretch out and kick my practice balls while Derek leans against his car, texting. He doesn't offer to help retrieve the balls. Every once in a while he glances my way, but for the most part he couldn't care less about football or helping me. He's got his stupid phone held up to his face until I tell him I'm ready to head out.

I drive part of the way while Derek sleeps. When we switch back, I lean my head against the window and fall asleep.

"Ashtyn," Derek's deep voice wakes me up. "We're here."

I open my eyes, blurry from sleep. Derek gently shakes me again. I blink a few times to focus and notice that Derek is looking down at me with beautiful blue eyes he doesn't deserve. It's not fair that he has those eyes, because they confuse girls—confuse me.

Derek pulls up to the front entrance of Elite. My heart starts racing. This is it, everything I've been waiting for. Scouts will be here, taking back information to their coaches about who they believe are the best players to recruit. I look around and realize I'm the only girl.

A crowd of parents and teens are scattered across the lawn. Some are in the check-in line and others are laughing and joking around as if they've known each other for years.

Derek puts on a baseball cap and sunglasses. He reminds me of a movie star who doesn't want to be noticed.

He helps grab my luggage. "You gonna be okay?"

I don't look him in the eye. "I'll be fine."

"Listen, I would stay and wait until you get settled, but . . ." He glances at the football players milling around, then pushes the baseball cap farther over his eyes. "I'm gonna head over to my grandmother's place and see what's up with her."

"That's fine." I grab my bags out of his grip. "I guess I'll see you in a week."

He lets out a sigh. "I guess so."

It doesn't escape my mind that he hasn't touched me since we were in the tent. We're not arguing like usual, or interacting at all really. We're just . . . existing. He gives me a small smile.

"Bye, Derek."

"Bye." When I start walking away, he takes my elbow and urges me back. "Have fun. Kick some ass and show 'em what you got. You can do this, you know."

"Thanks."

"Listen, Ashtyn, I don't know what to say. Last night—"

I don't want to hear him say sorry again, so I cut him off. "It's okay. Just leave."

He nods slowly. I want to call him back as he gets in his car, to tell him that I need to make things right between us, but I don't. I can't. I told him to love me for one night, and he couldn't.

I watch as Derek's car drives away and disappears as it turns the corner. Whether I like it or not, I'm on my own.

I straighten my shoulders and move to the end of the check-in line. I'm aware of a couple of stares from players and some parents. I'm a girl playing a boy's sport, and while my team has gotten used to having a female teammate, some guys don't believe girls should play football. They think we're too fragile. I just have to keep my head held high and act like I belong here as much as they do.

Derek's words echo in my head: *You can do this.*

A couple of guys in front of me nudge each other, urging their friends to gawk at the lone girl in line. One turns to me and says, "Yo, cheerleading camp is down the block. You're obviously lost."

His friends laugh.

I push my duffel farther up on my shoulder. "*I'm* in the right line." I cock an eyebrow. "You sure *you're* in the right line?"

"Oh, I'm sure, baby."

I'm about to say some comment back to him when the guy at the registration table calls out, "Next!" and waves me over. "Name?"

I clear my throat. "Ashtyn Parker."

The guy scans me up and down. "You're the girl."

"Yep." The guy's a genius.

He hands me a new backpack, a water bottle, and a folder all with the Elite Football logo. "This has your schedule for the week and the key to your dorm room. Uniforms will be given out before practice tomorrow. Make sure you wear your name tag at all times," he says, slapping a sticker with my name on it on my T-shirt. He places the sticker awkwardly by my neck because he's obviously uncomfortable placing it anywhere near my chest like all the other players. "Cafeteria is on the first floor of the dorms, right by the lounge."

"Okay."

As I walk away, one of the coaches calls me over. "Welcome to Elite, Ashtyn," he says. "I'm Coach Bennett, the special teams coach. I'll be working with you this week."

I shake his hand. "I'm glad to be here, Coach. Thanks for the opportunity."

"In case you didn't know, you're the only female in the program. Since there are no showers designated for women, the showers for the rest of the players will be closed from five to five forty-five a.m. and seven to seven forty-five p.m. so you can have privacy."

"Got it."

"One more thing," he says. "We won't tolerate sexual harassment of any kind. If you feel harassed at any time, inform me or anyone else on staff. That being said, I hope you have a thick skin. Boys will be boys. Don't jump the gun, if you know what I mean."

After the harassment talk, I head to the dorm and find my room at the end of the hall. All the guys have roommates, but I've got a single. I drop my bags on the floor and sit on the edge of my bed. There's a small closet, a window, a twin bed, and a desk. It's basic, but it's clean and spider-free. And no Derek. I've gotten used to having him around and hearing his voice. Even now, I miss him.

It doesn't take long for me to put my stuff away. If I were a different girl, I'd sit in my room and hide until tomorrow, when the program officially starts. Instead, I head for the lounge to meet the guys I'm going to be playing with for the next week. I catch sight of Landon sitting with a couple of guys on one of the couches. I don't have any emotion besides a desire to show him and everyone else here that I'm competitive and I'm here to prove it.

No way I'm letting Landon think I'm intimidated. I'm captain of my team back home and represent them as well. This isn't just about me. I stand right in front of him. "Hi, Landon."

He glances at me, gives me a pathetic mumbling "Hi," then goes back to talking to the guys without introducing me. It's obvious he doesn't want me sitting with him, so I find an empty chair on the other side of the lounge. I try to start a conversation with a couple of the guys sitting around me. They give short answers, then walk away like I'm contagious or something.

I'm walking back to my room when I overhear a bunch of guys talking with their door open. If they were my teammates, I'd be sitting with them. I'm an outsider in unfamiliar territory. Why be timid now, when I know being a loner won't do me any good on the field tomorrow?

I straighten and am about to walk in the room to introduce

myself when I hear a guy say, "Did you see that chick in line this morning?"

Another guy gives a short laugh. "That dude McKnight told me she got in the program so they can have a token female. The girl is delusional enough to think she belongs here."

"She better not be on my team," one guy says.

The other guys express similar opinions and suddenly I'm not in the mood to make friends.

I rush to my room and throw myself on my bed. Normally I'd be ready to challenge the guys, to show I'm not intimidated by their lack of enthusiasm of having to play with a girl. Right now I don't feeling like proving myself and feel totally defeated.

For the first time since I got voted captain, I don't feel like one.

CHAPTER 41

Derek

I look up at the motorized gate that slowly opens after I announce my arrival over the intercom. Some people would be impressed by my grandmother's massive estate, but I'm not into flaunting money or status. This house does both.

I park my car in the circular drive and look up at the tall pillars flanking the oversize front door. I'm sweating, and it's not from the morning sun beating down on me. Meeting my grandmother on her own turf is like facing an unknown team in a playoff game. You can't really prepare effectively for the game and you're anxious until it's over.

A guy wearing a black suit and a serious expression is at the entrance waiting for me. "You with the Secret Service?" I ask, trying to lighten the situation.

He doesn't seem amused. "Follow me."

I'm led into the house. The place is filled with high ceilings and large corridors, reminding me of those fancy cribs showcased on television. The staircase is polished metal, and the furniture is overstuffed and likely overpriced, too. The guy in the suit stops in front of a room overlooking the swimming pool in the backyard. It's filled with white furniture and purple cushions. It's completely feminine and over-the-top. I wonder if Ashtyn would like it or prefer her lived-in, old furniture back home.

I wanted to stay with her this morning until she was settled in the dorm. That was before I saw a few guys who would have definitely recognized me. I wanted to tell her about my past, but what good would it do? Saying nothing and booking out of there before anyone recognized me was the easy way out and I took it.

I'm looking out the window at the big pool in the backyard, wishing Ashtyn were here with me, when I hear someone come into the room. I turn around and recognize my grandmother right away. She's wearing a stark white suit, her hair is all poofed up, and her makeup is overdone. I'm taken aback that she's tan and looks like she just came from a vacation instead of the hospital.

She holds her head high like a queen when approaching her subjects as she walks up to me with her arms outstretched. "Aren't you going to say hello to your grandmother?"

"Hello, Grandmother," I say with a deadpan expression. I don't mask the fact that I'm not her biggest fan, but at least I don't flinch when she walks closer and gives me one of those fake air kisses.

She holds me at arm's length. I feel like a bull being assessed, and I'm almost surprised she doesn't open my mouth to inspect my teeth. "You need a haircut. And new clothes. You look like a pauper in those ripped jeans and T-shirt that I'd no more use as a dishrag than wear on my body."

"Lucky for you it's my clothes and not yours."

She makes a *harrumph* sound. A lady in a maid's uniform walks into the room with a silver tray filled with little sandwiches and tea. After she leaves, my grandmother points to one of the wicker couches. "Have a seat and some refreshments."

I stay standing. "Listen, I hate to state the obvious, but you don't look like someone on her deathbed. You said you were dyin'."

She sits on the edge of a chair and takes her time pouring tea into a fancy cup. "Bless your heart. I didn't *exactly* say I was dying."

"You said you were havin' treatments. You have cancer?"

"No. Sit down. The tea is getting cold."

"Diabetes?"

"No. The sandwiches are made with cheese imported from the south of France. Try one."

"Parkinson's? Lou Gehrig's disease? A stroke?"

She waves her hand in the air, dismissing all the ailments I listed. "If you must know, I was resting."

"Resting? You said you were *diagnosed*. You said seein' me was your last *dyin'* wish."

"We are all dying, Derek. Every day we're alive is one day closer to our death. Now sit down before my blood pressure rises."

"You have a blood pressure problem?"

"You're about to give me one." When I don't move, she sighs

heavily. "If you must know, I had a little procedure. I spent some time recovering at a spa in Arizona until the twentieth."

Procedure? I've fallen into a trap and was manipulated into coming here. As she reveals little bits, the truth suddenly dawns on me. I'm a fool. "You had plastic surgery."

"I'd like to call it going in for a tune-up. You should be familiar with that term, seeing as your father always did like to fiddle with his own cars instead of bring them to a professional."

"If that's supposed to be an insult, you're off the mark."

"Yes, well . . ." My grandmother looks up at me without an ounce of shame. "What I'm getting at is that it's not easy to see yourself getting older. You're my grandson, and the only family I have left. I've been a widow for ten years and your mother is gone. You're the last Worthington."

"I'm not a Worthington. I'm a Fitzpatrick."

"Yes, well, that *is* unfortunate."

Truth is, she's so used to acting like Texas royalty I don't think she realizes how arrogant she sounds. "I don't think my dad would agree with you."

She clears her throat as if she's got something stuck in it. "How is that Army man doing these days?"

"He's in the Navy."

"Whatever."

"I'm sure he'd send his regards, but he's on a submarine for the next five months."

"He abandoned his new bride so soon after the wedding? Pity," she says in a monotone voice. "Derek, sit down. You're making me nervous. It's bad enough you won't cash your trust fund allowance checks and I have to resort to sending you cash."

"I didn't ask for a trust fund, or an allowance." My grandparents set it up when I was born. I think it was their way of luring me to Texas with the hope I'd work for Worthington Industries one day. "By the way, Sunnyside Nursing Home says thank you for your generous donation."

My grandmother sighs. "I got the thank-you card. I am already a benefactor to many charities. The money is for *you*, Derek. You might dress like one, but I don't want you living like a pauper. Now sit down and eat."

"I'm not hungry. Listen, *Grandma*, in your letter you said you had somethin' important to tell me. Why don't you just spill it and get it over with, because truthfully this grandson-grandma bonding thing ain't workin' for me."

"You want the truth?"

Duh. I hold up my hands, urging her to come out with it already. I'm ready to leave here and book a hotel for the week.

"I want you to come live with me." She doesn't blink and she doesn't have a smirk on her face. I think the woman is serious. She might not be deathly ill, but she's obviously delusional.

"Not gonna happen. You're wastin' your time."

"I have a week to change your mind." She takes a calculated sip of tea, then sets the cup on the table. "You will give me a week, Derek. Won't you?"

"Give me one reason I shouldn't walk out that door right now."

"Because it's what your mother would have wanted."

CHAPTER 42

Ashtyn

It's the first day of practice, where we'll be assessed and placed onto teams for scrimmages. I wake up when my alarm rings at five and head to the showers. There's a big sign on the door of the bathroom:

5:00 a.m.–5:45 a.m.
CLOSED FOR FEMALES ONLY

Someone crossed out FEMALES ONLY and wrote FREMONT'S BITCH instead. The words cut deep.

I stand under the hot shower. I want to go home. Maybe Landon was right, that I got accepted to Elite because I'm a girl and they wanted to fill some sort of quota.

What am I doing here?

I leave the bathroom and pull off the sign. I'm not about to tattle for a stupid sign calling me Fremont's bitch. I'd lose respect for not being able to take a joke. Five guys are already standing in line with towels around their waists, waiting to enter. One of them is Landon. He snickers when I walk past him and says something to the guy standing next to him.

Back in my room, I glance at my cell phone and notice I've got five texts.

Jet: Find us a new QB who'll transfer to Fremont, even if you have to sleep with him! Take one for the team. JK (kind of)

Vic: Don't fuck up! jk (kind of)

Trey: Don't listen to Jet or Vic. (Monika told me to write that. She's sitting next to me.)

Monika: Good luck! XOXO

Bree: R cute guys there? Txt me pics!

They remind me that I have a job to do now that Landon turned out to be a jerk and abandoned our team. If I can get scouts to come to Fremont and watch me play, every player will get a chance to be seen. I can't give up or back down.

My phone rings right before I head outside for practice. It's Derek. I ignore the call. I have so much to say to him, but I can't say it now. I need to focus on football this week, nothing else.

On the field, the head coach blows his whistle. While the

players gather around, he gives a lecture on sexual harassment. Way to make the guys resent me even more . . . All eyes are on me and I just want to disappear until it's over. I don't even hear the pep talk before we do calisthenics and drills, because I'm still aware of all the stares. It's a closed practice, so parents and scouts are not allowed to attend today. None of the guys stand near me or talk to me.

The kicking coach, Coach Bennett, has the kickers work on technique for a long time, then in the afternoon has us kick the ball starting from the goal line. He increases the distance by a yard after every successful kick. I'm the best of the group, until Coach Bennett assigns the quarterbacks as holders so we can practice kicking and they can practice a trick play in a fake field goal situation.

Landon is assigned as my holder. He saunters over to me with an arrogant smirk on his face. I would ask Coach Bennett to assign me another holder, but nobody likes a player who complains. What would I tell him, that Landon is my ex-boyfriend and I don't want to play nice with him? He'd probably laugh in my face, then send me packing.

Football isn't for the weak, physically or mentally.

I can do this. I look around at the other kickers who are called on first. They're all at the top of their game, like specially trained machines who know what to do and when to do it. A bunch of guys I've only heard about but never met are on the field, mini celebrities with big egos to match their talent. I can imagine everyone here playing at the college level and beyond.

When Bennett calls me and Landon up for our turn, I get ready for the snap and attempt to execute a perfect kick right through the middle of the goalposts, but Landon tilts the ball at the last second and the ball tumbles on the ground after I kick the tip of it instead of the sweet spot. He does it so subtly that nobody else besides me can tell, unless you had a video camera and could replay it in slow motion.

"You whoring around with Derek?" Landon mumbles when I get back in position for a second attempt.

I ignore Landon and focus. This time, when the ball is snapped to Landon, he lets go of his hold on the ball at the last second so I miss it completely and fall hard on my ass.

"Oh, no! You okay?" Landon asks with fake concern. He holds his hand out to help me up, but I swat his hand away.

"Hold the fucking ball so I can kick it!" I yell as I get to my feet.

He twists his fists in front of his eyes. "Boo-hoo. Feeling sorry for yourself because you and your team are gonna suck without me?"

"McKnight, on the bench. Hansen, replace McKnight as holder!" Bennett calls out.

As Charlie Hansen jogs on the field to replace Landon, the two quarterbacks slap hands as they pass each other.

I get in position and Hansen takes the snap. At the last second, he tilts the ball slightly so I can't kick it right. It's an epic fail. I can hear snickers on the sidelines from the guys watching.

At dinner I sit alone at one of the tables. I'm sore, tired, and defeated.

The next two days are repeats of the first. I'm assigned a team, but none of the guys talk to me. I'm perfect when I'm kicking off the tee, but when the guys are holding the ball for me nothing I do will work. Somehow Landon has managed to sabotage me.

After evening practice on Wednesday, the head coach, Coach Smart, calls me into his office. It's in the main building near where I registered the first day. As I enter the office in full football gear, Coach Bennett is standing next to Coach Smart with my stats for the day.

"What's the problem, Parker?" Coach Smart asks me. "We brought you here because we saw potential. Not many female players make it past the high school level, but we thought you had what it takes to beat the odds." He points to the stats. "To say we're not happy with your performance so far is an understatement."

"I'm not happy with my performance, either. The guys are sabotaging me."

There's no sympathy or understanding—just a coach itching to get more out of his player. "You gotta figure out how to play through whatever drama is going on behind the scenes. There's always gonna be guys who want to create trouble and make other players look bad. It's up to each individual to rise above it and figure a way to make it work. We've got scrimmages the rest of the week, and a big game on Friday night. There'll be parents, scouts, the media . . . a full house. You want to go home and give up, Parker, just say the word."

"I don't want to go home."

"Did you come here for a reason?"

I nod. "Yeah, Coach, I did." I had just forgotten what it was.

"All right, here's the deal." He leans forward. "If you want to play Friday without embarrassing yourself and this program, you have two days to get it together and figure out how to make these guys want you on their team."

I swallow, but there's a lump in my throat. "Yes, sir."

After leaving his office, I tell myself it doesn't matter why or how I got here—I'm here and need to prove myself now more than ever. *You can do this.* I silently repeat Derek's words in my head over and over, hoping I'll soon believe it.

I'm about to walk out of the building, when I stop to check out the pictures of players on the wall who've attended the Elite program and have gone on to have solid NFL careers. They even have a wall of fame with pictures of their top players.

I stop and blink at one of the photos on the wall. No, it can't be. Below it is a small gold-plated plaque engraved with the words DEREK FITZPATRICK "THE FITZ"–MVP. Above the plaque is a photo of a player leaping over a bunch of linemen for a touchdown.

MVP at Elite? It can't be the same Derek Fitzpatrick who couldn't throw a football in a spiral to save his life. The same Derek Fitzpatrick who makes my insides melt every time I'm with him. The same Derek Fitzpatrick I almost made love to in the tent.

I step closer to the picture. There's no mistaking it—it's Derek. His eyes, his intense focus . . . that cocky, lopsided grin. His features are so familiar to me now.

I've known Derek for weeks. I've slept in the same bed with him. I've fallen for him . . . and yet he's made sure I never saw the real him that hides behind a bunch of lies.

The burning feeling in the middle of my chest is fueled when I think about Derek just standing there listening to me while I stressed over the fact that Landon ditched us and we're left without a decent quarterback. He knew I'd do just about anything to find a solid quarterback for Fremont. Yet he never even hinted he was a trained quarterback, an MVP.

Coach Bennett comes up to me. I gesture to the offending picture. "How good was he?"

"Fitz? He was the best quarterback I've ever seen. There are some guys who are born to play football. Fitz was one of 'em. Blew everyone away with his talent and ability to read the defense."

"What happened to him?"

Coach Bennett shrugs. "He quit playing and never came back. Shocked the hell out of us, that's for sure. Haven't seen anyone with that much natural talent since."

"What about Landon McKnight?"

Coach Bennett nods. "McKnight is decent."

"He's an all-state player and almost went undefeated last year," I tell him.

"The goal is to be undefeated, not almost undefeated. Right?"

I nod.

"With enough training and practice, McKnight is definitely on his way." He taps the picture of Derek. "As a freshman and sophomore, Derek Fitzpatrick led his team to the state championship."

That statement lingers in the air. Derek went to State. Wow. What would it be like to play in the state championship? Derek knows.

Back in the dorm, I pull out my cell and search "Derek Fitzpatrick Football." The first thing that comes up is a news article about a boy football prodigy who'd had the attention of Division I schools since he was fourteen. By his sophomore year in high school, he'd gotten three offers for full scholarships to college after he graduated. Another article's title is *Derek Fitzpatrick, Prodigy Quarterback*. At the end of the article is a picture of the boy wonder himself.

I follow links to article after article, one more impressive than the next. It's hard to think the person who dominates my thoughts had a secret past he never revealed. Did the thought of playing for Fremont with me ever cross his mind these past few weeks?

The betrayal cuts deeper than Landon's ever did. Landon and I dated, but I know now that it was superficial. He never really loved me. I was trying to fill a void in my life, an emptiness that I'd been living with. He played me for a fool and schemed with Bonk from Fairfield.

Truth is, Derek has played me for a bigger fool. *You can do this*, he'd said. Did he mean it, or was it another one of his jokes?

We agreed to stay out of each other's lives, but that's not going to happen. I call a cab to come get me. Back home, Coach Dieter always tells us to play clean.

I disagree. It's time to play dirty.

CHAPTER 43

Derek

'm staring at the expensive designer suit the butler Harold laid out on my bed. I'm sure my grandmother told him to place it there so she can keep trying to mold me into the grandchild she always wanted. I've been here for three days now, and I've been counting down the days until I can pick up Ashtyn and head back to Illinois. I abandon the suit and find the old lady in her oversize dining room.

She takes one look at me and frowns. "Derek, make your grandmother happy by changing into something other than those rags you call clothes. Didn't Harold bring up the suit I bought for you?"

"He did, but I'm not wearin' it." I reach out and take a piece of bread off the large buffet, but she slaps my hand away. "Wait for the guests."

"Guests?" A sinking feeling settles in my chest. "What *guests*?"

She looks way too proud of herself. That fake smile she's

trying to hide is an indication that she's up to something. "I've arranged a little get-together with some of the teenagers in town, that's all." She takes my face in her hands. "I know many single debutantes who have impeccable bloodlines, Derek."

"Bloodlines? You plannin' on setting me up with a mare? C'mon, isn't that a little old-fashioned, even for you?"

"Do you have a lady friend?"

"If you mean a girlfriend, the answer is no. I'm not lookin' for one, either."

"Nonsense. You need to be fixed up. It's as simple as that." She walks with purpose to the opposite side of the room. "You're tall, handsome, and you happen to be the grandson of the late Kenneth Worthington. It's time you embrace the fact that you're the heir to Worthington Industries, the biggest textile distributor in the world. You, my dear grandson, are a catch."

"I don't want to be caught."

"That attitude means you haven't met a girl worthy of your attention. You'll want to be caught if the right girl comes along."

I grab a piece of bread from the buffet and take a big, obnoxious bite out of it. "Thanks for the offer, but I don't need to be fixed up," I say with a mouth full of bread.

Her top lip curls in disgust. "I thought you went to a private school. Didn't they teach you basic manners?" I open my mouth to answer, but she holds a hand up. "Don't answer with your mouth full. Just . . . go upstairs, put your suit on, and come down when you're decently attired. Guests will be arriving shortly." When I don't look the least bit interested in dressing up for her shindig, she flashes me a practiced, superficial smile. "Please, Derek. Humor me for one night."

"If you're gonna say my mother would have wanted me to wear that suit, I swear I'm walkin' out that door and never comin' back. Don't pretend to know anything about my mother, because you were the one who disappeared from her life."

"I know my daughter more than you think, Derek." When I shake my head and am about to tell her off, she motions me to follow her out of the room. "Come with me. I need to show you something."

My instinct is to act like a stubborn asshole and walk out, just to make a point. But a voice in my head urges me to stay and follow the old lady.

My grandmother leads me to a big room filled with enough books to fill a small library. She closes the door and slides one of the shelves aside to reveal a safe. With agile fingers, she carefully opens the safe and pulls out an envelope.

"Here," she says, sliding a letter out of the envelope and handing it to me.

I glance at the paper and immediately recognize my mother's handwriting. The letter was dated two weeks before my mom died. She'd been weak back then and knew she didn't have much time left. I'd asked her if she was afraid . . . I couldn't say the rest of my sentence out loud. "Of dying?" she asked. When I nodded, she took my hand in hers and said, "No. Then I won't be in pain anymore." A few days later she stopped talking and lay in bed all day, waiting to die.

My grandmother stands in front of me with her head bent as I read my mother's words.

Dear Mother,

    I remember when I was a little girl I didn't talk because I was shy, but you told the other moms I was too intelligent to speak. I found out you paid off one of the judges of the beauty contest I entered in junior high so I'd win. I never told you the manager at The Burger Hut said he couldn't hire me the summer before my senior year of high school because you wanted me to intern with Daddy at Worthington Industries instead.

    For a long time I thought you did those things to control my life. As a mom myself, I realize now that you wanted to create this perfect life for me because you loved me.

    Take comfort in the fact that I've lived the perfect life. Steven Fitzpatrick is my one true love. Derek is my little football star and an amazing son—he's funny and handsome like his father and strong-willed and wild-spirited like me. He's perfect.

    I have one request. Please take care of my son when Steven can't, Mom. Look after him, because I won't be around to do it much longer.

        Love always,
        Katherine

I fold the letter up and blink back tears as I hand it back to my grandmother. "I'll go change," I say.

No other words need to be said. I get why I'm here and why she wants me to stay.

A half hour later I walk down the stairs in the suit she bought me. I leave the tie upstairs and unbutton the top two buttons of my shirt as a statement that my mom's wild spirit lives inside me, and that isn't going to change anytime soon.

The foyer is crowded, full of teenage girls in bright-colored dresses and big hair. Knowing how my grandmother operates, she already has a suitable bride picked out and the prenuptial papers drawn up and ready to be signed.

Lucky for me, guys are also invited, so I'm not the only buck on display.

Ashtyn would laugh at a party like this, where you gain popularity points by how much money and status you have instead of how much alcohol you can ingest before you puke. I'll bet nobody here has ever played Fact or BS with Jell-O shots. Or shaved their ball sacs, for that matter.

"Derek!" my grandmother calls out as she winds her way through the mass of people milling around. "You forgot your necktie."

"No, I didn't."

She reaches out and buttons the top two buttons of my shirt. "It's customary to wear a tie when you're at a formal function. You look like the gardener."

I hold her face in my hands, like she did to me less than an hour ago. "This might be a formal function to everyone else, but to me it's a dog and pony show. You want me to pretend to be one of 'em, this is what you get."

"Can't you pretend a little harder?" she asks, then leans in to say, "Cassandra Fordham and her mother have been staring at you since you came downstairs."

I unbutton the top two buttons again, then undo a third one for good measure. "Who's Cassandra Fordham?"

"Only the most beautiful girl in Texas. She wins beauty pageants, has incredible skin tone, and plays the piano."

Skin tone? Beauty pageants? Those attributes don't hold a candle to a girl who knows how to get down and dirty on the field and in a tent. "Does she play football?"

"Football?" My grandmother laughs. "Girls don't play football, Derek. They watch it. And yes, I'm sure Cassandra Fordham is a fan of the game. She's a Texan, born and raised. Football is in our blood. She's right there." She does her best not to make it obvious that she's pointing to the girl in an off-the-shoulder yellow dress. The yellow rose of Texas.

My grandmother slips a hand through my elbow and leads me toward Cassandra Fordham. I'm aware that most eyes are on me. Obviously Cassandra has been pegged the most desirable girl in the room. Since I'm the guest of honor, I have the feeling it's customary that I get first dibs.

"Mrs. Fordham, Cassandra, I'd like you to meet my grandson, Derek Fitzpatrick," my grandmother says in an assertive voice.

Cassandra is model pretty. She's got a small, perky nose and blue eyes that practically light up when she smiles. She does a small curtsy-type move. "How are you enjoyin' Texas so far, Derek?"

"You want the truth?"

My grandmother subtly elbows me and busts out a fake laugh. "Derek has been entertainin' me all week. Y'all should see him play tennis. We've been playin' every afternoon after lunch. He's a natural."

I haven't stepped foot on the tennis court since I've been here.

"I play, too," Cassandra says in a sweet feminine voice. "Maybe we should play sometime."

My grandmother nudges me again. "Of course he will. Right, Derek?"

"Right."

After some more small talk, my grandmother asks Mrs. Fordham her opinion on her new artwork in the living room and leaves me standing beside Cassandra. I feel like I've stepped into a time warp. Everyone talks and eats while soft music from a four-string quartet plays in the background. It isn't long before Cassandra grabs my elbow and starts introducing me to the other girls and guys at the party.

I get a break when she excuses herself to go to the restroom. I walk in the dining room and grab a bite. As I find a seat at the table, a bunch of girls surround me. I'm not gonna lie—the girls are hot. Texas has some of the prettiest girls I've ever seen in my life, and I've lived a bunch of places. I briefly wonder how they stay so thin when the food here is rich and fattening. Then I look down and notice that their plates are full of food, but they don't actually put any of it in their mouths. It's a scam, if you ask me.

Ashtyn would pile her plate high and enjoy the food without worrying what the guys here would think. Every day I've called her, but she hasn't answered. This morning I left her a text message telling her to call me. She hasn't.

After eating and wandering around talking to a couple of guys about football, their main topic of conversation, Cassandra appears at my side. She spurts impressive football stats like water, but it's as if she's been groomed to know about the sport without actually liking it.

I duck out and sit on one of the cabana chairs, hoping to be left alone. Reading that letter from my mom changes everything. When I read her words, it was like she was talking to me from the grave. She called me her football star. Man, that slashed open a wound that'd been stitched closed for a while now.

My privacy doesn't last long, because female hands cover my eyes and Cassandra's high voice whispers in my ear, "Guess who?"

CHAPTER 44

Ashtyn

As I walk up to the front entrance of the Worthington mansion with a mission to confront Derek, it suddenly dawns on me that I should have changed. I just threw on a pair of long shorts and my practice jersey, which has grass and mud stains on it from today's practice.

I ring the doorbell. A tall man with a grim expression answers the door. "May I help you, miss?"

I peek inside. The mass of people standing around in dresses and suits emphasizes the fact that I'm underdressed. If I cared, I'd call the cab back and leave. But I don't care. I'm on a mission, and nobody's going to stop me. "I need to see Derek Fitzpatrick."

"And who may I ask is calling?"

"Ashtyn." When that doesn't seem to satisfy him I say, "Ashtyn Parker."

An older woman with striking blond hair and diamonds

around her neck comes to the door and stands beside the guy. She's wearing a light blue tailored dress with a matching jacket. When I look into her sapphire eyes, I get a jolt of recognition. Those are Derek's eyes . . . this is Derek's dying grandmother.

Except she doesn't look like she's dying.

She looks healthier than most people I know. She eyes my football jersey and purses her lips like she just ate a sour lemon. "Who are you?" she asks in a haughty tone.

"Ashtyn Parker." I should have brought my name tag from Elite.

She tilts her head and focuses on my bare legs. "Miss Parker, my dear. Are you aware that you're wearing boys' clothes?"

Umm. How do I explain to a woman so impeccably dressed that I came here straight from football practice? "I play football. I had practice all day, and didn't have time to change before I came here. Derek and I drove here together from Illinois." When she doesn't look impressed, I add, "His dad is married to my sister." That might earn me some credibility.

It doesn't.

"My grandson is indisposed at the moment, Miss Parker," she says. "If it's not urgent, you can come back another time."

She's trying to intimidate me. It's working, but I still stand my ground. I have to find out why Derek lied to me.

"I'm sorry," I tell her. "I don't mean any disrespect, but I need to see him now and I'm not about to leave. It is urgent."

Derek's grandma finally opens the door and gestures for me to enter the house. "Follow me," she says, then orders the guy who opened the door to find her grandson and escort him to the library. She leads me through the crowd of teenage partygoers. This place is huge, like a museum. Some of the girls are staring at me and whispering to their friends.

I stop dead in my tracks when I catch sight of Derek and some girl through one of the huge windows leading to the massive backyard. She's got her arms wrapped around him, and my heart feels like it's being dragged over a cheese grater. It hasn't even been a week since we were in the tent, about to make love. Knowing that he could quickly hook up with another girl less than a week later makes me nauseous.

I squeeze my eyes shut and hope the girl is just a stupid figment of my imagination. I wish her to disappear. I should know better than for any of my wishes to come true, because they've never come true in the past. I open my eyes and, sure enough, she's still there.

"Miss Parker, dear, don't stare. It's bad manners," Derek's grandmother chides, then takes my elbow and leads me to a room with two couches, bookshelves filled with books, and a huge marble fireplace.

"I didn't mean to interrupt your party," I tell her, trying to tell myself that it doesn't matter that Derek is with another girl. I have no hold on him. I'm here to confront him, not make him fall in love with me. The fact that I fell hard for him is something totally out of my control and that just sucks for me. I look at his grandmother and hope she can't see right through me. "It must be hard for you to host so many people in your condition."

"Condition?"

I squirm. "You know, being so sick and all that."

"I'm not sick, dear."

"You're not?"

"No." The woman sits on a small couch in the middle of the room with her feet crossed at the ankles. She places her hands neatly in her lap. "Sit down, Miss Parker."

I awkwardly take a seat across from her. Do I cross my legs at the ankles? I'm in unfamiliar territory. The woman has an air of authority and superiority about her. She's eyeing me with keen eyes, as if she's judging my every move. I cross my gym shoes at the ankles but imagine I look like an idiot.

"Tell me about the relationship you have with my grandson."

"My relationship?" I almost choke on the word.

"Yes."

"I'm, um, not sure what you mean."

She leans forward. "I assume, Miss Parker, that since you came here on an 'urgent' matter you and Derek are *familiar* with each other."

"I wouldn't really say that. Most of the time Derek tries to annoy me and I ignore him. That's of course when we're not arguing, which we do quite often. He's a player and manipulator and he has a big ego. He's got this annoying habit of running his hand through his hair when he's frustrated. And he practically stole my dog. Did you know he's obsessed with smoothies? He won't eat a Skittle or anything with a preservative in it to save his life. It's not normal—*he's* not normal."

"Hmm. Interesting."

I'm so wound up, I'm not finished with my tirade. "And he lied to me. Did you know he used to play football?"

Derek's grandmother nods. "I am aware of that, yes."

"Aware of what?" Derek says as he walks in the room. I hadn't noticed before, but he's wearing a suit, as if he's going to a wedding. Or a funeral. He steps back in shock when he realizes that I'm in the room. "Ashtyn, what're you doin' here?"

The past few days I've missed seeing his face every day. When the guys were giving me a rough time this week, I thought of his words: *You can do this.* But the truth slapped me in the face as soon as I looked up at that MVP wall . . . and now he's standing here in front of me right after he was in the backyard with that girl.

I can't think straight. I want to ask about the girl, but just the thought of him with another girl makes my insides tighten and I can't manage to get the words out. Instead, I focus on the reason I came here in the first place. "You were a *fucking* prodigy!"

Derek's expression is grim. "How'd you find out?"

I walk up to him and poke a finger into his chest. "Your picture is plastered on the MVP wall at Elite. Ever hear of a Google search? You are such a liar!" My heart is racing when I add, "And I can't believe you're hooking up with someone after what happened between us."

"Ahem!" Derek's grandmother clears her throat loudly. "Miss Parker, obviously you have a lot on your mind and would like to hash this out. I'm just not sure this is the proper time or place to have this conversation. Derek, why don't you invite her to come back tomorrow to discuss football *and such*."

"Now's fine," he tells her.

"Yeah, now's fine," I say. "I don't care what you do or don't do with girls, Derek. I didn't come here to talk about anything else but why you lied to me about playing football."

"I didn't lie, Ashtyn." He doesn't look the least bit guilty. "Listen, I'm not sayin' I didn't leave stuff out."

I laugh heartily. "*Leave stuff out*? Oh, that's rich. You outright lied. I remember plain as day you said you were an *average* football player. Average, my ass." I huff a few times, trying to gather my wits as I tell myself to stop shaking. "I read that you played *varsity* as a freshman and led your team to two *state* championships. Do you know what I'd do to get my team to State? Just about anything, and you know it."

"I don't play anymore. And no matter what you think, I didn't hook up with anyone else since we were together."

Derek's grandmother steps between us. "May I remind you both there's a party going on just outside that door. A party that just happens to be in your honor, Derek."

"A party that I never asked for, remember?" Derek counters, then says to me, "You want to talk about lyin', let's put everythin' out on the table. You're not innocent, either. You told me you were okay with a one-night stand. That couldn't be farther from the truth and you know it."

My heart skips a beat. I can't look at him or respond, because I might be tempted to admit the truth.

"I don't want to make this about you and me," I tell him. "It's about football. You can't just stop playing when you're, like, amazing at it. Actually, some people are amazing at it. You're . . . how did they describe it? *Exceptional*. Not only that . . . one article said they'd 'never seen a young quarterback like Fitzpatrick, who could read players and adjust his strategy during plays like a pro.'"

He laughs, dismissing the assessment. "They might have exaggerated a little. You sure you came here to talk football? I think you came here because you missed me. Why haven't you texted me back?"

"Don't change the subject. I read at least five articles online. They all say approximately the same thing. You were MVP at Elite. I've seen the caliber of the players there. They're the best of the best, the guys who'll no doubt be starting in the NFL after college. Play with me, Derek. One last season."

"I'm goin' back to the party." Derek opens the door, but holds out a hand before leaving. "You want to join me, Sugar Pie?"

I look down at my football jersey. "I'm not dressed for a party, and you didn't answer my question."

"I answered it. You comin' or not?"

He walks out of the room when I don't join him, leaving me alone with his grandmother. "Well, that was . . . entertaining, to say the least," she says.

"I'm sorry to have bothered you." Feeling like I just lost a glimmer of light in my pathetic life, I pull out my cell. "I'll call a cab and be out of here in—"

His grandmother pulls the phone out of my hand and turns it off. "You should stay."

"Excuse me?"

She hands the phone back to me. "I've decided that you should stay here for the night. Attend the party and see what the night has to offer."

"I'm not exactly dressed for a party and it's obvious I've bothered you enough."

"It's a shame I didn't host a costume party." She grabs the edge of my grass-stained jersey with the tips of her thumb and forefinger. "Didn't your mother teach you to look in the mirror before you leave the house?"

"My mother left when I was ten. She didn't teach me much."

"And your father?"

I shrug. "He's kind of in his own world."

"I see. Well, you might as well get over the fact that you're not going back to that football camp tonight. I'll have Harold drive you back first thing tomorrow morning." She walks to the door and clears her throat. "Take a shower and make yourself decent. A neighbor of mine owns a boutique in town. She'll bring over something acceptable for you to wear."

Derek's grandmother leads me upstairs to a bedroom with an attached private bathroom. She tells me to hurry and wash up. I get the distinct impression that I better not disobey her. I don't want to attend the party, but she doesn't seem to care about my opinion. All I want to do is convince Derek to play for Fremont, but that doesn't look like it's about to happen.

After a quick shower, I call Coach Bennett and inform him I'll be back in the morning for practice. I hang up and notice a short, white strapless cocktail dress neatly spread out on the bed. How did Derek's grandmother get it so fast? On the floor is a pair of red stilettos. The whole outfit looks expensive and elegant. I step closer and notice the dress still has the tags on it.

Reaching out, I turn over the price tag. The dress is *seven hundred dollars*. I'll bet everything in my closet adds up to seven hundred dollars, and I don't even own a pair of stilettos. There's no way I can wear a dress that expensive, or shoes with heels this high.

I touch the silky fabric of the dress. I've never felt anything so soft in my life and wonder what it would feel like against my skin. Dropping my towel, I hold the material up to my body and look at myself in the mirror. Bolstered by the fact that nobody is watching, I unzip the garment and squeeze into it. I imagine being a princess and having this dress as one of many in my vast wardrobe of designer clothes.

I look in the mirror and hardly recognize myself. The dress hugs my curves and my breasts press against the material so they're pushed up and give me more cleavage than I usually have. It makes me feel sexy and, dare I think it, powerful.

Derek accused me of being here because I missed him. The truth is, I've thought about him too much. Thoughts of him have invaded my mind. I wish they'd go away. Every time I need encouragement, I think of his words. Every time I feel alone, I think of when we kissed and he smiled at me.

Prodigy quarterback.

Derek could save our team. He said he doesn't play anymore.

Did he even contemplate picking up a ball again? If I had the power to make him fall in love with me, would he change his mind and join the Fremont team? I look at myself in the mirror, then slip on the stilettos.

There's only one way to find out.

CHAPTER 45

Derek

My grandmother, who's been flitting around like a butterfly, is suddenly ignoring me. I've tried to get her attention three times since I left her and Ashtyn in the library. I know Ashtyn hasn't left because I've had my eye on the front door the entire time.

I finally run into my grandmother when she rounds the corner on the way to the dining room. "Where is she?" I ask.

My grandmother puts her hand to her chest. "You startled me. Don't sneak up on an old lady like that. You could've caused a heart attack."

"Your heart's fine. Where's Ashtyn?"

"You mean that poor girl who dresses like a boy?"

I nod. "Uh-huh."

"The one you called Sugar Cake?"

"That'd be Sugar *Pie*."

"Oh, that's right." She removes a piece of invisible lint off my suit jacket and takes her time buttoning my shirt back up. "You're transparent, Derek. Just like your mother was at your age."

"If you're thinkin' what I think you're thinkin', you're wrong."

"Then you won't mind that I invited *Sugar Pie* to stay the night."

I don't want Ashtyn anywhere near my grandmother. She's up to something. Everything the woman does is calculated and deliberate. She's not just being nice to Ashtyn by inviting her to stay here tonight. I can tell by the gleam in her eye that she wants information out of Ashtyn; information about us. That's as dangerous as giving secrets to the enemy.

"I'll drive her back to the dorm," I tell her.

She waves her hand in the air. "Nonsense. It would be in bad taste to make the poor girl go back to a dorm room with questionable amenities when we have more than enough space right here."

Oh, hell. It's useless to argue because it's obvious I'm not winning this argument. "Where is she?"

"In one of the guest rooms. And I might have given her a dress to wear. She can't possibly attend one of my parties dressed in that filthy football jersey and shorts. Bless her heart."

Oh, no. Did she have to pull out the "bless her heart" phrase again? Those words are like a loaded gun in Texas, where that phrase could either be an insult or a term of endearment, depending on the tone or intent.

"Stay out of my business, Grams."

"And what business is that, Derek?" When I don't answer, she pats my chest in a patronizing manner. "Don't call me Grams ever again. You just remember to be a gentleman, like a Worthington host should be."

"I'm a Fitzpatrick."

She raises a brow as she starts walking away. "Bless your heart."

I glance up, wondering if my mother is laughing her ass off right now or cursing the day she wrote that letter to my grandmother.

I start talking to a bunch of guys as I scan the place wondering if Ashtyn will appear anytime soon. For all I know she's locked herself upstairs and isn't coming down. This is definitely not her scene, where the girls are overdone and overdressed and the guys put on a smile and a suit. If this were a mud-wrestling match, she'd probably be jumping in the ring right about now.

A streak of white on the staircase catches my eye and I freeze. Whoa.

It's Ashtyn, wearing a short white dress that hugs her curves, and bright red stilettos that show off her long legs. I'm frozen in place and can't take my eyes off her. She catches the attention of my grandmother, who gives her a nod of approval.

"Who *is* that?" one guy asks.

"Never seen her before," another says.

A guy who was introduced to me as Oren gives a low whistle. "Damn, she's hot. I call first dibs."

Nobody's getting first dibs on Ashtyn if I have anything to say about it. Without hesitating, I walk over to her. The tops of her creamy white breasts are popping out, no doubt tempting every guy in the place, and those sexy shoes she's got on are what fantasies are made of. "What're you wearin'?" I ask in a harsher tone than I intended.

"Oh, you like it?" She twirls around slowly, giving me, and the guys still watching her, a 360-degree view. She almost trips on the heels and grabs my shoulder to steady herself. "Your grandmother let me borrow it. And the shoes, too. How cool are they?"

"I liked you better in the football jersey," I mumble.

"Why?"

"Because it's you."

"Maybe *this* is me." She heads for the buffet. "I'm starving. As you know, doing drills all day is hard work."

"Yeah, I know. Don't you want to go back to the dorm?"

"Trying to get rid of me?" She absentmindedly takes a gourmet cookie from one of the silver trays and starts eating it.

"No. I'm tryin' to keep those guys over there from hittin' on you."

"Why would you do that?" She takes another bite. And another. And another. She licks frosting off her lips. If her intent is to drive me insane, she's doing a damn good job of it.

"Because I . . . care about you," I tell her.

"Oh, please. Those are empty words. I've heard those words from my mom, my sister, my dad, and even Landon. They mean nothing to me."

They mean something to me. "You think I'm bullshittin' you?"

"Yes. I saw you with that girl with the yellow dress tonight.

Did you tell her you cared about her, too?" She's so riled up she keeps munching on the cookie as if it's the last one she's ever gonna have. When she's done, she slaps her hands together and wipes off the crumbs. "I think I'll go over by the staircase and meet new boyfriend prospects. They look like clean-cut, *honest* boys."

Her words are meant to slice right through me. "Don't let the suits fool you," I tell her.

"Like you fooled me about your football experience?"

Before I can tell her I'm not the answer to her prayers when it comes to recruiting a new quarterback for Fremont, Ashtyn puts her shoulders back. Does she realize it only manages to push her breasts out more? Everyone here is going to get more than an eyeful. She turns her back to me and walks toward the guys, who are still watching her with interest. I follow, not because I think she needs protection . . .

It's because I sense she's about to do something really, really stupid.

CHAPTER 46

Ashtyn

A crowd of boys are standing together in a huddle in the corner of the room. Their eyes are on me, and I do my best imitation of a runway model as I make my way over to them. I'm not nervous around guys, so why am I feeling agitated and clammy all of a sudden? There's a tingling, itchy sensation running down my neck. I ignore it, even though it's driving me nuts.

I put a hand on my hip and smile. "Hey, guys. I'm Ashtyn."

Two of the guys furrow their brows and immediately walk away. Another guy shoves his hands in his pockets and steps back. "I'm Oren," he says nervously. His eyes dart from side to side, as if he's looking for a way to escape.

"I'm, uh, Regan," the fourth guy says. Regan is totally focused on my chest with his eyes totally bugged out. I'm still clammy, but I'm tempted to point to my face and say, "My face is up here, buddy!"

Oren waves to someone across the room, then mumbles, "My girlfriend is over there. I better go check on her."

Regan suddenly pulls a phone out of his pocket. "I got a call. Sorry." But I never heard it ring or vibrate.

I'm standing alone, wondering why I just managed to scare away four guys in less than thirty seconds, when Derek comes up behind me. "Strike out?"

I look and feel sexy in this crazy minidress and shoes, but no boy will talk to me. Besides Derek. I'm trying to make him jealous. How can I do that when four guys sprinted away like I had a disease? I need Jet here. He'd have no problem pretending to flirt with me and would happily make guys think I was a great catch. Or Victor, who'd stand next to me like a bodyguard and make sure nobody sprinted away from me.

I whirl around to face Derek. "Did you come to rub it in my face?" I ask as I rake my nails down my neck and clear the itchiness in my throat.

"Whoa. Ashtyn?"

"What?"

His eyes are focused on my chest.

"Cowboy, my face is here. Stop staring at my boobs."

"I'm not lookin' at your boobs." He gestures to my chest and says, "You're havin' some kind of allergic reaction."

"No, I'm not," I say defiantly before clearing my itchy throat again. But . . . I examine my arms. They feel hot and as I look closer I realize they're red and splotchy. Oh, shit. "Yes, I am."

The only way I know how to flirt with Derek is to challenge

him and beat him at his own game. But it's practically impossible to argue when you're in the middle of an allergic reaction.

I look down at my arms, which are tingling and irritated. And my neck . . . it's like a hundred little mosquitoes bit it at the same time. My throat is really starting to itch now. The most unlady-like noise comes out of my mouth when I attempt to ease the discomfort.

Derek looks panicked. "Seriously, can you breathe?" he asks. "Or should I call 9-1-1 right now?"

"Of course I can breathe. I'm not gonna die, Derek. Just a dose of Benadryl should help." I back up against the wall behind me and rub my shoulder blades against it.

Derek quickly takes my hand and leads me to his grandmother, but I stumble a few times. I'm not used to walking in high heels.

"Do you have Benadryl?" he asks his grandmother. "I think she's allergic to something in a cookie she ate."

"She's allergic to cookies?" his grandmother asks, her voice full of skepticism.

I scratch my arms, trying to relieve the itchiness. "I'm allergic to purple."

"The caterer put a *W* on the cookies in purple. It's a regal color."

"Regal?" Derek shakes his head. "We're not royalty."

"Exactly. So at the last minute I told her to change it to yellow, so she put yellow frosting over the purple frosting to mask it." His grandmother has a worried look on her face as she quickly tells Derek where to find the Benadryl.

"Come on," he says, moving me through the crowd as I try not to scratch my neck even though it's itching like crazy.

I stumble again. "Derek, wait. I can't walk fast in these heels."

I give a little squeak of surprise when one of his arms slides under my knees and the other supports my back as he picks me up. Normally I'd order him to put me down, but I'm too agitated and uncomfortable to be strong right now. I wrap my arms around his neck and lean into him. I'm suddenly surrounded by the scent of his cologne and I breathe it in.

"You smell like a guy," I mumble into the crook of his neck.

"You don't," he says back. "You smell like flowers."

"I think it's the soap your grandmother had in the shower. It was pink, with little pieces of flowers in it. It was like bathing in a bouquet of roses."

I don't know how he manages to carry me up the entire staircase without stumbling or stalling, but he does it. Is he aware that everyone is pointing at us? If he is, he obviously doesn't care.

We reach the huge master bedroom, and he nudges open the door with his foot. The place is huge, with a sitting room next to the bedroom and a bathroom beyond that. Expensive paintings are scattered on the walls and the carpeting looks plush, like you can sink your toes into it. Derek sets me down in the bathroom and rummages through his grandmother's medicine cabinet.

"Stop scratchin'," he orders, taking my hand and holding it at my side.

"I can't help it. I swear that's the last time I eat a cookie."

"You should have gone for the fruit." He finds the Benadryl box and hands me two pills. "Here, take these." After I down the pills with water from the sink, Derek crosses his arms on his chest. "If your condition doesn't improve within a half hour, I'm takin' you to the hospital."

"I'll be fine."

"That's what you said the night we hooked up, and look at where we are now."

I glance at the walls. "We're in your grandmother's bathroom."

"I'm not being literal. Stop scratchin', Ashtyn. You're makin' marks all over your body."

I try my hardest to ignore the itching sensation, but that's like trying to ignore the boy standing in front of me—practically impossible.

My breath hitches when he takes my hands and holds them behind my back. "Stop! You'll make yourself bleed."

He's keeping a small distance between us, but why? Did all his feelings for me fade once he dropped me off at Elite? I need to fight to get those feelings to the surface, to remind him how amazing it was when we were in the tent.

My thoughts are all confused, and the itching doesn't help matters. I'm supposed to be mad at Derek for lying to me about his football experience and at the same time I'm determined to make him fall for me in an attempt to make him play football again. My real feelings are pushed aside right now, because if I acknowledge them, it'll break me apart inside.

I know Derek likes me, but just how much? He's desperate to keep his distance and doesn't want to admit that we had something more than just a casual hookup—something that I know can grow to be more than that.

I squirm in his grasp. "I'm still itchy."

He glances down at my neck and chest. "Be patient and let the Benadryl work," he says.

"I'm not a patient person." I moan in frustration.

"I know." He releases my hands. "Here, let me help. You've already done enough damage . . . there's scratch marks all over your neck. People are gonna think someone assaulted you."

"The only thing to alleviate an itch is to scratch it."

"Yeah, and the only thing to make your skin more irritated is to rake it with your damn nails. If you promise to stay still, I'll help you."

"What are you gonna do?"

"Keep your hands to your side and trust me."

Trust. There's that ugly word again. "Seriously, my skin itches. You wouldn't understand because you're not having an allergic reaction to purple frosting."

"Shh. You talk too much. Close your eyes."

"No."

"You're stubborn."

"Thank you."

"It wasn't meant to be a compliment."

I stare him down, but then as the itching gets worse I give in and wait patiently for his remedy.

I suck in a breath when he traces my neck in slow, rhythmic circles with the tips of his fingers, making my skin tingle instead of itch. I throw my head back and keep my eyes closed, giving him full access. "You remind me of a cat right now," he says in a low voice.

He traces my jawline, the outline of my neck, my chest . . . dipping lightly inside the top of my cleavage peeking out of the dress before venturing back up again. His fingers are like a caress and I'm getting light-headed and dizzy, so I reach out and grab on to him.

The sensual touch of his fingers is sending little jolts of electricity through my veins.

"Mmm . . . ," I moan.

His fingers linger over my shoulders before repeating the process all over again. "You're enjoyin' this too much, Sugar Pie."

"That's right, so keep doing it, Cowboy."

His laugh is deep and hearty, just like him. "Yes, ma'am," he says in a heavy southern accent. After a while I can feel the soft sensation of his fingers being replaced by his soft, warm lips. His breath soothes my skin as the itching subsides.

My insides turn into liquid fire as I pull him closer.

"What are you two doing?" his grandmother's voice booms from the doorway.

I whip my head up and lose my balance, but Derek catches me solidly in his arms. How are we going to explain this one? It's not like the woman is blind. I had my eyes closed, but his grandmother didn't. There's no escaping the fact that Derek's lips were on my neck and I was urging him closer.

"I was helpin' her," Derek explains.

"Uh-huh," his grandmother replies unconvincingly. She narrows her eyes as she holds out her finger. She wags it at both of us. "I wasn't born yesterday. I know there's some hanky-panky goin' on between you two. Come now, Derek. A bunch of guests are fixin' to leave. You're the guest of honor and need to say your good-byes. You can finish *helping* Ashtyn later."

Derek checks the blotches on my arms and chest to make sure they're fading. "You want to join me downstairs or stay up here?"

The itching subsides some. I look in the mirror and cringe. My skin is still all blotchy. This night isn't how I imagined it going down. I was ready to play dirty, but I didn't imagine it would be like this. "Maybe I should just go back to the dorm."

"No." Derek shakes his head. "You'll stay here tonight. I'll drive you back to Elite in the mornin'. Okay?"

I walk to my designated room while Derek and his grandmother spend the next hour saying good-bye to the guests. My hockey jersey and shorts have been cleaned and are lying on my bed. I hang up the dress, then put on my jersey and slip under the down comforter. I feel like I'm sleeping on a marshmallow mattress, it's so soft. It cocoons me as I sink into it and turn on the TV.

Derek's grandmother is the first one to knock. She walks in the room looking elegant and totally put-together even after hosting a party with at least seventy-five to a hundred people. Not a hair is out of place.

I must look like a mess. "Thank you for letting me borrow the dress. It's beautiful."

"Don't thank me. It's yours to keep."

"I couldn't."

"Yes, you can and yes, you will. Don't argue with an old, stubborn lady like me. You won't win." She leans over me to check my neck. "How's the itching?"

"I think it's all better," I tell her.

Satisfied that I'm not still having a reaction to the purple cookie frosting, she sits in a chair next to the bed. She puts her hands in her lap and looks at me with those Derek-lookalike eyes. "So . . . I know something is going on between you and my grandson. Care to tell me what it is?"

I turn off the TV and give her my full attention. "Umm . . . I'm not sure, actually. Maybe you should ask Derek."

"I did."

"What did he say?"

"My grandson is not cooperative when it comes to sharing details about his life, bless his heart."

"That's because you'll use it against me," Derek chimes in as he appears in the room. His suit is gone and is replaced with sweatpants and a T-shirt, looking more like the Derek I know.

He walks to the foot of the bed and gestures to my neck. "How you doin'?"

I lift my head up to show him my chest. "Better. It's gone except for a few scratch marks."

"Good."

It's too easy to get lost in the way he looks at me, those eyes that say so much more than any words can.

"I need to go check on the staff and make sure all the food is packed up," his grandmother says, getting up from the chair and walking out of the room. "Leave this door open."

When his grandmother leaves us alone, Derek lifts the covers and says, "Scootch over so I can sit next to you."

"Your grandmother said you need—"

"I know what she said. Move over."

I do. It feels good to have him here with me now, but even though physically we're close, mentally we're worlds apart.

I turn the TV on again and try to lighten the mood. "I need a TV in my room back home. This is awesome."

We don't say anything else for a long time. Some movie is playing, but I'm not paying attention to it because I'm too aware of Derek sitting next to me.

"I didn't hook up with that girl you saw me with tonight," he says. "She wanted me to take her upstairs and ditch the party, but I didn't."

"Why?"

For a long time he doesn't answer. But then he takes the remote and presses the mute button. He rakes a hand through his hair, and I hold my breath for his response. He turns to me, those piercing eyes of his capturing mine, and he says, "Because of you."

CHAPTER 47

Derek

The number-one rule in football is to not let your opponent know what your game plan is. I just revealed mine.

Just because I can't stop thinking about the girl doesn't mean I'm the guy who's gonna make everything right in her life. "I don't want to hurt you."

"Everybody I care about hurts me," she says. "I've become used to it."

"I didn't intend to join the list."

"Because you don't want to care about anyone who might actually have real feelings for you?" She gives me a small, vulnerable smile.

"Listen, shit happened in my past that I just can't let go of . . . not yet, at least."

"I've been through shit, too, Derek. Most of my life is spent trying to wade through it." She holds her hands up in frustration. "I'm fighting all the time for *everything* and I don't see you fighting for *anything*. It's like you want to keep punishing yourself for some unknown reason."

"You're right." This independent girl, who plays football and has a thicker skin than most guys I know, makes me want to share stuff with her that I've never shared with anyone else. I take a deep breath and let out what I've been holding inside for so long. "The day my mom died I got a call after school from one of the nurses at the hospital. She said my mom had been askin' for me all day." I throw my head back and wince, because the memory still fucking hurts. I'd do anything to turn back time and do that day over again. "I went to practice first, Ashtyn. I put football before my mom . . . I put it before everythin' else. When I finally got to the hospital, she was already gone."

Two days later I stood there watching as they lowered my mom's casket into the ground. I failed her. Her death was so permanent, so final. I'd never get a second chance to make it up to her. "I vowed I'd never play again after she died."

"It's not your fault she died, Derek." Ashtyn places her hand on my arm, her long feminine fingers warm and comforting. I wish she'd been standing next to me at the gravesite so I wouldn't have felt so alone that day. Instead, I figured if I stopped caring about anything and everyone, I'd eventually stop feeling anything at all. It worked.

Until I met Ashtyn Parker.

"It'll be okay," she says. "One day." She slips farther under the covers and lays her head on one of the oversize pillows, facing me. She reaches out and grabs my hand.

"You're tired. Want me to leave?"

"No." She's still got a grip on my hand. As her eyes close and she drifts off, she doesn't let go of my hand.

"Just so you know," she mumbles as she drifts off to sleep. "I did really crappy at football camp this week. Landon convinced the guys to sabotage me, but your words stuck in my head."

"What words?"

"You can do it."

I'm sitting on the bleachers watching Ashtyn do drills in the combine and play during the Friday scrimmage. She has no clue I'm here and I'm trying to stay invisible so none of the guys recognize me—I'm wearing dark sunglasses and a baseball cap while sitting behind a bunch of parents and scouts.

She's stretching on the sidelines, completely focused. In the first quarter of the game, Ashtyn missed two field goals. I watched the ball holders closely. They tilted the ball when she approached so she'd kick it at an awkward angle. More than a couple of parents in the bleachers laughed at her, and others complained that this is why a girl doesn't belong playing football.

The more the guys sabotage her, the more I have the urge to run on the field and replace the holder so Ashtyn can show everyone watching that she deserves to be here. But she wouldn't want that. She wants to fight her own battles.

I lean forward on my elbows as I watch the game. The guys are working hard, every one of them trying to get noticed by the scouts in the stands. McKnight is the quarterback on Ashtyn's team. He's a solid player and I can see why Ashtyn would want him on her team. But he's got an ego and taunts the opposing players when his team scores instead of focusing on the next play.

"Derek! Derek!" a woman's shrieking voice echoes loudly from the sidelines.

Oh, no. Please, no.

My grandmother is causing a huge scene, holding a bright purple sun umbrella and waving her hand like crazy to get my attention. She's wearing a big purple pantsuit that matches the umbrella. At first I ignore her, hoping she'll go away when I don't respond. Fat chance of that. She's got the attention of everyone in the stands and on the field.

"Who *is* that?" one of the parents asks no one in particular.

"Elizabeth Worthington," a guy sitting in front of her answers in a loud whisper. "She's the owner of Worthington Industries. Very influential lady. Her grandson trained here until his mother died. Quarterback."

"Oh. That's so sad."

Great. I've become the subject of parent gossip. I cringe as my grandmother walks up the bleachers and loudly bellows, "Yoohoo, Derek!"

All the spectators, including the scouts, are gawking and whispering among themselves. I might as well have come here with a sign on my head in fluorescent blinking lights saying DEREK FITZPATRICK.

My grandmother has no clue the commotion she's caused as

she takes a seat next to me. "Please tell me why I had to learn from Harold where you'd gone this morning."

"Because I didn't want you to come here and make a scene."

"Nonsense." She cranes her neck as she scans the field. "I can't see Ashtyn from these nosebleed seats. Where is she?"

"She's the one on the sideline next to the kicking net. I swear if you wave to her I'm ordering you to leave."

She keeps her hands down. "Okay, okay. Don't get so cranky."

"What's with the sudden interest in football?" I ask her. "You never came to Elite when I was trainin' here."

She shifts in her seat and keeps her eyes on the field. "That's what you think."

"I never saw you."

My grandmother turns to me with a mischievous smile. "Maybe that's because I didn't want to be seen." She clears her throat and turns her attention back to the game. "I've made mistakes in the past that I don't intend to repeat." She glances at me sideways. "You would be wise to do the same."

Mistakes. I've definitely made my share.

After the game, a crowd of scouts surround us and bombard me with questions. So much for being invisible. I tell them I have no plans to play football again, but a few of them give me their cards and tell me to call them if I change my mind.

My grandmother says she's going to wait for Ashtyn to get out of the locker room, when I catch sight of McKnight walking toward the dorm. I meet up with him in the common area, ready to confront him about sabotaging Ashtyn.

"Holy shit," fullback Justin Wade says. Justin and I were roommates my third year here. "It's 'The Fitz' in the flesh. Yo, Fitz, where ya been?"

A linebacker named Devon slaps me on the back. "Shit, man, I can't believe you're back. I thought you'd still be on the fast track to playin' in the NFL for sure. When I heard you'd stopped playin', it shocked the hell outta me."

"My team got creamed in the scrimmage," Justin says. "We sure could've used you—"

"I'm not here to play," I tell them.

"Wait a second," Landon says. "*You're* Derek Fitzpatrick?"

"The one and only, dude," Justin chimes in.

"A legend around here," Devon adds, then tells Landon, "He's the one I was telling you about the other night."

"No way. I can't believe this." Landon shakes his head as if he's still trying to figure out how I can be the guy in the pictures gracing the MVP wall at Elite. "Why are you here?" he asks.

"Just checkin on Ashtyn."

"Why, 'cause you want her for yourself?" He gestures to the doorway. "You've wanted to get into her pants the second you laid eyes on her, man."

I give a short laugh, the sound reverberating across the room. "You don't know shit, McKnight."

"I know *everything*." He leans forward and whispers in my ear. "If I tell her I'll play for Fremont, I can have her back with a snap of my fingers."

I push him away from me.

He pushes me, then throws a punch.

With my blood at its boiling point, my fists are flying. He doesn't miss a beat and fires back, so both of us are going at it. My adrenaline is running at an all-time high, and he can't get a good shot because I'm all in and don't want or need to stop fighting anytime soon.

A bunch of guys try pulling us off each other, but I resist and shrug them off.

Until I hear Ashtyn scream, "Derek!"

I turn toward her voice, see her shocked expression, and get clocked in the jaw. Damn, that hurt. McKnight has a solid right hook.

If that isn't bad enough, the coaches start rushing in. Coach Smart, the head coach and the one who runs the Elite program, gets in between us. "What the hell is going on here?"

McKnight wipes blood off the corner of his mouth with the back of his hand. "Nothin', Coach."

"Doesn't look like nothin' to me." He steps between us. "Derek, what the hell are you doing here starting trouble with one of my players?"

His players. I used to be one of his players. "Sorry, Coach."

He barks orders to one of the assistant coaches to tend to McKnight, then grabs me by the front of my shirt and pulls me into the empty hallway. I think he's about to kick me out, but instead he gets in my face like he used to do when I was on the field. "You used to be a role model to these guys, Derek." He grabs my chin, making me wince in pain, as he examines my bruises. "What's goin' on with you?"

I shrug.

"Where's your old man?"

I shrug again. "In the middle of the ocean somewhere."

He nods, as if somehow my father being deployed explains why I just got in a fight. He shakes his head. "I heard you got kicked out of that academy in California. So you're getting in trouble instead of playing ball?"

Ashtyn is standing at the door, glaring at me with anger and resentment. My grandmother and her umbrella are behind her.

"You know you should still be playing, don't you?" Smart says. "You can't just forget everything you worked hard for."

"I didn't forget it, Coach. I don't play anymore. End of story."

"Your story can't end, Derek, because it never even started," he says.

"This discussion is over, Coach." I came here to fight for Ashtyn, not me. This isn't about me.

"Not yet. You know I have zero tolerance for fighting," Coach says. "You can fight on your own turf and own time, not mine."

"I'm leavin'," I say.

"Don't leave." McKnight suddenly appears in the hallway with a few of the guys standing behind him. His posse. He holds out his hand. "Sorry, man. No hard feelings."

I shake my head in disgust and walk past him. I open the door and am about to walk out when I hear McKnight's voice. "That's all right, Derek. We all know you're afraid you can't live up to your legend status."

"My grandson isn't afraid," my grandmother chimes in. She pokes her umbrella in McKnight's direction.

I squeeze my eyes shut. When I open them, I glance at Coach Smart. And McKnight and his posse. And my grandmother. And finally Ashtyn. Every one of them is wondering what I'll do.

In the end, I do what I've been doing since my mom died.

I walk away and don't look back.

CHAPTER 48

Ashtyn

can't just let him leave. My dad drives off when things get tough and he wants to escape. I won't let Derek get away that easy, so I stand in front of his car and block his path as he's about to drive away.

He rolls down his window. "What're you doin'?"

"Get out of the car!" I yell. When he does, my blood boils and I storm up to him with long, purposeful strides. "You just fucked everything up for me!" I growl, then shove my hands into his chest.

"Stop yellin'," he says, glancing at the others around us.

"No, I won't stop yelling, because I'm royally pissed off. You know I'm fighting my *ass* off here, Derek. I'm fighting to be treated like one of the guys. I'm fighting to prove to everybody that I belong here." I'm getting emotional and don't care that everyone within a hundred yards can probably hear my rant. "I've been fighting since the second I came to Elite. Get it in your thick head that I don't want you to fight for me. It just makes me look weak. I need to fight for myself, or it doesn't count. But dammit, Derek, when are you gonna fight for yourself?"

"Not gonna happen."

I swallow the knot in my throat and say, "My mom left when I was ten years old. She didn't give a shit about me, and I have to live every day knowing it. You're lucky. You know your mom loved you."

"Lucky?" He gives a short, cynical laugh. "At least your mom is alive and you can talk to her. Do you know what I'd do to talk to my mom for just one minute? One lousy minute! I'd cut off my arm to have just one minute with her."

"What do you want out of life?" I ask, challenging him to answer. I need to pull it out of him. "What's your goal? Besides pretending not to care about anything, which I know is complete crap."

"Don't have one."

That's bullshit. "Everyone has a goal."

He's averting his gaze because he knows if he looks at me I'll see right into his soul. The wounds that should have healed by now are still raw because of the massive amount of guilt he's carried with him since his mother's death. He keeps punishing himself for that one decision he made a long time ago.

I know he wants to fight for something . . . deep down he's got a basic, intense desire to compete. It's killing him that he's ignoring his instincts and instead is determined to keep himself a ghost of who he can be.

Joining the military after he graduates is Derek's way of feeding that competitive fighting spirit . . . he was fighting for me back at the dorm, but my conflict with Landon isn't Derek's fight to win—it's mine.

Landon called Derek a coward. Suddenly it wasn't about me anymore, and Derek walked away.

Derek defiantly crosses his hands on his chest. "Please move so I can leave."

"Listen to me." I lower my voice and say softly, "Shit happens, Derek. Life goes on, whether you want it to or not. People die, whether you want them to or not. Don't make up some bullshit in your head that you quit football for your mom. She gave you life. You think she'd want your spirit to die right along with hers?"

"Don't bring my mom into this."

"Why not? Quitting won't bring her back. You say you don't have a goal? That's bullshit! You need to go for what you want and not hold back. When you figure it out let me know, because I'll bet my left nut you have a goal but won't admit to yourself what it is."

The corner of his mouth twists upward. "You don't have a left nut, Ashtyn."

"Yeah, well, you're acting like you don't have one, either." I don't mention the obvious—that if he doesn't fight for himself, it's useless to fight for us. "You need to forgive yourself."

There's a long, brittle silence before he says, "I can't."

He looks past me and I turn around. His grandmother is standing across the parking lot, pretending not to be paying attention to our conversation. When I turn back, Derek's running a hand through his hair. "My grandmother wants me to come live with her. I decided it's probably best for both of us if I stay in Texas and go to school here. I'll get you a plane ticket back to Chicago on Sunday."

I let his words sink in as deep sorrow fills my chest. "Is that what you want?"

"Yeah," he says, his face stoic and unemotional. "That's what I want."

CHAPTER 49

Derek

I drive around the rest of the day, my mind trying to wrap around the idea that I'm staying in Texas and moving in with my grandmother. When I arrive at her house, I find her sitting on a small bench in the foyer waiting for me.

"Where were you?"

"Out."

She nods slowly. "I talked to Ashtyn after you left. She's pretty upset."

"Yeah, well, she'll get over it."

"Hmm."

I look at her with a mixture of frustration and annoyance. "What's that supposed to mean?"

"I just think you're not being rational right now." She sighs loud and slow. "She said you're moving in with me."

"Oh, yeah. I forgot to tell you that I'm movin' in. Congrats, you got what you wanted." I start walking up the winding staircase to the second floor.

"I want you to be happy, Derek. That's what I've always wanted." She hesitates before saying, "It's what your mother would have wanted."

"How do you know? She's not around to ask now, is she? Want to ask my dad what he thinks? Oh, yeah. He's not around, either," I say, sarcasm dripping from every word.

"Well, regardless of who's around, you have to go back to Chicago to pack up your things if you're going to move in with me."

At the top of the stairs, I call out, "Get movers to do it."

"Nonsense." She stands tall and puts her regal nose in the air. "I've already arranged for the corporate jet to take us back to Chicago."

I stop dead in my tracks. "Us? Who's included in 'us'?"

"You, Ashtyn . . . and me."

No, no. "Sorry to break the news to you, Grams, but that's not how it's goin' down."

"Yes, it is. It's a done deal and everything is already arranged. Harold will be picking up Ashtyn on Sunday at Elite and she'll meet us at the airport." She crosses her arms and gives me a dignified stare that dares me to challenge her. "And *that's* how it's goin' down."

CHAPTER 50

Ashtyn

'm sitting in front of Coach Bennett and Coach Smart on Sunday morning for my final evaluation. I fight the urge to bite my nails as they review my stats and performance this past week. They're also supposed to share any feedback from the scouts who were present at the scrimmages.

"It was a pleasure having you at camp this week," Coach Bennett starts. "Both Coach Smart and I are impressed by your determination and drive."

But not my performance.

Coach Smart nods in agreement. "You're the first female accepted to our program, Ashtyn. We knew there would be challenges, and you faced them head-on. That takes courage, and I admire that in my players."

Coach Smart takes time to go over my stats with me and I cringe. "Your stats this week are not impressive, Ashtyn," he says.

"The feedback from the scouts and coaches wasn't what you were probably hoping for, but Coach Bennett secured an interview with the Northwestern coach next week. No promises, but at least they agreed to talk with you."

Just the thought of being able to talk to a Big Ten football coach should make me excited and happy. I don't know what's wrong with me. It's like as soon as Derek told me he was moving to Texas, suddenly everything feels so . . . off.

"No matter what happens, all of us at Elite have faith that you'll accomplish whatever you set out to do." Coach Bennett smiles warmly and holds out his hand. "We will definitely be following your team stats this coming season and wish you all the best."

I shake both of their hands. "Thank you both for the opportunity," I say, then gather my duffel from the dorm and wait for the limo to pick me up. I got a call last night that Mrs. Worthington is chartering the corporate jet.

I sit on the small airplane next to Derek. His grandmother insisted on coming with us. She says she wants to help Derek pack his stuff up. I heard Derek protest, but she just ignored him.

It's hard not to feel Derek's presence beside me. When we arrive home, Julian runs up to Derek with a big smile and my sister brings out cookies with the words WELCOME HOME in yellow frosting. I can't eat them. All they do is remind me of the night at his grandmother's house when Derek finally revealed everything he's held inside for so long.

"I'm Brandi. You must be Liz!" Brandi says excitedly. Mrs. Worthington flinches when my sister calls her Liz instead of

Elizabeth or Mrs. Worthington, but Brandi doesn't notice. "It's *so* nice that you came here for a little visit. Derek, isn't having your grammy here just *the best*?"

"Not really," he says.

Mrs. Worthington whacks him with her purse. "My grandson is lacking in social graces, but I intend to fix that."

"Where's Dad?" I ask, changing the subject.

My sister points to the den. "Watching television."

I peek into the den. "We're back, Dad."

He nods as if I'd just come back from going to the grocery store.

"Derek's grandma's here, too," I add, then gesture for him to get up and greet her.

He gets up, meets Mrs. Worthington for a brief moment, then walks back to the den and starts watching TV again.

"Not a social fella," Mrs. Worthington mumbles as she walks around inspecting the rest of the house.

"My dad's kinda introverted," I explain.

"Hmm." Mrs. Worthington takes one bite of Brandi's cookie and spits it out in her napkin. "Dearie, are you trying to poison us, or just break our teeth?"

Brandi laughs. "I admit I'm not the best baker."

"Obviously." She pats Brandi on the cheek. "We must get you some cooking lessons, dearie. Before you kill my grandson."

Brandi giggles, thinking that Mrs. Worthington is joking. I don't think she's joking at all, but it's probably best that my sister is clueless.

A low bark echoes through the house before Falkor comes running up to me and gives me slobbery kisses. "And this is Falkor."

"Eww. Ashtyn, dear, please . . . get that animal to stop giving you a tongue bath. It's very unsanitary."

Derek kneels down and Falkor abandons me without a second thought. My dog rolls onto his back while Derek rubs his belly and tells Falkor how much he missed him.

After Mrs. Worthington is settled in my bedroom and the rest of us are in the kitchen, Derek breaks the news to my sister and Julian that he's moving to Texas.

My sister's smile fades.

"But you're my brother," Julian cries out. "I don't want you to move to Texas. Don't leave!"

My sister looks shocked and her eyes are glassy. "I'm sure Derek has thought long and hard about his decision, Julian," she says in a dull and sad voice. "He needs to do what he thinks is best."

"Sorry, buddy." Derek reaches out to Julian, but my nephew ducks out of his reach and runs upstairs. Derek has a grim look on his face as he follows Julian upstairs.

"I failed my husband," Brandi murmurs. Her arms fall to her sides. She looks totally defeated. "I fail in everything."

"That's not true." I walk up to her and put my arm around her shoulders, comforting her. "You're a great mom to Julian. He's a great kid, Brandi. You didn't have any help and he's so smart and sensitive."

She shrugs as she wipes away tears running down her pale, heart-shaped face. "You already pointed out that I've been a shitty sister. I'm obviously a horrible stepmother. I should have just stayed in California."

"No." I hug her in earnest now as tears fall from my eyes, too. When she hugs me back, I choke back sobs. Derek will take a part of me with him when he leaves, and I don't think I can face the despair alone. I'm tired and sad and don't want to be strong anymore. "I need you, Brandi. I need my big sister and I'm so, so glad you're back."

"Are you okay?" she asks, holding me at arm's length, surprised that I'm crying along with her.

I shake my head. "No."

She wipes the tears from my cheeks and gives me a sorrowful, knowing look. "This is about you and Derek, isn't it?"

I nod, unable to say the words out loud.

She holds my face in her hands. "I'm here for you, baby sister. I'm sorry, I feel like this is all my fault."

"What's this kumbaya moment all about?" Mrs. Worthington asks as she walks into the kitchen. "I swear I feel like I'm in a funeral home with all the crying going on. You know what heals everything?"

"What?" Brandi asks.

I wipe my tears and wait for her answer.

"Spa treatments." She takes her phone and dials a number. "Harold, do that Googly thing and find me a reputable spa in Fremont, Illinois. Make an appointment for three people for a massage and facial tonight." She hangs up the phone, but then calls back a second later. "On second thought, make it an appointment for four. Ashtyn's father is grumpier than I am and definitely needs help."

"Liz, I don't think my dad will go to a spa," Brandi says when she hangs up the second time.

"Yes, he will," Derek's grandmother says without hesitation. "*Nobody* says no to a Worthington. And if you call me *Liz* again, I might just have to rip those overly dyed extensions out of your head."

CHAPTER 51

Derek

Ashtyn told me I needed a goal. I finally have one, although it's not really a goal but a mission. I've decided to clean the shed before I leave. It was dirty and neglected when I first arrived here, but I gave it new life. I'd already given it a paint job and fixed the broken slats on the roof and walls. This morning I decided to clean the inside of the shed so it'll look brand-spankin'-new. I cleared out everything, and then went to the hardware store to buy new shelves that won't fall off the wall and plywood to replace the old floor. I even tiled the top of the workbench so it was clean and usable again.

I saw Ashtyn leave the house this morning with Victor, who picked her up for practice. She's not talking to me. Julian isn't, either. I told him I'd come visit him every few months, but that didn't matter. He told me to leave him alone and he hasn't looked at me since. That was two days ago.

I stand back and survey my progress. "Not bad for a day's worth of work." Falkor, panting beside me while vigorously wagging his tail, obviously agrees with me.

"What in God's name are you doing, Derek?" my grandmother bellows from the porch. She walks over to me in the grass that needs to be mowed again. At least the backyard isn't a large patch of weeds and looks halfway decent.

"I'm cleanin' out the shed."

"Hire someone to do that."

"Why hire someone when I can do it myself?"

She holds up a powerful finger. "Because it helps the economy. When you hire someone, they have more money to buy things. It's basic economics, Derek."

I have to give my grandmother credit for creativity. She really does believe the nonsense that spurts from her lips.

"Well, *basically* I'm doin' it myself," I tell her.

She sighs. "Well, fine. Just . . . wash up afterward so you don't look like a street person."

I laugh as she walks away. To be honest, my grandmother is damn entertaining, and every now and then she does something that reminds me of my mom—like the way she sleeps on the very edge of her bed or the way she covers her mouth when she laughs. On the other hand, when she acts like a high-class snob, it's completely annoying and embarrassing. While she intends to turn me into a clone of her while I live in her house for the next nine months until I graduate, my intention is to take the snobbery out of her. It'll be a challenge, that's for damn sure.

At five o'clock, my grandmother announces that she's taking the whole family into the city for dinner. Supposedly she made reservations at The Pump Room, which she said is some fancy place where celebrities in Chicago eat. Gus has learned in the past two days that it's better to follow my grandmother's orders than to fight her. I think she's what he needed all along, a crazy lady to make him interact with the family instead of escaping it. I would go, but to be honest, looking at Ashtyn all night across a table and knowing I'm leaving her in a few days isn't what I'd call a fun evening.

I've managed to clean out the entire shed when it's suddenly dark outside. I get a flashlight from the house and put the shelves up, then hang all the tools back on the wall.

"Stop, or I'm calling the police!" a familiar feminine voice says from behind me.

Ashtyn is standing in the doorway, holding her signature pitchfork like it's a weapon. It's dark, but the small glow of the flashlight shines on the metal in her hands.

I give her a small smile and walk up to the pitchfork so it's an inch away from my chest. "You really don't want to stab me," I tell her.

She lowers the weapon. "You're right."

I take the pitchfork out of her hand and toss it outside, far away from my foot. "What are you doin' here? I thought you'd gone with everyone else to the city."

"I decided to stay." There's no mistaking the seductive tone of her voice.

She steps closer. From the small amount of light, I can tell she's wearing a hockey jersey and nothing else. My eyes rake over her half-clad body, unable to look away.

I swallow, hard. It's dark and the flashlight is losing battery fast. When I met Ashtyn, I had no clue what she'd do to me. Every time I'm near her, I want to push her away and pull her close at the same time. She talks like a jock but has a body like an angel. She knows I'm leaving, but she's here with me now . . .

"Why did you stay home tonight?" I ask.

The flashlight flickers, then it goes completely dark when she reaches out for me and whispers in my ear, "Because of you."

CHAPTER 52

Ashtyn

I sat on my bed for an hour before I gathered enough nerve to come to the shed tonight. I know Derek's leaving, but I want him to remember what it felt like to be with someone who loved him unconditionally. I tell myself not to be emotional, to be happy that we could have this one last night together. I never imagined I'd fall so hard for someone, especially after knowing him for such a short time, but I have.

I never believed in love at first sight, until I met Derek. It's all-consuming and delicious and wonderful and exciting. At the same time, it makes me nervous and self-conscious and emotional. Love exists. I know it does, because I'm madly, deeply, hopelessly in love.

Wrapping my arms around Derek's neck, I feel his hands on my waist as he pulls me close. We kiss, and I open my mouth to deepen the intimacy. His tongue is lost in my mouth and mine in his.

"Once we start this, I'm not gonna want to stop," he says in a hoarse, deep voice.

"Me neither."

Without another word, I close my eyes while his fingers hook onto the bottom of my jersey, and slowly, tantalizingly, he slips the material over my sensitive skin and tosses it aside.

It's dark. We can't see anything, but I can hear the sexy rasp of his breathing and feel the slow, sensual feel of his hands on my skin.

I reach out and roam my fingers over the muscles of his biceps and trace the hard, solid lines of his perfect, defined abs and pecs. "I lied to you," I tell him as my fingers move over the waistband of his shorts and follow the line of hair that leads downward.

"Mmm . . .'bout what?"

"I said I wasn't affected or impressed by your body." I kiss his neck and the musky scent of maleness envelops my senses. I move my kisses lower, to his chest, his abs, and lower. "I lied."

He throws his head back, and his hand weaves into my hair as I show him how much I appreciate his body. From the ragged sound of his breathing I know he likes it. A lot.

"My turn," he says in a strained voice after a while. I let out a surprised shriek when he scoops me up and has me sit on the empty new workbench in front of him.

He kisses me senseless and I move against him, wanting more, wanting him, wanting this night to last forever. Our bodies are slick with sweat now, and we're both panting and struggling to make this last longer, but I sense we're both holding on by a thin thread. My hands roam over his glorious body while I taste his mouth and he tastes mine.

He replaces his mouth with the tip of his forefinger, lightly moving it over my lips before dipping his finger inside my mouth so I can suck on it.

I lean back while he removes his finger from my mouth and moves it gently and passionately over my body. At some point his finger gets replaced by his mouth and tongue. When I feel his hot breath on my slick skin, my entire body tingles.

"You don't know what you're doing to me," I pant.

"Yeah, I do," he says in a hoarse, deep voice as he removes the rest of his clothes. I hear the rip of a condom wrapper and my body goes still.

"Did you get that from your wallet?" I ask him.

"Yeah."

"I thought you didn't carry a condom in your wallet."

He chuckles, and I can imagine his lips are curved into a mischievous grin. "Secret compartment."

I'm sitting on the edge of the workbench as he stands between my legs and slips on a condom.

I brace my hands on his chest. "Derek?"

"Yeah?" he says, his voice strained as he holds himself back.

I'm glad it's dark, and he can't see my face now, all hot and bothered and nervous. "I don't know what I'm doing."

He puts my hand on him so I can feel his arousal. "Obviously, you do."

"No, I mean I've done stuff before . . . but not . . ."

"What? I had no idea." He lets out a long, slow breath before placing his forehead against mine. "We don't have to do this, Ashtyn. Your first time shouldn't be in a shed."

"I want to." I hold his face in my hands. "I love you, Cowboy. Unconditionally. And this is the perfect place to do it . . . the place we first met. Nothing could be more special with you, right here. Right now."

And so we do.

Derek takes it slow.

"You okay?" he asks as we move together. "I don't want to hurt you."

I'm so overwhelmed and so in the moment it's hard for me to process it all. It's like I'm in the middle of a dream and I don't want to wake up. "Don't worry about me," I say in a soft whisper.

"I always worry about you, Ashtyn. I know you can take care of yourself . . ." He grabs my butt with his hands, urging my legs to wrap around him as he lifts me off the workbench. "But sometimes it's way better when you let someone else take care of you. Come with me and let go of your inhibitions, Sugar Pie."

I close my eyes while Derek takes over. He's right. I've never felt so loved and cared for in my entire life. He's so gentle and patient and knows just the right thing to do and suddenly I'm crying out his name and he cries out mine. I know this dream won't last forever and a part of me will always want him as a permanent fixture in my life.

"You own a piece of me," he murmurs as he holds me afterward.

"Good," I tell him. "And just so you know . . . I'm never giving it back."

CHAPTER 53

Derek

In the past, I knew what I wanted and went for it with a vengeance. When I was younger, it was football. I did what I had to do in order to be the best.

The day after Ashtyn and I spent the night together in the shed, I'm on the plane headed back to Texas. My grandmother is sitting across from me with a stoic look on her face. I know she bonded with Brandi, Julian, and Ashtyn. Hell, I even saw her secretly feed Falkor scraps of food under the table when she thought nobody was looking.

After we land, Harold picks us up.

"Did you have a nice time?" Harold asks us.

My grandmother and I look at each other. "The weather in Chicago is atrociously hot and humid," she says in a haughty tone. "But Fremont is a charming town. With people who grew on me, I suppose. Right, Derek?"

"Right," I say.

I enter my grandmother's house and it just doesn't feel right. It's too big and too empty. At night, I stare at the stark white walls and know this isn't where I want to be.

Before the sun comes up, I walk downstairs and am surprised to find my grandmother sitting in the library all by herself. She's got my mom's letter in her hand.

"You can't sleep?"

She shakes her head and puts the letter down. "It's not for lack of trying. What about you, Derek?"

"I can't sleep, either." I sit next to her. "You miss my mom?"

She nods. "Yes. Very much."

"Me, too." I look at my grandmother and for the first time since my mom died, I realize what I want. I want to be there for Julian and Brandi, the family I never knew I wanted. I want to be close to my grandmother even though she drives me nuts. I want to show Ashtyn what it means to be loved unconditionally—because she's the only girl I want to be with and I don't ever want her to feel alone again.

I want to fight for her. And go for it with a vengeance.

It's been a long time since I set a plan in motion, other than a stupid prank, but that competitive instinct kicks in as if it were never gone in the first place. I feel excitement and blood rushing through my veins as I plot out what I need to do. It won't be easy—far from it. But I welcome the challenge.

"Grams?"

"Yes, Derek. Did I ever tell you that I hate when you call me that?"

"It's a term of endearment, because I love you," I tell her, getting me a jab in the ribs. "I want to go back to Chicago. And I want you to come with me."

"I'm a Texan, Derek," she says.

"Me, too. Think we can be Texans who just happen to live somewhere else?"

She thinks about it for a minute, then nods. "Yes. Yes, I think we can give it a whirl and try it. I'll have Harold help us find a decent house to live in that's not too far from Brandi and Ashtyn. Of course Harold and the staff will relocate with us . . . and I have to come back periodically to oversee Worthington Industries. You know you're the heir to the company, don't you?"

"You keep reminding me."

"Good."

This is more than fixing the mistakes I made in the past. This is bringing purpose back into my life, something I'd been missing. Ashtyn knew I had fight left in me . . . and she helped me realize that I have goals and dreams just like she does.

My grandmother is more than happy to help set my plans in motion. It takes a bunch of calls to some universities and coaches I once played with, and pulling some strings that only an heir of Worthington Industries can pull off. I fly back to Chicago when I know Ashtyn's got her interview at Northwestern University. I know she won't be at practice. As soon as I land, I head over to Fremont High.

I walk on the field, and the familiar scent of fresh-cut grass envelops me. The coach is in an intense conversation with one of the assistant coaches. "Coach Dieter," I say, jogging to catch up with him.

The coach turns around, his sharp blue eyes giving me a once-over. "Yeah?"

I swallow. Suddenly I'm nervous. How could my nerves be wound tight just by talking to a small-town coach? Probably because in the back of my mind, I know this is it and I can't turn back.

"I'm a transfer student," I tell Dieter. "I'm startin' here in the fall and—"

"Son, I haven't got all day. State your business."

I tell him, straight up, "I want to play ball. Quarterback."

He chuckles.

"Listen, I know you lost McKnight and your backup isn't exactly starter material." I can't afford to show any weakness, only determination and confidence. "I'll be better than McKnight on his best day."

Coach Dieter's eyebrows rise. "You sure are a cocky sonofabitch. What's your name?"

I hold out my hand. "Derek. Derek Fitzpatrick."

The coach takes my hand and shakes it. It's a manly shake, one of those hard ones that tests the strength of another guy and it's over before you know it.

"Where'd you play?"

"Started in Alabama, then played at Sierra High in California. State champion, all-state player—"

"What year are you?"

"I'll be a senior."

Dieter calls over one of the assistant coaches. "Derek Fitzpatrick, this is our DC, Coach Heilmann. Coach Heilmann, Derek here thinks he's a better QB than Landon McKnight."

The defensive coordinator gives a short laugh, then shrugs. "What the hell. I'd give him a tryout, Bill. At this point it can't hurt," the assistant coach says before leaving us alone again.

Dieter taps his pen on his clipboard. "What *can* hurt is egomaniac wannabes wasting my time." Before I can tell him about my stats, he says, "Follow me, son. Let's get you suited up and see what you got."

I follow the coach into the locker room, where the rest of the team is putting on their gear. He motions for me to wait outside the equipment cage while he grabs me pads and a helmet. After he hands them to me, I sit on a bench and check out my future teammates.

I catch sight of Victor immediately. He takes one look at me and storms up, facing me head-on with fierce hatred on his face. "Get the fuck out of here, Fitzpatrick. You think you can hurt Ashtyn, then suddenly have a change of heart and expect her to run back in your arms so you can take advantage of her again? That's bullshit, man. I don't trust you, and neither does anyone else on this team, so you might as well go back to where you came from."

"I'm not goin' anywhere," I tell him.

"Oh, yeah? You want to get to Ashtyn, you've got to get through every single one of us."

"No problem." Whatever it takes. I'm not backing down.

He pushes me. I push back.

We're about to get into it when Dieter blows his whistle. Everybody stops what they're doing and suddenly the entire locker room is quiet. All eyes are on me. Obviously if Victor considers me the enemy, they all consider me the enemy.

"Everyone on the field!" Dieter yells.

Shit, this is not going to be easy.

Jet pushes my helmet off the bench. "Don't expect any one of us to kiss your ass or fawn all over you because you're supposed to be some sort of master QB and all. We all watched Ashtyn cry for days after you left. It was fucked-up, 'cause she never gets that emotional. You got a death wish, this is the right place."

When I run on the field after suiting up, Victor walks right up to Dieter. "We want Butter in as QB, Coach."

Dieter doesn't even look up from his clipboard. "I'm not planning anything but a winning season. From my experience, there's nothin' like shaking things up to make a team stronger. Maybe a new QB will light a fire under your asses."

Victor is getting riled up now, because he's breathing hard and his fist is clenched on to the face mask of his helmet hanging at his side. "Coach—"

"Salazar, stop whining. Now get your ass over to calisthenics. You, too, Fitzpatrick."

Victor stalks over to the field where the rest of the team is doing jumping jacks. Dieter grabs my elbow as I walk past him. "He's not gonna make it easy for you."

"I'm not used to things coming easy," I say.

I better keep my mind on the game and not the girl who has invaded my thoughts and my life.

During practice, I'm ordered to shadow the current QB, Brandon Butter. After he runs a play, Dieter sidelines him and tells me to call the same play. My handoff to Trey Matthews is textbook, but he drops the ball as soon as his hands touch the leather.

"What the hell?" I ask Trey after he drops the ball a second time. "That was a textbook handoff."

He starts walking away. "For a prodigy, your skills are obviously lacking," he mumbles, then crudely grabs his crotch for my benefit.

"Fuck you. My skills are spot-on."

Jet isn't any help, either. He tries his hardest to catch the current QB's throws every time, even when they're way off target, but he practically runs in the opposite direction the second the ball leaves my hand.

The guys on the offensive line leave a hole wide open for Victor to sack me. He does, repeatedly.

"Dude, you suck!" Victor says to me when we're getting in formation. He chuckles, amused at my inability to show off my skills.

"I wouldn't suck if your teammates would do their job," I yell.

As the ball is hiked to me, I look for Jet but am immediately sacked by Victor again. None of my offensive linemen are protecting me.

"That was for Ashtyn," Victor says, shoving me to the ground as I try to get up. Then he puts a hand out to help me, but I don't take it. It's his damn fault I got sacked. With my frustration at an all-time high, I stand up and push him. He's a linebacker. I shouldn't be surprised that his feet stay solid on the ground.

"Want a piece of me?" he asks.

Jet appears between us. He grabs the front of my jersey and urges me away from Vic.

It's too late. "Give me what you got, Salazar."

I brace myself and keep my center of gravity as he attempts to shove me to the ground. Ha. The big guy thought he'd take me down without an effort, but I'm one stubborn motherfucker, my adrenaline is running high, and I refuse to be taken down. Frustrated, he removes his helmet and gets in my face. Dieter blows his whistle. I think he's been blowing it ever since I got sacked, but I'm ignoring it just like everyone else at this point.

"You can't expect to come here, snap your fingers, and make us work for you," Salazar says.

I whip off my helmet. "I've played with freshmen who could run circles around you."

He rushes me just as Coach Dieter blows his whistle again. It's not easy to fight with equipment on. We're rolling on the ground trying to get at each other.

"Break it up!" I hear Dieter yelling.

A bunch of guys force us off each other.

"Fitzpatrick, on the bench!" Dieter orders, motioning to the sidelines.

What the hell? I'm being singled out? Fuck that. "You've got to be kiddin'. Coach, it wasn't my—"

Dieter points to the bench, cutting me off. "I'm not gonna say it again."

This team . . . these *assholes* . . . are fucking up my chance. I sit on the bench, seething from every pore of my body as the players put in 110 percent for Butter even though he sucks.

"Fitzpatrick, get your butt over here!" Coach Dieter yells from across the field. "The rest of you, take a lap around the field, then you're dismissed."

I grab my helmet and walk over to the coach. "I didn't come here to be sidelined." I can't hide my frustration.

"Listen, Derek, despite what happened on the field I can tell you've got a good arm."

"If the team'll back me up—"

"They won't." He takes his hat off and leans forward. "I can tell them until my face is blue, but for some reason the guys don't trust you. My boys'll take a hit to protect Butter even if it means breakin' their bones to do it. You need to earn their respect and loyalty. Once you do that, we've got a real good shot this year. It's up to you. You up for the challenge?"

"Yeah, Coach."

"Good. Now go do damage control and fix whatever drama is happening off the field, then meet me back here for practice Monday morning."

In the parking lot, Salazar is about to get on his motorcycle. He stiffens when he sees me.

"I'm tryin' to get Ashtyn back," I tell him.

"Good luck with that," he says with a shake of his head. "Not gonna happen."

"Dammit, Salazar . . ." Time to let it all out, because there might not be a second chance at this. "I love her." I open my arms out wide. "Why do you think I'm doin' all this? It's for her, it's for us, it's for me. Shit, I don't know. Maybe you're right and I'm the biggest asshole who ever walked the earth. But you know more than anyone how she feels about me. If I have a remote chance of winnin' her back . . . I've got to do this. Hell, I don't blame you for wantin' to beat the shit out of me. She wants a winning team, Salazar. I want to help give that to her. Help me give that to her."

He lowers his head and sighs. "You hurt her, Fitzpatrick. She cried in my arms like a fuckin' baby, man. She's like a sister to me and I will *not* let you hurt her again."

"I don't intend to. I hate to ask you this, but I need your help."

"With what?"

"I need to borrow tapes of every game Fremont's played for the past three years."

"Every game?" Victor narrows his eyes like he did that first day we met. He looked at me like I was the enemy on a rival team. "Should I trust you?"

I look him straight in the eye and say, "No. But I'd really appreciate it if you did."

CHAPTER 54

Ashtyn

take a deep breath as I sit in front of the coaching staff at North-western. It's considered the Ivy League school of the Midwest and one of the best football programs. I attended a seminar about the school and took an all-day tour of the campus. It's beautiful here, right on the shores of Lake Michigan. I can't help but wish Derek were here to say *you can do this*.

Derek. As much as I try to push the memories of us together to the back of my mind, I can't. He's become a part of me, whether he feels the same about me or not. When I close my eyes and think about him gently touching my face, running his hand through my hair, or just holding me because he knows I need to be held, I actually feel a calmness I haven't felt since my mom left.

I want to fly to Texas, grab him, and tell him how much I want him to choose me. But if I do, I won't be letting him choose his own path. I don't want to ever feel like I forced or coerced him to be with me. He obviously wasn't ready for a commitment, at least with me. I just want him to be happy. If he's happy without me in Texas, I need to be okay with it.

Who am I kidding? I'll never be okay with it, and I miss him so damn bad. He's my best friend, the one who taught me that I'm worthy of being loved. He made me feel confident that my mom was the one who was losing out.

For the first time in my life, I actually believe it.

"While we're impressed with your performance last year and you received a wonderful recommendation from Coach Bennett at Elite and Coach Dieter at Fremont, we're just not ready to offer you any kind of assistance or a scholarship," the coach says. "We have a lot of kickers to consider, Ashtyn. You're on our watch list, but to be honest, there's a bunch of players ahead of you and we want to be realistic. But we thank you for your time and interest in Northwestern. It's a great school, and we'd love to have you as a student here."

I nod, thank them for considering me, and the meeting is over in a matter of minutes. Once I'm back in the elevator on my way down to the first floor, a deep pang of sorrow settles into my chest at the realization that one door is closed.

They don't think I'm good enough.

When the elevator opens, I hear a familiar cranky old lady say in a commanding voice, "I'm telling you that I don't need an appointment with the coach! I need to see him now."

Derek's grandmother is wielding her umbrella like a sword in front of the doorman's face. The woman looks ready to slice the doorman in two, or at least whack him on the head if she doesn't get her way.

"Ma'am, it's against policy to let you in the elevator without an appointment."

"You are *obviously* a nincompoop when it comes to recognizing authority," Elizabeth Worthington barks out, frustration and agitation laced in her voice. "Now get out of my way so I can see my . . ."

Mrs. Worthington lowers her umbrella and clears her throat the second she sees me. "Hello, Ashtyn."

Just being in the same room with the old lady, even when she's threatening someone, is supremely comforting. "Mrs. Worthington, what are you doing here?"

"This heathen doorman has vexed me to no end," she says. She sighs in annoyance while she reaches into the purse hanging from her forearm and pulls out a monogrammed handkerchief. She dabs invisible sweat off her forehead.

It doesn't escape my attention that she hasn't answered my question. It's a habit she obviously picked up from her grandson. Or maybe it's hereditary, and they were both born with the trait.

But I'm not about to let her off the hook. "I thought you went back to Texas. What are you doing here?"

Mrs. Worthington places her handkerchief back in her purse and pulls out a clean one. "That, my dear, is a very good question." She clears her throat again and says, "Quite honestly, Ashtyn, I heard you were here and I came back to be here for you. I've got a car outside waiting to take you home."

Me?

She came here for *me*?

Nobody comes back for me. They leave me, just like my sister, my mom, and Landon . . . even Derek, the one person who mattered most. But this old, cranky lady with a bad attitude came back for me.

"Don't look at me like that," she orders.

"Thank you," I whisper, my voice trembling.

The old lady pulls me aside and shoos the doorman away. She unfolds the clean monogrammed handkerchief and starts wiping tears from my face. "You're just a complete mess, and, well, you're pretty much hopeless and need guidance. I figure I'm the only one capable of turning you into a lady of any substance."

I still her shaky hand as she wipes fresh tears falling from my eyes. "I love you, too."

Her eyes are welling up as more tears stream down my face, but she blinks them back and composes herself. "Stop blubbering, because now you're turning me into a mess and I won't have it."

"I'm sorry I called you a snob."

"You didn't call me a snob."

"I thought it."

She purses her lips and taps her umbrella on the ground like a cane. "Well . . . truth is, I probably am a snob. Now let's get in my car and head back home, but first we need to eat lunch. I'm hungry."

A limo is waiting outside for her . . . for us. I sit across from her and notice her smirking, that same smirk that Derek has when he's being mischievous.

Later that evening, Brandi and Mrs. Worthington go out for dinner while I babysit Julian. After I put Julian to bed and am in my room talking to Victor about my interview at Northwestern, Julian comes in the room wearing his little pajamas with cartoon characters on them.

"I can't sleep," he says shyly as he stands next to my bed.

I hang up with Victor and look at my nephew. "Want to come sleep in my bed?"

He nods.

I lift my comforter and he climbs inside. He's sucking his thumb while his other hand wraps around me.

"I love you, Julian," I say as I kiss the top of his head.

He takes his thumb out of his mouth and looks up at me with adoring eyes. "I love you, too, Auntie Ashtyn."

CHAPTER 55

Derek

've never been nervous before a game. A calmness would come over me and I was able to block out all insecurities and self-doubt. I was able to focus entirely on the game. I had an over-abundance of confidence that I'd win. And I did.

I never thought there was a chance that I would lose.

But now, as I walk up to the house and see the shed in the backyard, I think about the odds against me. The thrill of antici-pation makes me sweat. What if I end up losing her? And as much as I keep telling myself I need to have confidence, I'm filled with self-doubt.

Everything I set up is in place, except for one thing.

I ring the doorbell, but nobody answers, so I walk into the house. Gus is sitting in his big leather chair, watching televi-sion. I sit on the couch, pick up the remote, and turn off the tele-vision.

Gus turns to me. "What do you think you're doing? I thought you moved to Texas with that bossy grandmother of yours."

"I need to talk to you, Gus. It's important." I put the remote back on the table.

The man sits up straighter in his chair and rests his hands on his stomach. "What do you want, Derek?" He glances at his watch. "You've got exactly three minutes."

For a long time I didn't care what people thought. Suddenly everything matters. Even if Ashtyn doesn't think her father's approval is important, it is. Probably more than she wants to admit.

I wipe my forehead and take a deep breath. I rehearsed what I was going to say, but all those words are forgotten. I look at Ashtyn's father, always looking glum, and clear my throat. "I've developed feelings for Ashtyn, sir."

He raises an eyebrow. "Since when?"

"For a while now."

He gives me a hard, cold stare. "You asking for my approval?"

"Yes, sir. Not that I need it, but I sure would appreciate it."

He looks me up and down, then sits back in his chair and sighs. "I haven't done right by her. If her mother was here, Brandi wouldn't have left and Ashtyn wouldn't have played football. I thought if I didn't make a big deal about it, she'd decide to quit. I failed."

"You still have a chance to make it up to her, Gus. She needs you. She's a strong, independent girl who'll fight for what she wants, but you'd make it a helluva lot easier for her if you were there to cheer her on. If you'd watch her, you'd see that she's a great football player. I cherish her, sir. More than anythin'. And I'm gonna be by her side whether you're there or not."

Gus nods. I think I just got his approval, but I'm not sure. It'll have to be enough.

I go back to Victor's house and change clothes. It's time. It's the fourth quarter and it's the last play of the game . . . in the Super Bowl of my life.

CHAPTER 56

Ashtyn

Mrs. Worthington is the slowest eater I've ever met. She insisted we go to a grill across the street from Millennium Park for lunch. The woman takes a bite of her burger and chews until her food is completely decimated before taking another bite. She keeps glancing at her watch every two seconds, like she's timing her bites. I just want to go home so I can close my eyes and pretend Derek is coming back. I know it's useless.

"So I've decided to rent a house in that Godforsaken town of yours," Mrs. Worthington says, then takes another bite.

Wait, I'm confused. "You're moving to Fremont?"

"I told you that you'd be hopeless without me." She gestures to my ears. "You should listen better, or get those ears of yours tested. You're family to me now. Contrary to popular belief, I look after my family. No offense, but your sister's a flake and your father could use a little pep in his step. Y'all need a little Texas influence, if you ask me."

This old lady is moving here to be with us, to keep an eye on us, and to make sure we're taken care of. Just the thought of it brings a tear to my eye. "What about Derek?"

She rolls her keen blue eyes that remind me of Derek's. "My grandson is a wild card. I can't keep up with him. One day he's moving to Texas, the next he's going back to California. For all I know he'll end up here in Chicago."

I don't tell her that's not about to happen. It hurts like crazy to admit it, but Derek made his decision to leave and he isn't coming back. I give her a small smile.

She checks her watch again. "I've got to go to the ladies' room. I'll be right back." She takes her purple sun umbrella off the back of the chair.

"Do you need help?" I ask, wondering why she'd need her umbrella to go to the restroom.

She waves the tip of it in my direction. "I might be an old lady, but I can surely get to the restroom without an escort."

I've already learned that arguing with Mrs. Worthington is useless. She heads to the restroom and I stare down at my burger. I ordered the one made with meat from grass-fed cows. Derek would be proud of me for my healthy choice. He has no clue how my life has been altered because of him. Everything I say or do brings up a memory of the time we spent together. Will the gnawing pain in my heart ever go away, or will I have a gaping wound in it the rest of my life?

In time I'll be okay, but I've resolved myself to the fact that I'll always have an ache in my heart that only Derek can heal.

A random woman with long brown hair sits in the chair opposite me, right in front of Mrs. Worthington's burger. I'm completely caught off guard. I'm about to tell her the seat is obviously taken, when recognition sinks in.

No. Way! It can't be . . .

"Katie Calhoun?" I blurt out.

She takes a French fry off Mrs. Worthington's plate. "So I hear Northwestern didn't offer you a football scholarship. That's too bad."

My mouth is wide open in shock. I couldn't talk even if I tried.

"Listen, Ashtyn," Katie says. "Can I be real honest with you?"

I nod slowly, still in shock.

"Don't give up." She takes another fry and wags it at me as she says, "I can't tell you how many people thought I would quit, but I never did. And even when I didn't get the full support of my teammates, I never gave up." She leans in and whispers, "I think you're stronger than you think. So does Derek."

Derek? Slowly the realization that he had something to do with Katie Calhoun being here settles in my brain. "He set this up, didn't he?"

She nods, then turns her chair around. "Watch the monitor," she says, pointing to the TV in the bar showing ESPN highlights.

Katie nods to the bartender, which is some sort of cue, but I have no clue what's going on. Suddenly, the TV screens go blank. Then, all of a sudden, "ASHTYN PARKER HIGHLIGHT REEL" comes on the screen, then fades out.

Highlight reel? But I don't have a highlight . . .

My eyes start to water and my heart does a little flip when footage of me playing my freshman year appears. Then footage of my sophomore year . . . and junior year. I watch each clip of me successfully kicking field goal after field goal, many times being rushed by my teammates afterward as they congratulate me.

Derek did this. He spent time going through every game and took snippets of my most memorable games. He even set the reel to music.

When the screen fades to black, I think it's over. Until the word "DEDICATED" comes on the screen and footage of me practicing during our road trip to Texas comes up. My hand flies to my mouth in shock. Derek wasn't playing games or texting when I was practicing. He was filming me with his cell phone while I yelled at him practically the entire time.

At the end, the screen is filled with the words "ASHTYN PARKER, KICKER."

Everyone claps for me. This was all set up by Derek. How did he find Katie Calhoun? How did he get her to come here? Why?

"You're talented, Ashtyn. I'm impressed," Katie says. After giving me a pep talk and answering a bunch of questions, she stands up.

"Do you know where Mrs. Worthington went?" I ask.

"She's at the bar." Katie waves to the old lady. Mrs. Worthington waves back with her umbrella.

While I'm still reeling in shock, Katie sets an envelope on the table and slides it in front of me.

"Good luck, Ashtyn," she says. "I'll be rooting for you."

Katie walks out. Nobody else in the restaurant knows who she is, even though she's one of the few females who've played football at the college level. She's a pioneer, a legend.

My fingers glide over the envelope. In Derek's handwriting it says, *After you read this, go across the street to* The Bean.

The Bean is this big silver metal sculpture in Millennium Park. I look over at Mrs. Worthington, who holds up our check and gestures for me to leave.

I shove the letter in my pocket and rush out of the restaurant. All I want to do is run up to Derek and wrap my arms around him. Surely he's here, by *The Bean*. It takes every ounce of energy for me not to run into the crowded city streets. I wait for the light with everyone else by the sidewalk, craning my neck.

I don't see him.

I rush across the street with the rest of the pedestrians when the light changes, while frantically searching for signs of the boy who suddenly has a goal . . . and I hope that goal is to be with me.

I told Derek to go for what he wanted, full force, and he did. The truth envelops me. I thought he left me, when all along he did what he thought he needed to do to prove how much he cares about me.

When I get to *The Bean*, my sister, Julian, Falkor, and my dad are standing in front of it. Julian has a box of Skittles in his hand, which he holds out to me.

"Derek told me to give you this," he says. "Open it."

I open the box and peek inside. There are no purple ones.

Brandi points to a tree in the distance. "We're supposed to tell you to wait by that tree over there."

"For what?" I ask.

My dad shrugs.

"Where's Derek?" I ask. I just need to see him, to talk to him, to say I'm ready to fight for him, for us. Together we can make this work. If I wait any longer, I swear I'm going to explode.

But neither my sister, my nephew, nor my dad is giving me any hints, so I follow their directions. When I get to the tree, there's a bunch of purple Skittles arranged in a big purple heart.

"Yo, Ashtyn!" Derek's voice echoes from across the park. "Heads up!"

Derek appears all the way across the park, wearing a Fremont High football uniform, complete with helmet and pads. In his hands is a football.

With expert precision, he tosses the football to me. It flies right into my waiting hands, but I'm too nervous and drop it.

He takes off the helmet. "You fumbled," he says with a grin. He jogs the distance between us so he's standing in front of me now, taking my breath away as I look into his mischievous, sparkling eyes and his gorgeous, chiseled features.

"I know."

"That was a perfect throw," he tells me. He threw that ball from way across the park, practically across the street and between a ton of people. And it was completely on target. "Why didn't you catch it, Sugar Pie?"

"Because I'm nervous and my heart is beating like crazy."

The side of his mouth quirks up.

I take in the football player in front of me. But he's not a football player. Maybe he was in the past, but that was before his mom died. I'm not going to push him into playing again. He told me his decision not to play was final, so . . . "What are you doing wearing that jersey and all that equipment, Derek? Why are you here?"

"I joined the team." He shrugs. "I figure that's the only way I can spend time with my girlfriend. She's the kicker for Fremont, you know. And she's a damn good one at that."

I reach up and touch his gorgeous face. "Thank you for making the highlight reel. And for finding Katie Calhoun. I have no clue how you did it."

"Let's just say your teammates like their captain a lot." He stills my hand with his own. "What about the letter?"

"The letter?" I fish it out of my pocket and hold it up. "I haven't read it yet." Finding Derek was more important than anything.

He motions for me to open it. I rip open the envelope and slide the letter out. When I read the words on the paper, the realization of what he did this past week hits me.

I lower the letter and look up at Derek. "You got me an offer from a Division I school."

"No. *You* got an offer from a Division I school. I just sent the highlight reel." He kicks the ground. "And made a couple of calls."

"You did it for me?"

"Ashtyn Parker, I'd do anythin' for you." He cups my head in his hands and leans in close. "I love you."

"You know what this means, don't you?"

"What?"

"That you have to fight to be first string. Right now Brandon Butter's got the top spot. I can't be dating the second-string quarterback. I have a reputation to protect, you know."

"Don't you have faith in me?"

"Oh, I have no doubt you can do it. After all, Cowboy, you did the impossible and made me fall in love with you."

"The impossible, huh?"

"Yeah."

He laughs. "From what I remember, you melted the first time you laid eyes on me in the shed."

"You're rewriting history, Derek. I seem to remember that I stabbed you the first time I laid eyes on you."

"That's because you were struck by The Fitz's good looks and charm."

"Get over yourself. I thought you looked like a thug. And if you refer to yourself in third person as The Fitz again, we're through." I scan him up and down. "Even if you are the sexiest boy alive in that uniform, and if we were at home I'd . . . I'd . . ."

"Do what?" he says, leaning down closer so his lips are touching mine.

I wrap my arms around his neck and kiss him.

When we come up for air, he says, "The Fitz is back."

"Yeah, well, tell him that his girlfriend is counting on a winning season."

He flashes me one of his irresistible grins and says, "He already won."

ACKNOWLEDGMENTS

Thank you to Emily Easton and the entire staff at Walker Books for Young Readers for braving the storm as I rewrote this book numerous times. I also want to express my sincere gratitude to my agent, Kristin Nelson, who really held my hand when I needed her unconditional support and encouragement. I am probably responsible for more than a few gray hairs on both your ends—sorry about that!

Karen Harris and Ruth Kaufman are not only great friends but amazing critique partners, as well. Without you two, Derek and Ashtyn would never have fallen in love. Seriously, words cannot express how thankful I am for your unconditional friendship and help. You both are selfless and amazing people who will remain lifelong friends.

My assistant, Melissa Jolly, helped me brainstorm ideas and acted as my sounding board and my additional critique partner when I needed it. Thank you a million times over for keeping me sane these past four years.

I can't forget Rob Adelman, who continues to show me that life is not about what you know, who you know, or what you look like. It's about how you can make fun of family members and the people whom you love most—Rob, I don't have to tell you that you are the epitome of greatness, because you remind me of that all the time. I love you.

My family definitely deserves a shout-out! Thank you to Moshe, Samantha (who is allergic to purple dye, like Ashtyn), Brett, and Frances—we are a crazy bunch, but I wouldn't want to ride this roller coaster of life with anyone else.

Finally I want to thank all my fans, teachers, and librarians who have supported me and my books—you are the reason I continue writing! I wouldn't be where I am today without you spreading the word to your friends, students, and colleagues.

As always, you can find me on Facebook and Twitter—see you there!

SIMONE ELKELES is the *New York Times* and *USA Today* bestselling author of the Perfect Chemistry trilogy, and the queen of romance. Her funny way of looking at the world shines through in novels that are bursting with sarcastic wit, edgy characters, and exhilarating drama.

www.simoneelkeles.com

@SimoneElkeles